THE FADI

To Alec

"May you know guidance,
strength, wisdom and love"

with best wishes,

Phil Allcock

Also by Phil Allcock:

THE FADING REALM

Stories of the Realm: 3

PHIL ALLCOCK

Phoenix

Front cover design by Vic Mitchell

ISBN 0 85476 318 X

Phoenix is an imprint of Kingsway Publications Ltd, Lottbridge Drove, Eastbourne, E Sussex BN23 6NT. Typeset by J&L Composition Ltd, Filey, North Yorkshire. Printed in Great Britain by BPCC Hazells Ltd.

For a very special friend: Joanie Yoder
With many, many thanks for all your help, prayers and
shining faith—and for the caring encouragement and
understanding that only another author can provide

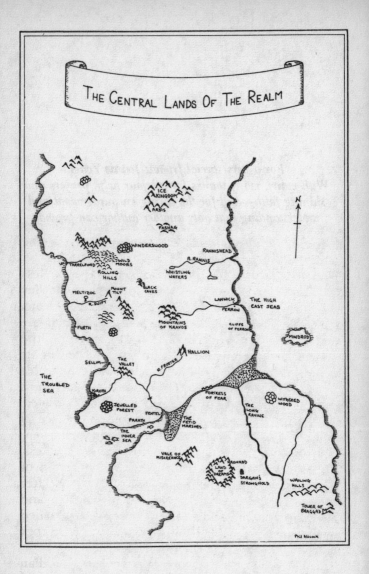

THE CENTRAL LANDS OF THE REALM

ICE KINGDOM
ARDIS
PASHAG
WINDERSWOOD
RANNISHEAD
R. RANNIS
TARRELFORD
WILD MOORS
ROLLING HILLS
WHISTLING WATERS
MELTIROC
MOUNT TILT
BLACK CAVES
R. SWIFT
LANNICK
PERRON
THE HIGH EAST SEAS
FURTH
MOUNTAINS OF KRAVOS
CLIFFS OF PERRON
MINDROD
HALLION
THE VALLEY
R. FROTTER
SELLIM
THE TROUBLED SEA
KIROTH
FORTRESS OF FEAR
JEWELLED FOREST
JEMTEL
THE FETID MARSHES
THE LONG RAVINE
WITHERED WOOD
PARATH
THE INNER SEA
VALE OF MISCREANCE
LAND OF DREAMS
ROHADD
DARGAN'S STRONGHOLD
WAILING HILLS
TOWER OF BRAGGAD

PHIL ALLCOCK

Stories of the Realm

This is the third and final book in the trilogy of Stories of the Realm, recounting the tale of Taz-i-tor, the Golden Sceptre of Elsinoth.

The first book, *The Will of Dargan*, tells how Kess and Linnil, the Quiet Ones, leave their peaceful valley home. Meeting Valor, a Mountain Guard, they learn of the theft of the Golden Sceptre of Elsinoth the Mighty (known to the elves as Toroth), creator of the Realm. The Sceptre has been stolen by Carnak, its Keeper, who killed Valor's father as he made his escape. Carnak takes the staff to the Southlands stronghold of Dargan the Bitter, a Dark Master. Dargan plans to use the Sceptre's powers to force all the people of the Realm to follow his will.

Meanwhile, guided by Meltizoc the Wise, Kess, Linnil and Valor seek help. They enlist the aid of Vallel and Vosphel, the golden-haired Water Crafter sisters; Hesteron, the tall and aloof Air Crafter; and Gatera, the huge Land Crafter. They are also joined by Merric, a wandering minstrel; and Rrum, a rock man they rescue from the Black Caves.

Led by Athennar, son of Tolledon (the Guardian of the Realm), the company sets sail for the Southlands, accompanied by Sash, the black leopard. As they cross the Inner Sea, they are attacked by a scorbid, and Vosphel dies as a result of its sting. The others reach the Southlands, only to be attacked and scattered by Athennar's cousin, Zendos, who is Dargan's apprentice. Zendos has previously kidnapped Athennar's love, Melinya.

After many struggles, during which they come face-to-face with their own fears, the company is reunited within Dargan's stronghold. Together they reach the Throne Room and reclaim the Sceptre. Meanwhile, Tolledon's army has captured the Fortress of Fear from the brutish Zorgs. The fortress is the only safe route between the north of the Realm and the south.

In the second book, *In Search of the Golden Sceptre*, Dargan thwarts the company's plans. Not only does he recapture the Sceptre, but he also takes Linnil prisoner, and escapes on the back of a winged Tark.

Most of the friends travel back to the Fortress of Fear, disconsolate. However, Rrum and a group of rock people return to Dargan's stronghold to destroy it. In one of the dungeon cells Rrum finds Carnak, who appears insane. He takes him to the fortress, and the company learns that Zendos is not dead, as they thought, but has escaped to the Ice Kingdom taking Melinya with him. As Zendos is the only key to the location of Linnil and the Sceptre, five of the friends (Kess, Athennar, Hesteron, Vallel and Valor) go in search of him. They are accompanied as far as the Mountains of Kravos by Gatera and Rrum.

As the five friends journey on, they are trapped in a fog by the Mistress of the Mists. Kess rescues Whisper, a prisoner in the mist, and Vallel and Hesteron use their Crafts to defeat the Mistress. Kess and Whisper then return to the Fortress of Fear.

En route, they capture two Zorgs, Gur'brak and Bar'drash.

Meanwhile, Gatera and Rrum meet the Wanderer, who tells them he has seen Tarks landing near the Ice Kingdom, carrying two people—possibly Zendos and Melinya. Rrum and Gatera set off to explore the area. Following a tunnel that leads into the heart of a mountain, they find a colony of imprisoned people. However, before they can help, the two friends are caught by thunder goblins and locked in a cell next to Melinya. Breaking free and rescuing Melinya, they hide in a cave on the mountainside, but the goblins find them.

Athennar, Hesteron, Vallel and Valor meanwhile meet Fashag, a surly gnome who is also a Fire Crafter. The four travel on to the Ice Kingdom. Once inside the city, they are caught by Zendos and imprisoned in tombs of ice. However, they are rescued by Fashag, and Zendos is defeated and killed—but without revealing Dargan's whereabouts. They leave the Ice Kingdom, and arrive in time to save Gatera, Rrum and Melinya from the thunder goblins.

During this time, Linnil has been held prisoner in a cave system underneath the Tower of Braggad. Dargan has been experimenting with the Sceptre, making plants fade; now he tests his increased powers on Linnil, forcing her to believe she loves him. To dishearten his enemies, he sends her back to the Fortress of Fear, knowing that she too will fade.

Kess and Whisper have meanwhile gone to the Jewelled Forest, guarded by Callenor and Marason. They are seeking a chest that contains a potion that could restore Whisper's strength. Marason is killed, but the three others find the chest, and Whisper is healed. They return to the fortress, only to find that Linnil is delirious and has started to fade.

Just as they are all losing heart, Meltizoc discovers details of the Globe of Truth, which is hidden deep within the dreaded Black Caves. The Globe could restore Linnil's mind, and enable her to reveal Dargan's hiding place. Four of the friends—Merric, Gatera, Rrum and Valor—vow to Kess that they will find it. Kess at last begins to see a glimmer of hope. . . .

1

A New Quest

'Wait!'

The command rang out in the still air as the four friends strode across the courtyard of the Fortress of Fear. Valor shrugged uneasily at Merric, while Gatera and Rrum stopped and looked around.

Athennar and Meltizoc hurried up to the friends. Before any of the four could speak, Athennar said, 'I can guess where you're going—to the Black Caves to try and find the Globe of Truth.'

Valor groaned. 'Don't try to stop us!' he warned.

Nodding in agreement, Merric added, 'Time is not on our side. Rather than stay and talk, we thought it better for a few of us to seek out the globe.'

'And you didn't think to ask if we had more information?' replied Meltizoc. 'Do you know where to look? And wouldn't it be better if you were able to stop at Hallion for extra food and rest? That will be easier to arrange if you are accompanied by someone who knows his way around Hallion.'

'You?' asked Valor, unable to keep the impatience from his voice.

The wise man chuckled. 'I think that Athennar might be a more logical choice.'

Smiling, Athennar added, 'We must all work together—the future of the Realm may depend on it.'

'But what of Melinya?' asked Merric.

Athennar's smile faded. 'She needs rest—she is still weak from her imprisonment. I hate to leave her, but she will be safe here. Meanwhile, I must continue to do everything in my power to ensure that Dargan is defeated—otherwise there will be no future for us to enjoy together.'

'And Hesteron and Vallel?' asked Valor.

'They, too, guessed that you would try to leave. However, they are weary from our adventures in the Ice Kingdom, and will stay here to provide company for Kess and Whisper—and in case they can be of service in any other way. Now, if you will wait a few moments more, I will fetch Windrider.'

Gatera patted his great girth as Athennar strolled away. 'At least we might get some decent food on the journey!'

A groom soon appeared, leading Valor's and Merric's horses, followed minutes later by Melinya and Athennar, who was leading his proud white steed, Windrider. Before he mounted the horse, Athennar took both of Melinya's hands in his. She seemed a pale fragile flower beside him. 'I must go, but you must stay, my love. I can't risk losing you again so soon.'

'You are always in my heart,' she replied. 'My prayers will be with you. Go, and serve the Realm well.'

Looking thoughtful, Meltizoc addressed the company once more. 'In the Great Tome of Neldra, there is a rhyme which may help you to locate the Globe more accurately—'

Valor snorted. 'Your first rhyme wasn't exactly a resounding success!'

Meltizoc smiled patiently. 'If you think back, you may remember that it provided the key which helped to release you from Dargan's control!'

Colouring as he remembered his imprisonment in Dargan's stronghold, Valor fell silent.

'As I was saying,' continued Meltizoc, 'the rhyme may help. First, however, you need to be aware that the only entrance to the correct maze of underground tunnels and chambers is from the central cave.' Pausing, he pulled out a small scroll, reading it before passing it to Athennar.

'Through water, wind, and the awesome fire,
Then slowly down the steps that seem to take you higher;
The truth is held by age, and age to age is spanned—
But youth must use the truth to help an aging man.'

'Humph!' snorted Valor again.

'Take care not to despise that which is untried,' Meltizoc counselled him. 'Now, be away, all of you, and may Elsinoth guide your footsteps!'

The heavy gates at the front of the fortress were opened, and the five friends passed through, unaware that a lonely face watched them from a window high above.

Kess sighed, then withdrew from the window. *Well, they're gone*, he thought, *and my hopes go with them.* Would they be successful? And even if they were, would they be in time to save Linnil? She was very weak, and he had no idea how much longer she would last. His mind flickered back over the events of the past few months, sifting through the fragments, trying to make some sense of it all. Anger and futility gnawed at him, threatening to overwhelm him.

A light knock came from the door, and Whisper's face peeped round. 'I thought I'd just come and see if you know what's happening,' she said. 'Some of your friends seem to be leaving.'

'I know.'

'But why?'

'Because they want to help Linnil. They're going in search of the Globe of Truth.'

'Oh.'

'Would you have done the same?'

Whisper flushed. 'Why, of course. I mean—'

Frowning, Kess turned away. A gulf had opened up between the two of them since their return from the Jewelled Forest: a gulf that he felt unable—or unwilling—to cross.

'Kess, you can't go on blaming me for drinking the contents of that phial we found! I said I was sorry— you don't realise just how desperate I was to live!'

'Not as desperate as I am for Linnil to live!' muttered Kess.

'But surely you can understand—'

'Understand what? You won't even tell me who you really are! You expect me to trust you without any basis for that trust! What's more, you've deprived Linnil of the one real chance she had!'

Whisper bit her lip in frustration. 'I suppose I do owe you an explanation. I couldn't tell you before we found the phial, though, in case you refused to help me.' She hesitated, then lowered her voice. 'The truth is, I come from a land far across the seas.'

Kess looked at her in surprise, but Whisper's silver eyes were gazing down at the floor, transfixed.

'I am the daughter of a great chieftain; a mighty warrior called Ifrac. Our land has been through a time of many difficulties. I was sent with a group of warriors to find other lands and to—er—recruit more people to fight for us.'

'Recruit?' said Kess. 'Don't you mean capture?'

Whisper shrugged. 'Perhaps. Anyway, our boat was caught in heavy seas, and began to break up. The other warriors were all swept overboard and drowned. I alone managed to cling to a part of the boat, and was eventually washed ashore on the coasts of your Northlands.'

'The "other" warriors?' mused Kess. 'So you are a warrior, too!' A vivid scene flashed into his mind—his recent dream of Whisper fighting on a distant shore. He remembered, too, how vital and strong she had become since drinking the 'healing of the body' potion.

'In my land, to survive one must fight. In the last few years, however, I have had much time for thinking. There are perhaps better ways to solve problems . . .'

'Why didn't you tell me all this before?' Kess asked.

'Would you have believed me? And if you had, would you have helped me?'

Kess shook his head. 'I don't know.'

'I couldn't afford to take that risk. I was alone in a strange land, and had been held prisoner by the Mistress of the Mists for so long. Can you blame me for wanting to escape; for striving to live?'

Grudgingly, Kess shook his head again. 'I suppose not. But what now? Do you still intend to kidnap people to help your father?'

Whisper smiled ruefully. 'By myself? I think not! Besides which, I owe you my life—twice now. If I can repay that somehow, then I will. Can we be friends once more?' She offered her hand.

Kess looked at it, but didn't shake it. 'Perhaps,' he murmured. 'Perhaps.'

A little while later, Kess sought out Hesteron and Vallel. He found them strolling along the battlements, surveying the northern plains beyond. The Quiet One realised that they were probably thinking of their homes, many days distant. The thought made him long for the comfort and security of his own Valley home, left behind so long ago. Those carefree days spent by the Cleansing Pool with Linnil and Narfic were gone for ever.

'Good meeting!' said Hesteron. 'How's Linnil?'

'About the same,' Kess replied. 'I only hope the others can find the Globe of Truth. You should have travelled with them—and gone on to your homes. There is little enough to do here, except worry.'

Vallel put a reassuring hand on his shoulder. 'We were too tired to go north; and if we had visited our homes, we wouldn't be here if you should need us.'

'No,' added Hesteron, 'and having started on this quest, we would both prefer to see it through. The friendships that have been forged within our small company mean much to us. As Vallel said, while we are still needed, we will stay.'

Kess nodded gratefully.

Vallel added, 'And try not to worry! Aren't you the one who has shown us that we need to trust in Toroth—or Elsinoth as you call him? He won't let us down!'

'I don't know any more,' muttered Kess. 'Sometimes I find everything so difficult to understand. Perhaps even Elsinoth is just a figment of my imagination.'

'Have you already forgotten how your cry to Elsinoth saved us in the Vale of Miscreance? Or how we were all rescued from the perils of the Mists? I'm sure, too, that Vosphel glimpsed his face even as she died. She was so at peace. . . . ' Vallel's voice trailed off wistfully.

Kess nodded in sympathy, but didn't reply. How

could he believe in Elsinoth with Linnil still lying near death in her bed? Where was *her* peace?

His thoughts were interrupted by a shout from one of the elven archers nearby.

'A Tark!'

A small pinprick of black gradually grew larger as they watched. They could just hear the harsh cry which gave the creature its name: 'Tarkkk! Tarkkk!'

The Tark glided high above the fortress, circling slowly as if teasing the archers. One or two loosed off arrows, but Tolledon, who had joined the group on the battlements, told them to hold their fire. 'The creature isn't stupid—it's keeping out of range.'

Gasping with exertion, Meltizoc arrived. Hesteron found a large lump of stone for him to sit on while he regained his breath.

Kess was still watching the Tark, and suddenly glimpsed a cloaked figure astride it. 'Dargan!' he hissed between clenched teeth. How he wished he could get his hands on the loathsome Dark Master.

'Yes,' wheezed Meltizoc in agreement. 'He is probably just amusing himself; reminding us of his supremacy.'

The Tark wheeled suddenly, and then sped off northwards. The company watched until it was out of sight.

'Where do you think it's going?' Vallel asked.

'Who knows?' Meltizoc replied grimly. 'On some errand of evil, I have no doubt! Perhaps Dargan has just found out that Zendos went to the Ice Kingdom. If he doesn't realise the sorcerer is dead, he might be going there to wreak his revenge.'

'I hope not,' replied Tolledon, 'for the sake of the Tissirim. I would hate them to suffer any more.' He turned to his archers. 'There is little more we can do at the moment. Post a few extra men, and keep watch.

Inform me immediately if the Tark returns.' The elves bowed formally and Tolledon retreated down the steps, followed by a puffing Meltizoc.

Wending their way through a narrow band of trees, Athennar and the other travellers also heard the cry of the Tark in the distance. Dismounting rapidly and leading the horses beneath the wide, spreading branches of a large oak, they watched as the creature and its rider flew overhead.

A cold shiver ran down Valor's back. 'I thought the Northlands would be free of Tarks,' he said.

'Then you reckoned without Dargan—a dangerous thing to do!' replied Athennar, leading Windrider out on to the trail once more. 'We'll have to be extra vigilant from now on: it appears that Dargan is growing bolder by the moment.'

'Perhapps he is too confidentt!' grated Rrum.

Merric patted the little rock man on the back. 'I hope that you are right, my friend,' he said.

Sighing, Valor leaped onto Sundust. He wished he could believe what Rrum had said. To him, it appeared that Dargan had every right to be confident—as every day took him closer to his goal of controlling the Realm. How could their little expedition hope to stop him? How could anyone hope to stop him?

2

Assault on Hallion

Dargan had taken great personal delight in sending the girl—Linnil—back to her friends: knowing that they could do nothing to help her; knowing that instead of giving them hope, it would produce seeds of despair.

Then, emerging from his dark underground hiding place, he had started searching the area outside the castle. The Tower of Braggad was perched on a rough rocky outcrop, leading down to a desert-like plain. This suited the Dark Master admirably, as even his least intelligent scouts would be able to spot any unwelcome visitors while they were still far off. However, Dargan now sought areas of vegetation on which to test his new-found powers.

Impatiently, he gazed around. Poking out from the cliff-face at irregular intervals were the wiry arms of various shrubs and trees. Made hardy by their harsh surroundings, they would be ideal objects on which to test his strength.

Grasping the Sceptre, he struggled up to the nearest plant—a coarse bush with sparse leaves, growing out of a crack in the rock. After some hours of effort and exploration, using his mind to probe ever deeper into the thick woody stems, he managed to control and twist the bush's growth. With a grunt of satisfaction, he returned to the tower to await developments.

Within a day, the bush was weakening; growing paler. By the end of the fourth day, it had faded into nothingness. Dargan snorted in triumph at this small victory. It signified far greater things to come: while he had been awaiting the results, he had learned to project his increasing power over greater distances, until his evil thoughts could blight a whole section of the cliff-face at once. To his surprise, not only trees and shrubs began to fade, but also one or two of the smaller rocks. He couldn't have been more delighted.

Some of his other experiments had, however, met with far less success. With Linnil gone, the Dark Master was impatient to test his powers on other 'thinking' creatures. Unfortunately, only his slaves were to hand, and they proved to be unpromising subjects. Most were Zorgs, and their characteristic stubbornness and rather dim natures meant that they could only respond to the simplest of mental commands. This just made Dargan impatient, causing him to lose control of their wills altogether. He constantly had to calm himself before starting the frustrating process all over again.

As his experiments continued, an idea began to form in his mind, fed partly by his thirst for revenge and partly by his craving to exhibit his power to those who would appreciate its implications. Although he was not yet ready to try out his control over groups of humans (the girl, after all, had been weakened considerably by her time as a prisoner), he wanted to give the Northlanders a reminder of his might: yet another claw of despair to tear at any hope they had left. He knew just what to do to hurt them most: he would pay a little visit to Hallion! Even the well-guarded centre of the Realm would pose no problems for a Tark—he could just fly in and fly out again.

And so it was that he coaxed the trusted Targul into taking him once more into the skies above the Southlands. Flying steadily northwards, they eventually reached the Fortress of Fear. Knowing that the elves would see them, Dargan delighted in persuading the Tark to circle overhead. The sight of the scurrying figures below—one or two of them even shooting a few futile arrows up into the air—brought an evil laugh to his lips, even though the sound was snatched away almost before it was formed.

After taunting them for a short time, he urged the Tark on again, delighting in pitting its strength against the harsh talons of the wind. He cackled wildly as it raked through his hair. It was an exhilarating feeling: soaring over the lands of the Realm, soon all to come under his dominion. A surge of power flooded through him, and he threw back his head in triumph. His! All his!

As he flew onwards, he failed to notice five tiny figures below, partly obscured by the straggling trees. Unaware, he sped on towards Hallion.

Dusk was beginning to drain the sky of colour as Dargan directed Targul to land on the grassy plain near the Falls of Hallion. His eyes glinting with satisfaction, he gazed around. Then he tugged the Sceptre from his cloak and, holding it tightly, allowed its energies to flow through him. He focused them on the grass and plants all around. He could sense the vibrancy of it: so much living material that it threatened—just for a moment—to swamp him. Then he quickly regained control.

After battling for some hours, he felt satisfied that he had achieved his objective. Stumbling slightly in the darkness, he made his way back to Targul. He mounted quickly, and urged the Tark upwards and over the Falls into Hallion itself.

The sheltered vale seemed very quiet, but Dargan took no chances. He landed in a small clearing, well away from the main signs of habitation. The task he had set himself would take most of the night, and he wanted to avoid interruptions as much as possible.

The thought had scarcely passed through his mind when he heard the sound of footsteps running lightly between the trees.

'Who's there?' asked a voice.

'Why, it's only me,' Dargan replied, assuming the tones of an old crone. 'I'm just gathering a little firewood, my dear.'

'Firewood? At this time of year?' The voice came closer, and the lithe figure of a young elf appeared from the trees.

Dargan watched him closely from beneath the hood of his cloak. 'Um, yes, my dear. I get so cold, even in the summer.'

'Perhaps I can help you then.' The elf still sounded a little suspicious.

'Why, that would be most kind!'

Drawing nearer, the newcomer stopped as Dargan threw back the hood of his cloak. Before he could react, the elf was gripped firmly by the Dark Master's mind control, and fell heavily to the ground, as if struck by a heavy object.

'How convenient!' mused Dargan. 'Targul, here's a ready-provided meal for you. Feast well—you will need your strength for the return journey!'

The green eye slits glowed in anticipation as the creature shuffled over to the prostrate form. There was a brief, piercing shriek, then silence as the Tark settled down to its grisly task.

Satisfied that no one else was nearby, Dargan started the long process of channelling his will into the land all around. The cool night air wafted around him, rippling through the folds of his cloak, but he ignored it. Gripping the Sceptre, he withdrew into himself, allowing its power to touch him, surge through him. Then he redirected it outwards, letting it seep into the grass all around him, sensing it creep into the proud trees. His will probed and analysed each branch and twig, each leaf, each cell: drifting, changing.

Around the hillsides his power roamed, devouring all in its path: twisting, shifting. It was an immense task, but somehow he summoned all the reserves of strength he had built up, and persevered.

The pale light of morning was caressing the tree-tops before he had finished. Slowly, gently, he withdrew into himself, gathering together his depleted resources. Then, with a gasp and a groan, the Sceptre fell from his numb fingers, and he collapsed to the ground, exhausted.

Some time later, Dargan dragged himself to his feet. He felt completely drained, but knew he couldn't risk staying there much longer. The Hallion people would soon be awake and active. Picking up the staff, he staggered over to Targul and wearily struggled on to the creature's back. Then, with a single word of command, the Tark rose into the morning skies.

Despite his tiredness, Dargan chuckled to himself as he looked down. Soon the valley below would be bare—all the trees and plants gone for ever! That would teach his enemies to meddle! It was just a foretaste of what they could expect when he had fully mastered the Sceptre. Urging Targul to greater heights, he sped southwards towards the frugal comforts of his tower.

Two days later, Athennar, Merric, Valor, Gatera and Rrum approached Hallion. The journey had been easy, and the friends had soon relaxed in each other's company. Gatera strode along, his huge bass voice occasionally booming out a marching song, while Rrum wheeled and tumbled alongside. Merric sometimes chose to ride, sometimes to run free, his fingers plucking at some of the taller grasses as he passed.

Valor spent much of the time riding alongside Athennar. The Hallion man had begun to teach him some of the secrets of Animal Crafting, and Valor thirstily lapped up the knowledge.

As they trotted across the grassy expanse towards the Falls of Hallion, a rider came galloping towards them at great speed. Recognising the man as one of Hallion's trusted archers, Athennar called the company to a halt, and waited.

The horse stopped a few yards away and, flinging himself from the saddle, the man rushed straight across to Athennar.

'Sire, Hallion, it's—' the man gulped and coughed.

'Steady! Take your time,' coaxed Athennar.

'Apologies, sire. Good meeting to you all—at least, I wish it was a good meeting. I have grave news. Two days ago, a Tark was seen flying from Hallion in the early hours of the morning.'

'A Tark!' interrupted Valor. 'It must have been the same one we saw on the day we set out!'

Athennar nodded grimly and motioned the man to continue.

'A little later, we found an elf—drained—in the forest at the far end of the vale.'

'Drained?'

'He had a look of sheer terror on his face—yet at the same time his eyes seemed completely empty. It was awful. But that's not all, sire—the whole vale seems to have been placed under a curse.'

'A curse?' queried Athennar.

'Well, that's the only explanation we have. It's the trees; the flowers; the plants. There's something strange about them.'

'What do you mean—"strange"?'

'It's hard to say exactly. But they seem to have an air of unhealthiness about them. And the most peculiar thing is—and I swear that this is true—one or two of the smaller plants even appear to be fading.'

Athennar grimaced. 'We believe you,' he said. 'But I'm afraid that what you call a "curse" is something even more sinister. It appears that Dargan can even change the face of the land—no doubt he wants it to be barren and empty, a sorry echo of his own heart.'

Turning to his companions, he continued, 'We have to succeed—and soon. Otherwise, all that we love will be lost for ever.'

3
Journeying On

It was a subdued procession that made its way across the plains leading to the Falls of Hallion. At one point, Athennar pulled Windrider to a halt and slid to the ground. He examined the grass all around and muttered to himself.

Remounting, he motioned the company onwards. In answer to Merric's questioning gaze, he said, 'It's not only in Hallion where the plants are suffering. I had an uneasy feeling that something was wrong here as well. Now I'm sure. The grass is beginning to fade—only very gradually, but I can already see that it has lost some of its vitality.'

The minstrel gazed at the green expanse all around. To him, it still seemed bright and alive. 'Are you certain?' he asked.

Athennar nodded curtly.

They soon reached the Falls, and the signal was given for the water to be diverted into its underground channel. They rode quietly up through the passage, each of the travellers preoccupied with his own thoughts.

There was little to cheer them when they reached the open air of the Vale of Hallion. They met several small clusters of people; each group discussing the recent events in hushed tones. Athennar exchanged greetings with several friends. Then he asked the messenger to guide them to the area where the elf's body had been discovered.

It took some time to reach the small clearing, and Merric was troubled to see Athennar's worried expression as he surveyed the forests they were travelling through. 'Can you also see the fading here?' he asked.

'I can sense it,' was the short reply.

When they arrived at the clearing, the horses shied slightly and then halted, refusing to go further. The friends dismounted, and the messenger pointed to a flattened area of grass where the elf had lain. Some yards away was a circle of yellowed grass, spreading outwards towards the trees.

'This must have been where Dargan stood,' muttered Athennar, crouching down to examine the spot. 'Is there no end to his evil? He must be sure of his power to strike at the very heart of the Realm!'

Merric slowly nodded his head. 'He grows stronger with each passing day. Linnil is our only key. We must find the Dark Master—and to find him, we must seek out the Globe of Truth. It is our only hope. Dargan must be halted, before it is too late.'

'Perhaps it's already too late,' grumbled Gatera.

Rrum looked up at his huge friend and said, 'No! Itt is *nott* too late! We are still alive! We can defeatt the evil one!.'

Athennar sighed, then straightened. 'You are right, Merric. We must find the Globe—or at least, you must find it. I have things to organise here—Tolledon will want a full report of all that has happened. You can rest in Hallion tonight, and be on your way early tomorrow. I will follow on as soon as I can.'

The next morning, the reduced company set off once more on their journey to the Black Caves. A sombre mood still hovered over them—they had all been dismayed by the changes that seemed to be occurring in Hallion. The sheltered vale had always been regarded as a haven of safety: now it had been tarnished at a single stroke by Dargan.

To compound their misery, the skies turned a dull grey, and a steady drizzle of rain began to fall. The grey turned to black, and the drizzle to a downpour. Driven by a hard wind, it lashed at them, but they lowered their heads and battled onwards. Even the normally good-tempered Gatera scowled as he trudged alongside the drenched horses.

They considered sheltering from the storm, but the countryside was very open, with little to protect them from the rain's fury. Searching out a safe hiding place would delay them too long, so they decided to struggle on.

After a miserable night spent huddled beneath the scant shelter of a few rocks, they were greeted by the dawn, rising in a soft golden glow. The rain had ceased, and from a nearby tree came the cheerful chirping of birds.

'Oooh!' groaned Gatera, easing his cramped limbs. 'I feel like I'm made out of stone!' Then, seeing Rrum grinning nearby, he quickly added, 'I didn't mean that, my little friend! Don't start thinking of me as your next meal!'

Merric smiled. 'The cure for aching limbs is a little breakfast, followed by a healthy walk. That will help us all, and will also allow the horses a little more rest.'

Valor snorted. 'They never warned me about this

sort of torture when I was training to be a Mountain Guard!'

Chuckling, Merric picked up his lute and played a merry tune. The minstrel was missing Linnil, but felt himself relax a little as his fingers rippled over the strings. Music, which had so often comforted and encouraged him, lifted his spirits once more.

The early promise of the dawn was fulfilled by a lovely sunny day. They made good progress, and by late evening had reached the outlying hills of the Mountains of Kravos. Rather than stop for the night, they decided to continue as far as Gatera's home. The thought of shelter, a welcoming fire and good food far outweighed any feelings of tiredness.

A few hours later, they tramped wearily into the little dell where Gatera's family lived. As they emerged from the trees circling the dell, a powerful voice called out.

'Stop! Come no further!' The dying flames of a small fire wavered as if troubled by a breeze.

Valor reached for his sword, but Gatera chuckled. 'Would you keep your own husband from the warmth of the fire, Mardilla?'

A large shape detached itself from the shadows, and the friends smiled too as Gatera's wife stepped forward to greet them.

'Good meeting to you all!' she said warmly. 'Apologies for my caution: these are strange times.'

'Indeed they are!' agreed Merric, stepping forward and shaking her hand. 'I trust that we find you in good health, Mardilla—and the children also?'

'We are all well, thank you,' she replied, as Gatera gave her a big hug.

'I'm sorry for leaving you for such long periods,' he said sheepishly. 'I wish I could spend more time with the children.'

'There will be time enough for that when your task is done,' answered Mardilla. 'Meanwhile, you must fight for the safety of us all.'

Gatera smiled gratefully. 'And now I will fetch more wood to stoke up the fire. We are all weary.'

'And hungry too, I expect,' teased his wife. 'I will heat up some stew—it will at least make sure that your stomach's rumblings don't keep us awake all night!'

Gatera cuffed her playfully and then climbed back up the slope in search of firewood, accompanied by Rrum.

'He is a fine man,' murmured Merric.

'Yes,' smiled Mardilla, her eyes twinkling in the glow of the fire.

The company awoke late the next morning, refreshed from a good sleep. Valor, who had risen earlier than the others, had prepared some breakfast, partly helped and partly hindered by the Land Crafters' two boisterous children. The youngsters were rather shy at first, but soon resorted to chasing each other around the dell, scattering cooking utensils and leaping over piles of wood.

Gatera arrived and joined in the game. After a while he caught the children, and sent them into a nearby cave to play. Then he settled down by the ashes of the campfire as the rest of the company arrived, yawning and stretching.

'This afternoon, we must press onwards to the Black Caves,' he boomed.

'Indeed,' agreed Merric, 'but I would hear more of these caves before we venture any further. What do you know of them, Rrum? It was in one of the caves that we first met you!'

'I do nott know much,' grated the little rock man, 'though I have heardd many rumours. Itt is saidd thatt

the firstt caves were formed centuries aggo by a groupp
of Northern Rrokki, who were seeking sheltter andd a
new home. Slowly, very slowly, they ate their way intto
the hillside. Eventtually, they broke intto a maze of
natural passages. They foundd many thinggs; thinggs
of beautty and of danger. Many never retturned from
exxploring the passages. Mostt of the older Rrokki
decidded itt was nott a safe place, and leftt. They
moved south, many arriving att Rronadd. A few stayed
att the caves. Itt is saidd thatt they were joined by a
few Moor Men, but I do nott know. I have nott heard
of anyone who has seen them—andd none came to
my rescue when I was tied upp in the cave.'

Gatera nodded. 'What you have said, my little
friend, agrees well with what little I have heard. I
remember Hesteron saying that the Black Caves are
feared, and that several Air Crafters disappeared
when they explored them. He also said that there was
a rumour of a great maze of tunnels, and of a huge
central cavern with a burning floor.'

'Meltizoc spoke of "water, wind, and awesome fire",'
added Merric. 'I wonder what he meant?'

'I expect most of it is superstition!' scoffed Valor.
'And those who explored may have died because they
were careless—perhaps they fell down gaps in the
ground or something. If there was some evil creature
in there, I'm sure it would have emerged from the
caves by this time—in which case, someone would
have seen it! Otherwise, the dangers we face
are probably just natural ones that abound in
underground passages.'

'Do not take such matters too lightly,' counselled
Merric. 'Have you already forgotten how we suffered
in the tunnels beneath Dargan's stronghold?'

Valor shrugged and fell silent.

'We need to be prepared,' continued Merric. 'It is

well that we brought ropes and torches with us. Even so, we must take great care when we reach the caves. We know not what might await us.'

Two days later, the small group arrived at the Black Caves. Valor gritted his teeth as he remembered his fight with the leader of the band of Zorgs—and his own unwitting folly in taking Dargan's 'eye' and strapping it across his chest. How careless he had been—his actions had allowed the Dark Master to follow all their movements for several days.

Now the caves appeared as harmless black holes. The bodies of the Zorgs were nowhere in sight— perhaps having been dragged off by wild animals. Merric and Valor saw to the horses, then the companions walked slowly towards the caves.

'What did our wise friend say?' asked Gatera.

'He said that only the central cave leads to the maze,' replied Merric.

'Well, what are we waiting for?' said Valor. Without looking for a reply, he headed for the middle cave.

4

The Black Caves

'Valor!' Merric's voice was uncharacteristically stern. 'Wait! We must act as one. Do you not remember the barak you killed in the caves? There may be more of the creatures! If we go forward together, we will be more able to resist any attacks.'

Valor grudgingly waited for the others to join him, a slight scowl on his face. He fidgeted impatiently, anxious to be doing something rather than standing still with time to think. As soon as he thought too much, he became depressed: haunted by memories of Linnil fading slowly; of the recent taint upon Hallion; of Dargan misusing Taz-i-tor, the Golden Sceptre of Elsinoth.

His friends joined him, and they lit their torches and stepped cautiously into the central cave. Valor shivered. It felt cold and damp after the warmth of the sunshine outside.

The torchlight flickered around the chamber as the company crept towards the darkness at the back of the cave. Within moments, the walls drew in to form a wide passage. This in turn narrowed until they were walking two abreast, Valor and Merric in front, followed by Gatera and Rrum. The little Rrokki seemed unconcerned by the possible dangers of their quest, and frequently paused to investigate changes in the rock walls.

The passage eventually opened into the side of a tunnel which had much rougher walls. Peering at them, Rrum said, 'This is where the Rrokki mustt have brokken through intto the maze!'

After a brief discussion, they turned right. The tunnel roof began to slope downwards, making progress difficult. Merric and Valor had to crouch down as they walked, and Gatera was reduced to crawling. Rrum meanwhile ambled happily alongside.

Within a short distance they reached the end of the tunnel, blocked off by a huge rockfall.

'I hope this wasn't the route we were supposed to take!' muttered Valor.

Rrum examined it, and then reported, 'No. This has been here a very longg time.'

Turning around, they retraced their steps. As they did so, Valor was sure that he caught a brief glimpse of two sharp eyes, glinting in the darkness ahead. As soon as he looked at them, the eyes disappeared. He glanced at Merric.

The minstrel nodded. 'Yes, I also saw them. Have your sword ready!'

The return journey along the tunnel was even more uncomfortable, taken at a half-crouch, and holding both swords and torches. They were all relieved when the roof once more sloped upwards and they could stand erect.

Stealthily approaching the point where the tunnel was joined by the passage from the cave, they were still taken by surprise when a bristling furry body sped out of the entrance, snapping and snarling.

A barak! thought Valor, readying himself. As the vicious mountain bear raced towards him, he tried to swing his sword, but it clanged off the wall of the tunnel. In haste, he tried to jab at the creature. It was like trying to spear a fly.

The next moment, the beast careered into his legs, knocking him to the ground. He dropped his torch and sword. At the same time, he heard Merric give a shout of dismay. Then something landed on top of him, winding him. It was the troubadour! Pushing him off and struggling to his feet, Valor looked for his sword.

Meanwhile, there was a loud bellow from Gatera. A hard furry object came flying through the air, knocking Valor down again. When he finally managed to stand up, a little groggily, he could see the body of the barak lying on the passage floor.

'Sorry!' said Gatera sheepishly as Valor rubbed his head. 'Only it clawed my leg, so I picked it up and threw it as far away as possible!'

'Are you hurt?' asked Merric, who had also clambered to his feet. He had been trodden on twice by Valor.

'Just a scratch,' replied Gatera, showing some deep red gouge marks near his ankle. He seemed unconcerned about the angry wounds.

Valor cautiously examined the barak for any sign of life, but its neck was broken.

'Shall we continue?' suggested Merric.

They edged past the entrance passage and on down the tunnel. It weaved erratically onwards, but fortunately they were able to walk upright.

After several minutes, and still on the alert for further barak attacks, they reached another obstruction. Both the floor and the ceiling dipped suddenly, and a cold underground river swept across their path.

The only way onwards was to cross it—but the roof
of the cave sloped down to within a foot of the water.
They couldn't tell how deep or wide the river was.

'This must be the way!' said Valor. 'We haven't
passed any turnings.'

'Then one of us must test the river to find whether
or not it is safe to cross,' Merric replied. 'I will—'

But he was too late. Valor, putting down his
weapons, backpack and torch, was already climbing
down into the water.

'It's bitterly cold!' he shouted.

The other three watched anxiously as he moved
forward. The water reached his waist, then his chest,
then his shoulders. Keeping his head clear of the
water, he struggled on. Soon he was out of sight of
his companions. They waited anxiously as the minutes
passed. Then, with great relief, they greeted him with
a cheer as he re-emerged.

'It's safe!' he gasped. 'You won't need to swim—
you can just keep your head above water all the way
across. Gatera will have to bend a little, and Rrum
may need some help, but we should all manage it.' He
waded back up the bank and collected his belongings.
'Anything that might be spoilt by the water can be
rolled up in our leather blankets and held above our
heads,' he suggested. 'If I go ahead of you, I'll re-
light my torch when I reach the other side. The glow
should guide you safely through the river.'

He doused his torch and, taking his blanket from
his backpack, rolled it around his sword, provisions,
torch and rope.

The others followed suit, Merric reluctantly leaving
his lute propped against the cave wall, as he didn't
want to risk damaging it in the water. The troubadour
waited until Valor had time to reach the other side,
then doused his torch—Gatera and Rrum had already

wrapped theirs in a blanket. The river gleamed with the golden reflections from Valor's torch.

Merric stepped in first, bracing himself against the chilly waters. Gatera followed; he had offered to carry Rrum to the other side, but the rock man had declined.

'I will gett across,' he said.

Gatera knew better than to argue with the stubborn rock man, so he waded after Merric, bending low to avoid the roof of the passage. Even so, he still banged the back of his head as he tried to keep his mouth above the water.

Soon he was sitting on the opposite bank beside Merric and Valor, waiting for Rrum to appear. There was no sign of him.

After several anxious minutes, the Land Crafter muttered, 'I'm going back!' Taking a torch, he eased his way back into the river, again stooping as the roof lowered. When he reached the other side, he lit the torch. Rrum was nowhere in sight.

Casting caution aside, the big Land Crafter bellowed, 'RRUM! Where are you?' The echoes rolled away down the tunnel, but there was no reply. Gatera shook his head. He was completely baffled by the Rrokki's sudden disappearance.

There was a splashing noise behind him, and Merric struggled out of the river to join him. 'I heard your cry,' he said. 'Where can he be? Surely he has not left us again, as he did when we were near the Land of Dreams?'

'No,' replied Gatera slowly. 'He would have said something. There's no reason for him to go so suddenly and mysteriously. Either he's been captured or—'

'Or he has been swept away by the river,' finished Merric. 'There is a strong undertow, and although he is sturdy, he is also small.'

'Aye,' agreed Gatera. He stamped his foot in anger, and the vibrations rumbled along the tunnel floor. 'I can't even go in search of him—I don't know where to look!'

Then he gritted his teeth with determination and muttered, 'I can at least search the river!' Plunging back into the cold water, he waded halfway across and then turned downstream. The river disappeared into a hole in the side wall. Taking a deep breath, Gatera submerged himself and crawled forward to investigate. He could see little, so groped around himself as he moved forwards, but found no sign of Rrum. After a few yards, he knew he would have to turn back before he ran out of breath.

However, the tug of the water was stronger than he had realised. It took all his strength to make progress, and his lungs were bursting by the time he broke back into the tunnel. With a huge gasp, his head burst out of the water, almost hitting the rock ceiling, and he took several big gulps of air. Then he waded back to the bank to join Merric, who looked at him questioningly.

'No sign,' Gatera said gruffly. 'If he was swept away, he'd never make it back again—the current's too strong. I only just managed to struggle back myself.'

Merric nodded, then voiced the fear that Gatera had left unspoken. 'Then if he has not been captured, he must surely have drowned.'

The huge Land Crafter hung his head and nodded wearily.

'Come,' said Merric, 'we must rejoin Valor. I fear we can do no more for Rrum. We have no choice but to complete our task.'

Silently, Gatera followed as the troubadour plunged once more into the river.

5

The Cavern of Winds

Valor was waiting patiently at the other side of the river. When told the news about Rrum, he had to be restrained from diving into the water in search of the Rrokki.

'If I had trouble fighting the current, you would have no chance,' warned Gatera.

The three disconsolate friends took one last look at the river—hoping that the little rock man might suddenly appear—then turned and started on the next stage of the journey along the tunnel.

The air was still surprisingly fresh. At times there almost seemed to be hints of a breeze. They passed several side passages but decided to keep to the main route. Slowly the tunnel began to narrow, and from ahead they could hear a faint moaning sound. Drawing their swords, they advanced cautiously. The moaning became louder: it was long and drawn out; a lonely, desolate wail. The breeze that they had only sensed before now came swirling along the passageway.

Creeping around a corner, the three friends saw a

strange sight. The tunnel led into a large cave which
was broken up into a honeycomb of natural arches.
A pale yellow light throbbed within the rock of the
arches. As they edged their way forwards, the trio
realised the source of the wailing—a strong wind
weaved its way through the chamber, fluctuating in
step with the pulsating glow.

'Meltizoc's rhyme spoke of passing "through the
wind"!' shouted Merric. 'I think we must strive to
reach the other side of the cave—we must head for the
source of the wind!'

Stepping out into the cave, the friends passed
through two or three of the strange arches without
any difficulty. However, the wind was becoming
stronger with every step, and soon they were fighting
to stay on their feet. As they struggled forwards, the
howling of the wind also increased. They were unable
to cover their ears against the chilling noise, as they
needed their hands to steady themselves. The wailing
became almost unbearable.

The arches they passed through seemed to be
formed from thick stalagmites and stalactites that had
fused together. Battered by the gusts, his jerkin
flapping wildly, Merric joined Gatera and Valor in the
partial shelter behind one of the columns. Being
lighter than either of his friends, he found it more
difficult to stay on his feet. However, all three were
sweating freely from their exertions. Their torches
had been blown out at an early stage, and they took
the opportunity to strap them to their backpacks,
freeing their hands. The glowing columns enabled
them to see sufficiently and also offered a little respite
from the draught, but Merric knew they would have
to proceed as soon as they had gathered their strength.
They had not come this far to be defeated by a heavy
wind!

The minstrel wished that Hesteron was with them. Perhaps the Air Crafter would know an easy way to tackle the wind, or even divert its fury away from them. As it was, they would just have to battle forward in the hope that it didn't get any stronger. It was difficult to concentrate their efforts, though, when the incessant wailing noise kept piercing every thought. It caused a persistent pain in his head.

Merric jumped as he felt a touch on his arm. It was Gatera. The Land Crafter made several gestures with his hands, which at first Merric couldn't understand. Then he realised that Gatera was offering to go in front, shielding the other two from the worst buffeting of the wind. It was impossible to argue, as his voice wouldn't be heard above the loud moaning sounds, so the minstrel nodded in agreement.

Moving out from the shelter of the column, Gatera swayed slightly before steadying himself against the harsh gusts. Merric and Valor stepped behind him, keeping close to his broad back. They were able to help him by pushing from behind as he made his way slowly forward.

However, the wind hadn't finished with them yet. As they eased their way between more columns, it suddenly changed direction, clutching at them with rough hands and tumbling them towards a different arch. They fell and rolled, struggled to their feet, fell again.

As he was about to get up again, Merric felt Gatera's restraining hand on his shoulder. The Land Crafter pointed urgently behind them. Just beyond the nearest arch was a wide gaping hole, its black mouth greedily awaiting new prey. Valor was already rising however and, plucked from his feet once more, stumbled and was blown through the arch. Clutching wildly for support, he managed to grasp one of its pillars. The deep void was only inches from his feet. A cold breath of anticipation seemed to come from the blackness.

Gatera crawled slowly back to the arch and grabbed the young Mountain Guard's arm. Slowly, his muscles straining, he dragged Valor away from the lip of the chasm. As they rejoined Merric, Valor smiled weakly, and signalled that he was unhurt.

The three lay flat on the cold floor for a while, recovering their strength. The force of the wind was reduced at this level: it was only when they tried to stand that they encountered its full strength. Motioning to the others, Gatera began to crawl his way forward, keeping as close to the ground as possible. Merric and Valor followed suit, worming their way from arch to arch.

It was a slow, painful and uncomfortable process. Occasionally they had to stop to cover their ears to get some relief from the never-ending howling.

Raising his head, Merric could see that they had nearly reached a large arch, beyond which was a dark tunnel. That must be the way out! He nudged the other two and pointed. Nodding, they redoubled their efforts. Mercifully the howling had begun to lessen.

Any relief they felt was short-lived. As they neared the arch, a cold blast swept into their faces, raising swirls of dust that made them choke. The wind swept round them, over them, seeking to turn and push them away.

Gatera turned round and shouted something to Merric. The minstrel struggled to hear the words before they were snatched away.

'Grab . . . belt!' The Land Crafter was pointing urgently to the thick leather belt around his waist. The minstrel nodded, and strained forward to grasp it. He could see Valor struggling to the other side of the

Land Crafter. Then, with a great heave, Gatera hoisted himself forward. Merric and Valor half-crawled and were half-dragged alongside, hanging desperately on to the belt to prevent the wind from sending them spinning across the floor.

Inch by inch, they clawed their way to the arch. With a final lurch, Gatera pulled himself through, heaving the other two after him.

The three lay on the floor, panting heavily. Then they looked at each other with amazement as a new truth dawned. There was no wind here beyond the arch—the air was perfectly still. Yet they could hear it blowing in the cavern; could still hear its distant moans.

'I . . . I don't understand . . . ' gasped Valor. 'Where does the wind come from? I thought it was blowing from this passage, yet there's not the slightest breeze . . . .' He stopped and shook his head in bewilderment.

'Aye, it's a mystery,' acknowledged Gatera. 'But I for one am thankful that we don't have to crawl any more!' He levered himself slowly into a sitting position, and dusted himself down.

Merric rose wearily to his feet. 'It seems unlikely that this is the last difficulty we shall encounter. Meltizoc also mentioned fire.'

'And Hesteron spoke of burning lakes,' added Valor. 'But we knew that it wouldn't be easy. We have at least survived the winds, so we must stand a chance of finding the Globe.'

'Aye. A better one than Rrum,' muttered Gatera. 'I only wish he had survived the water!'

'None of us can know our destiny,' Merric said quietly. 'We can only strive to follow the right paths. Are we ready to continue?'

'Lead on, my musical friend, lead on.'

They retrieved the torches from their backpacks

and lit them. The flames burned steadily, with barely a flicker. Satisfied, Merric led them into the tunnel. The passageway was wide at first, so they walked side by side, each engrossed in his own thoughts.

After a while the tunnel began to slope downwards. It curved gradually to the left, and they travelled cautiously forward down the long spiral: around any bend they could bump into an adversary or some other kind of danger. Gradually the air in the passage was losing its freshness. It was becoming dry and slightly stuffy. As they wandered forward, they realised that the whole corridor was beginning to warm slightly. The strange yellow glow they had seen in the cavern of winds began to pulsate from somewhere deep within the rocky walls. At the same time, they could hear new noises in the distance: sucking, gurgling sounds; both ominous and intriguing.

Moving onwards, they could sense the warmth on their faces now. The tunnel straightened out, and some way ahead they could see a flickering orange glow, complementing the throbbing yellow in the rock walls.

They worked their way slowly towards the glow, avoiding the walls of the passage, which had grown steadily warmer. When they reached the end, a curious sight met their eyes.

They were standing on a small platform at the edge of a huge cavern. Two other openings, one on either side of their tunnel, also led on to the platform. In front of them was a sea of bubbling lava, glowing orange, and slurping noisily. Dotted throughout it, like lumps of bread in a hot bubbling soup, were large rocks. At least, Merric thought they looked like rocks, though he realised they may have been what was left of the original cavern floor.

'Stepping stones!' grunted Gatera.

'Sorry?' said Valor.

'These rocks—they're obviously meant to be stepping stones over to the other side. If we are to get any further, we must cross this lake.'

'Are you sure we can't just go down one of these other tunnels?' asked Valor hopefully.

'I'm sure. They must just be other passages leading here.'

'We should rest before going any further,' suggested Merric. He pulled a flask of water from his backpack and offered them both a drink. Valor swallowed thirstily and then handed it to Gatera.

'It won't be easy to reach the other side,' said the Land Crafter, wiping his lips and returning the flask to Merric. 'One slip could mean the end. We must—'

He was interrupted by a warning hiss from Merric. A large, mysterious shadow was emerging from the mouth of one of the other tunnels. There was no time to flee. Drawing their swords, they stood side by side and awaited this new menace.

6

A Visit from Dargan

Dusk had snatched the last rays of light from the sky above the Fortress of Fear. Most of the occupants were inside, either making their preparations for sleep or already clutched tightly in its strong embrace.

Along the battlements, lonely figures paced backwards and forwards, keeping a weary vigil. There were some sixty men and elves on guard, but they were thinly spread around the perimeter of the vast, sprawling fortress. Some grumbled about their duties: even if enemies were waiting on the plains outside, only the keener-eyed elves would have been able to detect them in the thick gloom.

High up above, out of sight in the blackness of the skies, Dargan cackled to himself. He could see the guards, many of them being picked out by lights from within the fortress. This was going to be easier than he had expected! He selected the most suitable target—an elven archer whose patrol had taken him some distance from his nearest fellow guard. Pointing the figure out to Targul, the Dark Master gasped momentarily as the creature started its swift, silent descent.

Down on the battlements, Dargan's target, a young elf called Silrin, sensed rather than heard the Tark's approach. Some inner instinct made him look upwards as an ominous shape dived rapidly towards him.

To his credit, Silrin didn't panic, but had time to cry out, 'Tark!' Then, before he could fit an arrow to his bow, the creature swooped down, sending him sprawling. As he struggled to regain his feet, he saw the Tark land awkwardly on the narrow walkway.

Fear and revulsion surged up through the elf's heart: his own cousin, Sildar, had been horribly killed by one of these creatures recently. Quickly fixing an arrow to his bow, the young elf took aim and fired. The arrow glanced off the creature's leathery hide.

It was only then that Silrin realised the other threat: a dark-cloaked man had slid from the back of the Tark and now walked menacingly towards him. Even as the elf reached for another arrow, he saw the cold white of the man's pupils, and found that he couldn't look away. Captured by the gaze, he felt himself sinking. He tried to struggle but failed. Everything around him became a blurred and milky haze. The arrow slipped from his numb fingers, and he crumpled into a heap in front of the approaching figure.

Dargan chuckled, then sighed. He would have to hurry—he could already hear running footsteps, no doubt drawn by the wretched elf's cries. Bending down and grabbing Silrin's wrists, he hoisted him over his shoulder and struggled back to the waiting Tark.

'Stop!' a voice cried. A man in Hallion garb rushed towards him, sword drawn. The Dark Master wheeled, and the man, just feet away now, jerked as he felt the full force of Dargan's will. It was as if he had run

headlong into a wall, and he groaned, stumbled, and
fell.

Dargan gave a grunt of satisfaction, and lowered
Silrin to the ground as he reached Targul. The elf
would make an ideal subject for his further experiments! Unfortunately, the Tark had needed to feed
off the intruder they had encountered at Hallion, to
replenish its energy. Now it was strong, however, and
Dargan could use this new elf for his own purposes.

He noticed the bright green glint in the Tark's eyes
when it looked at the elf—but he was easily able to
control the creature; besides which, it would be
allowed to feast on their prisoner once Dargan had
finished with him. Tossing the elf across Targul's back,
he started to climb up after him.

Other shouts came from the battlements—more
guards were beginning to arrive. At the same time, a fat,
wheezing figure started puffing up some nearby steps.

In commanding tones, Dargan gave the Tark its
instructions. It flapped lazily downwards from the
battlements, knocking the portly figure from the steps
before rising up high and fading once more into the
blackness of the night.

A few days later, Kess sat at the side of Linnil's bed,
gazing at his sister's pallid face. Her eyes stared back
at him, unseeing, her thoughts locked away in a world
that he couldn't reach. Holding her hand, he looked
at it with concern. She was still fading. For some
reason, the process had slowed since she had been
given the liquid from the phial in Whisper's chest, but
it hadn't halted completely. Her flesh had a hint of
translucency: he could almost imagine that he could
see the bones within her hand.

'Hold on,' he urged her. 'The others may be able
to find the Globe—don't give up hope!'

Linnil stirred a little, but gave no answer. She spoke little these days, unless someone mentioned Dargan's name, when she would automatically begin to recite her feelings of 'love' for the Dark Master.

Looking down at her, Kess shook his head. 'Sometimes I wish we had never left the peace of our Valley,' he said quietly. 'We were safe there. No one bothered us and we could do as we pleased. Now where are we? In a cold fortress on the borders of a strange land, and in the middle of a fight that we seem to be losing! And where is Elsinoth in all this? Why doesn't he do something to help us?'

'You have to help yourself if you want to get anywhere!' said a soft voice behind him. 'Only weaklings trust in others!'

Kess jerked round to see Whisper standing behind him. He coloured slightly, and then replied, 'You didn't say that when you needed my help to get out of the Whistling Waters—or to find the chest!'

This time it was Whisper's turn to flush.

Two other voices came floating along the corridor and seconds later Hesteron and Vallel arrived. 'Good meeting!' they said in unison as they walked through the door.

'Good meeting,' muttered Kess. Whisper stayed silent.

'How is Linnil this morning?' asked Vallel, a worried frown creasing her smooth complexion.

'The same.' Kess shook his head and sighed. 'I hope the others return soon; she grows a little weaker each day, a little more withdrawn from reality.'

'They will return as swiftly as they can,' Hesteron reassured him.

Kess sighed again but nodded. 'What news of Meltizoc?'

'He's still unconscious. Tolledon thinks that when

the Tark knocked him off the steps, he must have struck his head badly on the ground.'

'Will he recover?' asked Whisper. Despite the wise man's suspicions of her, she had grown quite fond of him.

'We don't know,' Hesteron replied. 'The healers who are tending him still seem very concerned.'

'But he can't die!' blurted out Kess. 'We need his wisdom now more than ever! He's the only one who is able to translate the Tome of Neldra!'

Hesteron nodded his agreement. 'It would be a sad loss—he is a good friend. But don't lose hope yet! He may be old, but he also has a great inner strength which may see him through.'

Vallel squeezed his hand, and gave a smile of encouragement to Kess.

'Meanwhile,' Hesteron continued, 'Tolledon has doubled the guard on the walls, and issued more of the double-strength arrows we used against the Tarks in the battle for the fortress.'

'It's a little late for that!' Kess grumbled.

'Perhaps we have all been guilty of underestimating the power of our enemy. At least we can learn from our mistakes! If the Dark Master calls again, he will find us better prepared!'

'Always too late!' muttered Kess again. 'It's too late for Linnil, and too late for Meltizoc.'

'Yet they are both alive!' Vallel reminded him.

'You call this living?' hissed Kess, pointing at Linnil. 'Look at her! Sometimes I think she might be better off dead! At least she would be at peace! Why doesn't Elsinoth do something? Why do we always have to wait?'

Hesteron shrugged his shoulders. 'Perhaps he is at work even now—we just don't know it yet.'

'I don't think I know anything any more,' said Kess.

'All I do know is that my sister is dying, and there is nothing I can do about it, except to pray that she recovers.'

'Perhaps that is the greatest thing that any of us can do,' suggested Hesteron.

Gur'brak sat on the edge of his bed and scowled. He was tired of being cooped up in this cell in the heart of the fortress—although it was considerably more comfortable than the first one that he and Bar'drash had been given. Tolledon had kept his word when he had promised to help them if they told him what they knew about Dargan. Although the information Gur'brak had given him wasn't any help to the Guardian, he had still made sure that they were rewarded. They had been moved to a larger room which had two chairs, a table, two reasonably comfortable beds, a window overlooking the courtyard, and a shelf full of books.

The books were of little interest to the two Zorgs, as neither of them could read very well. However, they had both been pleased with the extra space—even though the room was still a prison cell, with a guard stationed outside the door.

Gur'brak couldn't understand the treatment they'd been given. He'd expected at least some rough handling; followed probably by various methods of hideous torture, leading eventually to their death. Instead, they had been fed well, and treated politely most of the time—except when they had tried to escape! He just couldn't figure it out.

The thickset Zorg had had plenty of time to think—especially as his companion spent most of the day and night asleep, sometimes accompanied by loud snores. Gur'brak was coming to the conclusion that these humans and elves weren't perhaps the vicious enemies he'd always believed them to be. He'd never really stopped to think about such things before—he'd had his orders, and had obeyed them unquestioningly— well, most of the time.

Now, having little else to do, he started thinking more about why he had always been a fighter. Perhaps there was nothing else he could do. Occasionally, though, he had thought that there must be other things in life besides orders and battles and more orders. Now he was beginning to envy the easy-going and cheerful manner of his captors. Several times he'd heard the names 'Elsinoth' and 'Toroth' mentioned, and that disturbed him even more. What if he'd been fighting for the wrong side all this time? What if this Elsinoth really did exist, and what if he was even stronger than Dargan? No doubt he'd soon get his revenge on the Zorgs for helping the Dark Master!

He looked over at Bar'drash, who was just rising from his bed, yawning noisily and scratching the scar that ran across his face.

'Nice to see you're awake!' said Gur'brak sarcastically.

Bar'drash just yawned again and rubbed his empty eye socket.

'You look about as lively as a dead toad!' grumbled Gur'brak.

'Well, there ain't exactly a lot to do around 'ere, is there?' said Bar'drash. 'Unless, of course, you've thought of another escape plan!' His eye glinted as he looked hopefully at Gur'brak.

'Naw. Besides which, why bother at the moment? We get good food, and we don't have to risk our necks fighting for Dargan!'

'Aw, c'mon boss—you said yourself that you didn't fancy staying 'ere for ever! We're still locked up, remember! Isn't there anything we can do?'

'Perhaps I should just ask them nicely if they'll let us go!' muttered Gur'brak.

'Yeah ...' said Bar'drash, grinning for a moment. 'Aw, no, it wouldn't work, boss!'

'You don't say!' replied Gur'brak. 'Well, if you haven't got any better suggestions, perhaps you'd better go back to sleep!'

Bar'drash shrugged, stretched himself once, then sank back on to his bed and was soon snoring once more.

Now what? thought Gur'brak. *If I'm cooped up in this cell for much longer with this idiot, I think I'll go completely mad!*

He scowled again, and lay back on his own bed. Perhaps Bar'drash had the right idea after all . . . .

7

Alone in the Caves

Rrum was surprised to find himself being bowled along by a strong current. As he was crossing the underground river, he had tripped over an unexpected rock at the point where the river's flow was at its strongest. Before he could regain his feet, he had been swept away. At first he tried to struggle against the current, but to no avail. Eventually he allowed himself to be carried along.

He was concerned about his friends, and hoped that they wouldn't try to follow him. None of them probably realised that as a Rrokki he could breathe underwater—though with some discomfort—for quite long periods of time.

After a while, the current eased. Feeling a little bruised and battered, Rrum half swam, half tumbled along. A dim light was filtering down through the water. Perhaps he had been swept outside! If so, he would soon be able to find his way back into the Black Caves and rejoin his friends.

One bank of the river was now becoming less steep, and the little Rrokki struggled towards it. Soon his head was above water, and a moment later he was scrambling out on to the bank.

As he squatted and regained his breath, he realised with some disappointment that he hadn't reached the open air after all. Instead, he was in a small cave. The light seemed to come from a blue fungus growing on the walls.

Standing up and shaking himself, Rrum grimaced. It seemed as if he was well and truly lost! Well, the only way he was going to get out of here was by walking. Waddling slowly across the cave, he noticed a passage at its far end. He hoped this wasn't going to lead to another dead end!

The passage was more dimly lit than the cave, as there were fewer patches of the fungus; but there was still enough light to enable him to see where he was going. He passed one or two dark holes in the wall, which may have been other tunnels, but as there was no light in them, he hurried on by. Once, going past one particularly large opening, he felt a strange cold sensation running down his back—as if something evil lurked there in the darkness.

On he trudged, the passageway twisting and turning before him. Once or twice he imagined he was being followed, but when he looked back he could see nothing. Rrum was used to travelling alone, but he would be glad when he could find his way out of this tunnel. On and on it went, never in the same direction for more than twenty yards. At one point he wondered if he'd turned around without realising it, and was heading back for the river.

At least there was a plentiful supply of food at hand. The loose rocks that were scattered over the floor of the passage tasted old and stale, but they gave him enough energy to carry on with his journey.

After some time, he sat down on the floor of the

passage to rest. He was just beginning to doze when again his senses alerted him to something menacing nearby. Opening his eyes, he peered back down the corridor. There was nothing in sight—but the nearest corner, some fifteen yards away, seemed to be growing ominously dark.

Rrum scrambled to his feet. There was very little that frightened him, but this had set his nerves jangling. If there was something nasty following him, he would prefer to be able to see it!

As he hurried away down the tunnel, the feeling of danger gradually passed. Up ahead he could see a brighter light reflecting off the passage walls. Picking up speed, he rounded the next corner to find himself at the entrance to a wonderful new cavern.

A dazzling display met his eyes. Great rocks of all shapes and sizes jutted out from the floor of the cavern. Hanging from the centre of the cave was a single, enormous stalactite, from which shone a bright white light. Embedded in the rocks throughout the chamber were thousands of tiny gemstones, which reflected the white light in sparkles of different hues. The whole cave glowed with vibrant colour, as if a rainbow had been broken up into millions of tiny fragments which had been scattered all over the rocks.

The little Rrokki gazed in wonder. Softly, he padded forward, looking first at one rock, then another. Everywhere he gazed there were reds and blues, yellows and greens, purples and oranges, golds and silvers. It was entrancing, almost hypnotic. He wandered slowly, almost as if in a dream, to the central stalactite.

It was smooth, and the purest white he had ever seen; like a single long tooth hanging from the roof of the cave. Despite the brightness of the light, he was able to look at it without hurting his eyes. The tip of the stalactite ended just above his head. Reaching up, he touched it gently. It was warm, and seemed to hum with light.

Reluctantly, Rrum forced himself to keep walking. Passing between two boulders, he found himself at the edge of a small pool. Encircled by the rocks, it too shone and glistened in myriad colours. The little Rrokki knelt and touched the surface of the water. A multi-coloured ripple spread away into the centre of the pool. The reflections of the rocks formed dazzling patterns which grew, then dissolved, then grew again—the shapes and tints changing as the ripple spread outward. He watched for minutes—perhaps even hours—entranced by the beauty before his eyes. He drank it in, letting the images soak through the whole of his being, revitalising him.

As he watched the rainbow colours, he felt as if Elsinoth himself was at work inside him; comforting and strengthening him for the journey ahead. Smiling, he turned and looked once more at the steady white glow of the stalactite. It was surrounded by a halo of bright colours. Rrum felt a new emotion stirring inside his heart: hope.

Eventually, with a deep sigh, he stood up. He worked his way slowly past the pool and continued towards an opening in the wall of the cave beyond. It seemed to be the only other exit from this sanctuary of peace and beauty. He stopped and took one last look at the radiant colours of the cavern. Then reluctantly, he turned and stepped into the passage.

The dim blue light of the tunnel looked weak and unfriendly after the splendour of the cave. Nevertheless, Rrum knew he would have to go that way. He knew also that the memory of the rainbow cave would stay with him for ever. For almost the first time in his life, he grunted a short prayer of thanks to Elsinoth before trundling into the passageway.

The new tunnel was straighter than the previous one and Rrum was able to make rapid progress, moving in a combination of somersaults and a fast, rolling gait. From time to time, he again encountered side passages leading off from the main tunnel, but none of these was lit by the curious fungus. The little rock man couldn't understand why it should be confined to the walls of this one passage, but he sped along, hoping to meet a tunnel that would somehow lead him back to his friends.

The floor of the passage began to slope downwards, at first gradually and then, with surprising suddenness, dipping down into darkness. Rrum was unable to slow down in time, and found himself tumbling, slipping and sliding down the long rocky slope.

When he reached the bottom, he groaned and picked himself up. After the battering he had received from the river, followed by this long fall, he felt as if he was one large bruise. Then he groaned again. There was no blue light down here—the fungus had stopped somewhere near the top of the slope.

For a moment, he considered turning back, but it was too long a journey—and he had seen no signs of a better route. Dusting himself off, he headed cautiously into the darkness of the tunnel.

Fortunately, he hadn't gone far when he noticed some light filtering into the passageway some distance ahead. He quickened his pace, and soon found himself inside another cave. This was smaller than the previous one, perhaps some twenty yards across. Out of one wall a great gush of water tumbled, feeding an underground river. He wondered if it was a continuation of the one which had swept him off his feet. Perhaps if he had stayed in the river, he could have reached this cave with little effort—though still with much bruising! Grimacing from the aches running through his body, he decided he was glad he hadn't— otherwise he would never have experienced the delights of the rainbow cavern.

The roof of the cave was a long, long way above him. In one section was a deep crack that disappeared upwards. It was through this cleft that some light filtered its way down from above. Rrum wished he could fly—up there was the open air; the countryside; the hills.

Strolling across the cave, he looked for any signs of an exit. There were none. He couldn't understand it—why should a passageway lead all this distance, just to end in a cave? Perhaps he had missed another turn near the top of the slope.

He was about to venture back to the entrance passage when something made him stop. Again that chill, strange fear swept over him. Whatever it was that was following him had found him at last—trapped in a closed cave!

Rrum sensed it coming closer; sensed a blackness filling the tunnel. Then, his nerves tingling, he saw it for the first time—a monstrous shape that lumbered silently forward on two huge misshapen legs. A cave-warg! It was like something out of his darkest nightmares. Childhood memories flooded back; his parents warning him that if he misbehaved, a cave-warg would come and take him away and gobble him up. He knew most of the stories were a mixture of legend and superstition; he had never really thought that such creatures might actually exist!

The cave-warg stopped for a moment. Rrum could sense its age; could sense, too, an ancient evil at work. A finger of cold fear again ran up and down his back. The creature's dark red eyes glinted with malice. The lower part of its face was completely taken up by a massive, protruding jaw that drooled at the sight of its prey.

Rrum stood, frozen, for a moment. Then, as the thing began to move forward, he backed away. The cave-warg followed. Rrum's sturdy Rrokki courage was waning in the face of such an opponent. He knew he couldn't hope to win any battle against the creature. It trudged closer and closer . . . .

Suddenly, he realised that there was only one possible means of escape. Turning, he somersaulted across the cave; then, without even pausing to look back, dived into the cold waters of the river.

Again he found himself being swept along by the current. This time, however, he welcomed its embrace. The swirling waters curled around him, tumbling him along playfully. Closing his eyes, he allowed himself to be carried along.

After some time, the current subsided, and the river widened out. Again Rrum was able to pick himself up and trudge slowly to the side. He found a little ledge running along above the river, and heaved himself up on to it. Carefully, he scrambled along in the dark, not sure where he was going, but relieved to have escaped the clutches of the cave-warg.

He had crawled along for a few minutes when the ledge widened, and he sensed a draught against his side. Feeling around in the dark, he could tell that it was an opening of some kind. He crawled into it, inching his way forward, hoping that it would lead somewhere. It did. After a few minutes, he was delighted to see a yellow glow ahead. Standing up, he started trotting towards it, and soon came out into another wide passage. At first he was unsure which way to go, but the light seemed to fade in one direction, so he headed the other way.

As he moved forward, he saw a deeper glow ahead. At the same time he heard some strange, menacing noises. He stopped for a moment, wondering whether to proceed or turn around. The memory of the cave-warg was still fresh in his mind, but his courage had returned. He decided to creep forward and investigate this new threat. Trying to be as quiet as possible, he eased his way forward to the end of the passage.

8

Of Fire and Flames

Gatera waited, staff in hand, as the towering shadow crept towards them. Raising the staff above his head, he prepared to deliver a mighty blow. The next moment, he was leaping up and down, nearly knocking Valor over.

'Rrum, you little rascal! Where in the Realm did you come from?' He grabbed hold of the little Rrokki and lifted him off the ground.

'Oww!' grunted Rrum.

'Sorry, my friend—are you hurt?' Gatera asked as he gently lowered him to the ground.

'Justt a litttle,' replied Rrum. He briefly explained his adventures, his eyes glowing as he described the rainbow cavern.

When he had finished, Valor said, 'Now what do we do?'

'Now we try to cross this burning lake!' rumbled Gatera. 'As I was about to say before our friend arrived, it could be very dangerous. I think I had better go first.'

'You?' queried Valor indignantly. 'Why? You're

the heaviest of us all! Surely if the rocks aren't safe—'

'Then I will be able to avoid them in time,' interrupted Gatera. 'You seem to forget that I'm a Land Crafter! I should be able to sense any danger and react more quickly than any of you. I also have a longer stride, so it will be less trouble to reach the next stone.'

So saying, he grasped his stout wooden staff in one hand, and leaned over the edge of the platform. Tapping the end of the staff against the first stone, he rested it there for a moment, and then gave a grunt of satisfaction. The next moment, he stepped across the bubbling lava to the stone. It wasn't very large, and his big, bare feet made it seem even smaller.

'The rock is cold, despite all the heat from the lava!' he called. Several other stones were within reach of the first one. Reaching forward again, he tapped one of them. This time, he gave a grunt of disapproval. He tried another and nodded. Before he moved on, he reached awkwardly into his backpack. Producing a lump of limestone, he made a mark on the rock on which he was standing. Then, stepping across to the new stone, he also made a mark on this.

It was a slow process, but he eventually picked his way forward through the maze of stones until he reached the other side. His friends had a clear trail to follow. Then, to their surprise, he strode back towards them.

'What are you doing?' called Valor. 'Why didn't you wait for us?'

'I think this is one place where my little friend will definitely need some help!' replied Gatera as he reached the platform. 'I don't intend to lose him again!' Picking up Rrum, who gave an uncertain and toothy grin, he held him awkwardly under one

arm and once more started back across the fiery
lake.

Merric and Valor looked at each other and shrugged. 'I believe it is now our turn!' the minstrel said.
'We must cross with care!'

Valor nodded, and leaped over to the first stone.
Some of the rocks were easy to reach, but others
required a rather longer jump, with little room for
error. On one such leap, Valor found himself
overbalancing as he landed. His arms flailed wildly as
he fought to stay upright. Then one of his knees
buckled, and he fell. Fortunately, the rock was one of
the larger ones. Even so, his head was within inches
of the bubbling red lava, and the scorching heat made
him jerk his face away.

Gatera, a few steps ahead, called back in concern.
The embarrassed Mountain Guard waved and,
scrambling back to his feet, continued his journey.
The light-footed Merric followed him with little
difficulty.

Although the rocks were cold, all the friends were
very hot by the time they reached the safety of the
other platform. The steaming lava had taken its toll,
and they felt uncomfortable and weary.

'Little wonder that no one has returned to tell of
anything beyond the burning lake!' said Merric.
'Without your skill, Gatera, we are unlikely to have
crossed it safely!'

The Land Crafter chuckled. 'I'm glad that my
crafting has finally proved useful! I was beginning to
think I was nothing but a large and rather useless
burden!'

'You have never been a burden, my friend,' Merric
replied, a grateful twinkle in his eyes.

Looking around, there only appeared to be one exit
from this new platform—a narrow opening, lit by the

glow from the burning lake. Having recovered some of their strength, they passed gratefully into the tunnel, eager to leave the heat of the cavern behind them. However, the temperature seemed to change little as they moved forward: the air in the passageway was still very warm, although drier than it had been in the large cave.

Unexpectedly, they came to some crudely cut stone steps. The companions began to descend, not knowing what to expect. However, their next challenge was not from any physical danger: it came from the effects of the steps upon their minds. Although they could see that the steps spiralled downwards, they began to feel as if they were climbing, and were soon panting from their exertions.

Gatera stopped and mopped his brow. 'This is no use!' he growled. 'These steps are making me dizzy!'

The others nodded in agreement.

'Did not Meltizoc's rhyme speak of going "down the steps that seem to take you higher"?' asked Merric.

'Aye.'

'Then we must trust his words! Although it may seem as though we climb, in truth we are descending. We must believe that!'

'Yes!' agreed Valor. 'Concentrate your thoughts on the steps everyone! Force your minds to recognise that we're going downwards!'

The others nodded again, and then started walking down the steps, proceeding slowly and uncomfortably. With great relief, they soon reached the bottom.

The tunnel stretched out before them. After a brief rest, they continued in single file, Valor in the lead and Gatera at the rear. Gradually a new glow—a richer, deeper red—lit the tunnel walls from a source some distance ahead.

They slowed as they approached the red glow. Each

of them sensed danger. Valor drew his sword, and Gatera fingered his double-headed axe, ready to wield it at the first sign of any attack.

As they emerged from the tunnel, they found themselves in a small, circular cavern. In the centre was a pool of crimson fire, the flames licking hungrily upwards. The friends stood around it, spellbound. There was something curious about the fire; something strangely hypnotic about the dark red flames, occasionally shot through with streaks of pink.

As he watched, Gatera felt a tingling sensation on the back of his neck. Turning, he almost swung his axe as he noticed a large, dark, threatening shape behind him. Then he laughed to himself—it was just his shadow, looming over him from the cavern wall. He was about to turn back when he noticed something strange about it. The dark head-shape of the shadow began to peel itself away from the wall, followed by the shoulders . . .

'Look out!' he warned the others as he watched in astonishment. Their shadows, too, were detaching themselves from the walls of the cave. As they prised free, he could see that their outlines were fringed by tiny, flickering flames. Gatera sidestepped, but his fire-shadow followed his movements. The Land Crafter felt another tingle, and could only gaze, wide-eyed, as the legs of his shadow pulled free of the floor, and its feet detached themselves from his own feet.

Valor, nearby, tried to stab his own fire-shadow, but his sword passed straight through it, glowing a sombre red for a moment. At exactly the same time a flickering arm grabbed momentarily at him and then withdrew. Merric meanwhile was trying to leap away from his shadow, while Rrum stood still, apparently entranced by the event.

Gatera, with a roar of frustration, again stepped to

one side. His fire-shadow echoed his movements. This time, the giant Land Crafter swept his axe downwards through the shadow. The axe sizzled, leaving behind a trail of crimson, and a bright flame licked along the blade and part way down the wooden handle. At the same time, Gatera felt a hot finger run across the front of his tunic. When he withdrew the axe, the handle was still smouldering slightly. 'Let's get out of here!' he bellowed.

A few yards away, Merric began to run back towards the entrance of the cave. His fire-shadow followed him and blocked his way.

Valor decided to try the other exit from the cave. This time, his shadow accompanied him, but made no attempt to stop him.

Gatera and Rrum meanwhile had followed Merric. Three fire-shadows—one huge, one medium, and one small and round—now guarded the entrance to the cave.

'Let us see what happens if I try to walk through them!' Gatera muttered. He strolled purposefully towards the entrance, but his fire-shadow stood resolutely in the way. Head down, the Land Crafter kept moving forward. The next moment he felt a searing heat, and staggered back again. Little flames leapt from his hessian doublet, and he hastily patted them out with his huge hands. The smell of his own scorched hair filled his nostrils. There was no way through!

'Valor has found a way!' called Merric, pointing to the other exit. Gatera and Rrum followed him as he ran to join the Mountain Guard. Again, their fire-shadows accompanied them, but this time allowed them to follow Valor into the new passage. Gatera had the uncomfortable feeling that they were not being allowed to escape, but were being carefully herded towards some greater danger.

The tunnel was short, and soon opened into a larger chamber. To one side, against the cave wall, was a semi-circular pit, from which scarlet tongues of fire flickered occasionally. Some feet above the pit was a stone platform, enclosed by bars of rock. A short flight of steps led up to the platform. Across the other side of the cave were two dark exits—one large and wide, the other a tall, narrow crack.

The company headed for the wide tunnel, but were soon stopped in their tracks. Their fire-shadows moved ahead, preventing them from going any further. They backed away, and two of the fire-shadows flitted behind them. They were almost surrounded! The flickering shapes closed in on them.

Gatera looked to one side, and suddenly realised what was happening. 'They're pushing us towards the steps!' he shouted.

The friends stood their ground, Valor and Merric with their swords drawn, Gatera with his blackened axe, and Rrum unarmed but rooted firmly to the spot.

The dark shapes, their edges still trimmed in minute dancing flames, advanced towards them. Merric and Valor tried to slice through them, but it was like trying to cut the air. Gatera tried swinging his axe around his head and then through his fire-shadow, but again it was useless. This time, there was the smell of singed hessian. The wooden handle of the axe burst into a red flame which shot along towards his hands. Alarmed, he dropped the axe. It burned fiercely, greedily for a moment. Then the flames died, leaving behind just the blade and a line of ash. Gatera grunted in dismay. He had cut the axe handle himself many years ago, and it was as if a trusted friend had been destroyed. Kneeling down, he picked up the blade and put it in his backpack.

However, there was no time to ponder their

problems. He felt his skin getting hotter as the shadow advanced. Backing away, he sensed his friends following his example. This was hopeless! Slowly but surely they were being shepherded towards the stone steps. Rrum tried to burst through the fiery barricade, but even his leathery skin was scorched, and he had to stagger back once more.

Valor tried spitting at his shadow. There was a sizzle, and a tongue of flame flicked back at him. Merric attempted to dive through the fire-shadows, thinking that his momentum might carry him to the other side. But it was like diving at a red hot blanket. The shadows both resisted and scorched him, leaving him groaning in pain on the ground until Gatera helped him to his feet. There was no alternative: slowly and reluctantly they were forced up the steps.

Gathering together, the shadows began to follow them upwards. As if in approval, a great spear of blood-red flame sprang up out of the fiery pit and then subsided once more.

Side by side, the friends stumbled backwards up the steps and into the stone cage. As they did so, two stone bars slid down from the ceiling, trapping them. Merric tripped over something and looked down to see a few charred bones scattered around the floor of the cage.

The fire-shadows, as if satisfied by their work, retreated down the steps. Then, to the amazement of the friends, they leapt into the blazing pit, and were swallowed up in its flames.

Gatera grasped two of the stone bars of the cage and heaved with all his strength, but he was unable to move or break them.

'Rrum!' said Valor urgently. 'Can you gnaw your way through these bars?'

The little Rrokki inspected the stone and nodded

doubtfully. 'It may be possible, but it will take some time.'

Gatera breathed a sigh of relief. Perhaps they would soon be free after all!

His rekindled hopes were soon dashed. A strange figure emerged from the narrow crack in the cave wall below. Its body was small and wiry, and bathed in flame. It made a strange hissing sound—rather like that from the steaming lava. The companions strained to make sense of the noises.

'Welcome! I am the one they call the Flame Massster. It isss long sssince I have been able to entertain anyone to the delightsss of my little cage. At lassst my hunger will be filled for a while—ssss.'

The creature drew nearer. Its shifting form, a mass of reds, pinks and purples, hurt their eyes.

'Do not think you can essscape—ssss,' it said, drawing a long-fingered hand across the bottom step. A tall curtain of flame sprang up, barring their exit even if they were able to break out of their stony cell.

'What do you intend?' called Merric, still nursing his wounds from his attempt to break through the barrier of fire shadows.

'Do not worry yoursssself—enjoy my hossspitality while you can—ssss—'

'But what are you going to do with us?' asked Valor, his face flushed with both anger and heat. 'We haven't done anything to harm you!'

The Flame Master gurgled horribly. 'Sssuch impatience! Your bodiesss offend me—they are too moissst. Here, you will be heated ssslowly, asss the flamesss dance underneath you—ssss.'

'And then?' asked Gatera.

'And then after a few dayss, when your bodiesss are dried of fluid—then, I will devour you!' The Flame Master let out a final hiss of glee and retreated once more to its lair.

9

The Trials of Athennar

A troubled frown creased Athennar's brow. It had been more than a day since his friends had left for the Black Caves, and he had been anxious to catch up with them. However, his departure had been delayed, as there were people he had to see; messengers to be sent to Tolledon at the Fortress of Fear; and the vale had to be inspected for any other signs of the damage inflicted by Dargan.

It was as if a blight had suddenly passed through the sheltered valley. Hallion—a haven of rest in the midst of conflict; a place of beauty and of peace—had been tainted, wounded even. The people of the vale went about their work silently. The usual sounds of singing were absent, and even the children were subdued.

Athennar gritted his teeth, and cursed Dargan as he prepared to mount Windrider. There was little else he could do now—the quest for the Globe of Truth was the most important task left. All else—indeed, the future of the Realm itself—probably hinged upon the success of the quest.

Nudging Windrider towards the passage that led out of Hallion, he made a silent vow to Elsinoth that the Dark Master would not go unpunished.

A few hours later, Athennar was travelling northwards when a dark shape bounded over a hill and raced towards him.

'Sash, you old scoundrel!' shouted Athennar in delight. A smile passed his lips for the first time in the last two days. Leaping lightly from his horse, he greeted his old friend.

'I was hoping you would find me!' he said, fondly stroking the black leopard's broad head. 'I have an important task for you!' He started speaking to Sash in the strange animal language he had learned over many years. The leopard looked at him intelligently, then licked his hand.

'Take this with you,' instructed Athennar. He pulled a small wooden disc from his pocket. On one side was engraved a picture of his own face. Tying the disc carefully around the leopard's neck with a thin leather thong, he gave her a final stroke.

'Now go; run swifter than the wind, my faithful friend!' he said. Sash looked at him once more then loped off northwards, and soon disappeared from sight.

Giving a satisfied grunt, Athennar remounted Windrider and again set off in the direction of the Black Caves. The country he was riding through was hilly, with occasional patches of scrub and woodland. As he was travelling along a narrow track through a particularly dense collection of bushes, two burly, bearded men leaped out in front of him. Bandits! The Animal Crafter was about to ride them down when a voice from behind called out, 'Don't even consider it! Get down—now!'

He looked round. Another man—clean-shaven, but as big as his companions—stood behind him, an arrow poised and ready to fire. Carefully, Athennar dismounted, his hand away from his sword.

'Well, what have we here?' chuckled the bandit leader, one of the two bearded men. 'A Hallion man, if I'm not mistaken!'

'You're not!' replied Athennar curtly. 'I am Athennar, son of the Guardian, and I would ask you to let me pass. I am on a journey of great importance!'

This merely brought great guffaws of laughter from all three ruffians. The one who had spoken stroked his beard thoughtfully. 'Son of the Guardian, eh? Then you'll be worth a coin or two, I'll warrant!'

Athennar frowned. He was regretting having sent Sash on ahead. Seeing that argument was useless, he called out in a strange snorting voice to Windrider.

'None of that!' warned the bandit leader, moving forward.

The next moment, there was a flurry of activity. Windrider, responding to Athennar's instructions, backed up, then struck out with his hooves, lashing at the bandit who carried the bow and arrows. One of the hooves smashed into the man's arm, and the weapons were sent flying. The man gave a piercing yell of pain. At the same time, Athennar drew his sword and, seizing the initiative, leaped towards the bandit leader before the fellow had time to move.

'For the Realm!' he cried, and lunged forward with a telling sword thrust. The man crumpled, clutching his side and moaning. Athennar turned to the other bearded bandit but, seeing the fierce look on Athennar's face and his fallen comrades, the man turned and fled into the bushes.

Sheathing his sword, Athennar sprang up on to Windrider. Looking down at the two remaining bandits, he said softly, 'I have no time now to teach you better manners. I will say just this: mend your ways. I will be passing this way again. If I find that you are still practising your thieving ways here, it will go ill with you!'

He was rewarded by a pained scowl from the bandit leader, who rolled out of the way as Athennar urged Windrider forwards.

Later that evening, he wound his way through a small stretch of woodland until he found a sheltered glade. Slipping gratefully from Windrider's back, he tended to the horse's needs before stretching his leather blanket underneath the spreading branches of an old oak tree. The night was calm and warm, and stars sparkled brightly in the sky. Soon he was asleep, content in the knowledge that Windrider would warn him of any approaching danger.

After a few hours, Athennar awoke. The sky was only just beginning to lighten, but he ate a hurried breakfast and then led Windrider out of the glade and once more on towards the Black Caves. A strange sense of foreboding had filled his dreams—harsh, vibrant, fiery images. Feeling the need for greater speed, he urged the horse into a gallop.

Three days later, after a tiring but uneventful journey, Athennar reached his destination. He had half expected to meet his friends on their way back; although he had made good time, they must have reached the caves at least late the previous day. However, as Athennar approached the caves, he was dismayed to find the horses tethered outside, untended. He talked softly to them, and led them to a nearby stream to drink. Then, watching all the time for signs of his friends, he made his way to the middle cave. Lighting his torch, he waited for a moment as the flame grew. Remembering what Hesteron had told him about the baraks that lived in the caves, he advanced slowly, the torch in his left hand and his sword in his right.

At the point where the passageway broke into the main tunnel, he pondered for a moment before turning left. On he strode until he reached the dip in the cave roof and the underground river. He was about to turn around when his eye was attracted by something that reflected the torchlight. Moving closer, he looked at the object. Merric's lute! The others must have somehow crossed this river—otherwise the minstrel would never have left the lute behind.

Wading across, arms held high, he gasped with relief when he reached the other side. For the moment, he slipped his sword back into its scabbard. Then, padding quietly forward, he continued the search for his friends.

After some time, he reached the cavern of winds, having been alerted beforehand by the distant moaning sounds. He paused at the entrance to assess the danger. In the distance, through the various arches, he thought he could see the exit tunnel on the far side of the cave. However, he decided not to take the direct route: if the winds were meant as a deterrent to visitors, then that would also be the most difficult path. Instead, keeping to the wall of the chamber, he edged his way along the side. The wind here was rough but bearable and the moaning, although persistent, was nothing more than an annoyance. He battled forward, until he reached the far wall of the cavern. Then he crept along the wall until he was near the arches that led to the exit tunnel.

This was the most difficult time: now he would have to face the full fury of the wind. Tensing himself, he pushed forward through the first arch.

At first the force of the wind almost lifted him off his feet. But Athennar's body had been honed to a rugged fitness by his travels through the Realm. Bending his head, he struggled with all his might against the wind. Inch by inch, foot by foot, he strained forward until he reached the next arch. Then he paused in the shelter of one of its columns for a while to rest. The noise was awful, but he tried to close his mind to it. Gathering his strength, he strode out into the arch and forced his way through and on towards the final arch.

Shaking with the effort, he collapsed thankfully over its threshold, wondering if the other four had made it this far. As soon as he felt stronger, he jumped to his feet and stepped forward into the tunnel. Strangely refreshed after his labours, he broke into a run. The urgent feeling from his dream had returned: his friends had need of him!

It only seemed minutes later when he reached the boiling soup of underground lava. For a moment, he looked at it in disbelief and dismay, but this turned to relief when he saw the recent limestone marks on the stepping stones. They must have been made by his friends—which meant they had at least made it this far!

His keen eyes picked out the trail across the burning lake; then, the sense of urgency encouraging him on, he leapt nimbly from stone to stone. Once he reached the other side, he paused for a moment, then raced along the tunnel that led to the fire caves.

When he reached the confusing steps, he almost fell down them as his mind reeled in confusion. Remembering the rhyme, he stopped, then closed his eyes and continued carefully downwards, a step at a time. Once he reached the bottom, he headed quickly towards the glowing caves ahead.

Running straight through the first cave with the pool of crimson fire, he failed to notice his fire-shadow. Before it had time to prise itself from the wall, he was racing on to the next cave. With a shock of surprise, he slid to a halt.

'Athennar!' croaked Valor weakly from the cell. 'Save us! We're frying!'

The Hallion man barely had time to take it all in: his friends imprisoned in the stone cage; the flickering tongues of flame licking up from the pit beneath it; the curtain of fire guarding the bottom of the steps.

'No! Save yourself!' shouted Gatera.

Athennar swung around to see a strange figure— his fire-shadow—advancing upon him. At the same time, the Flame Master emerged from his crack. Like his friends before him, Athennar was herded towards the steps. Under the Flame Master's control, the curtain of fire died down briefly, enabling Athennar to be forced up the steps. The Flame Master pulled a lever and the cage bars opened. The Animal Crafter was forced inside by his fire-shadow. Once there, the bars crashed down once more, and the Flame Master, dancing with glee, drew a new curtain of fire across the bottom step.

'Oh, no!' groaned Gatera, slumping against one side of the cage, licking his dry and cracked lips. 'While you were free, we had some hope of rescue. Now, truly, all hope is gone!'

10

Searching for Truth

The five friends crouched uncomfortably in their
stone prison. Merric was very quiet. His light frame
had particularly suffered from the constant heat
following his experiences with the fire-shadows.
Despite his wiry resilience, he felt as if all his strength
was being sucked from him; slowly, painfully. When
Athennar had arrived, the troubadour was feeling
very light-headed, and at first hadn't realised what
was happening. Valor, Gatera and Rrum were faring
slightly better, but all were parched and weakened
by the constant heat. Once Athennar had been
imprisoned, their hopes had also plummeted. He had
tried to encourage them, but even the solid Gatera
seemed to have admitted defeat.

'There is nothing we can do!' he grumbled when
Athennar coaxed him into thinking of ways of escape.
'There's no way out!'

'Never give up hope!' Athennar urged him.
'Remember that Elsinoth is with us!' Gatera just shook
his head; Valor scowled.

Unexpectedly, support came from Rrum. 'You are

rightt, my friendd,' he grated. 'The Mightty One has saved us before. He can do itt again.'

Gaining strength from the little Rrokki's speech, Athennar called out, 'Help us now, Elsinoth! We are your servants! We need your help!'

From one corner of the cage, a weak whisper came from Merric. 'Yes, Toroth, aid us!'

Then all five friends sank into quietness, each one deep in his own thoughts of loved ones; of the Realm; of freedom.

The minutes stretched into hours, and the hours passed slowly, each taking its toll as their strength and energy was sapped. Soon it would be all over—the Flame Master would come for them. Their only chance was to overpower him, but none of them really believed they could get near enough to succeed.

Athennar thought of Melinya: this latest parting had come too soon. In desperation, he clung on to the thread of faith, and to a faint hope—unspoken to the others, lest it should fail. He allowed himself to sink slowly to sleep, so that he could at least conserve some of his energy. Gatera was already asleep nearby, snoring loudly.

Rrum had tried several times to gnaw his way through one of the bars, but it had heated up as he had chewed away, and had burned his mouth. Reluctantly, he had to admit defeat.

Merric was dozing fitfully, dreaming of streams, forests and mountains. His sleep was rudely disturbed by a cry from Valor, who had been pacing up and down the floor of the cage. 'The Flame Master's coming!'

Wearily, Merric raised his head and watched the flame-covered creature approach. 'Where are you, Toroth?' his mind shrieked.

Back at the Fortress of Fear, Melinya stirred from her sleep. Rising from her bed, she wrapped a cloak around her. She pulled up the hood, stepped out of the room, and walked along the corridor until she reached a door that led onto the courtyard.

Passing through it, she flitted across to some steps and climbed up to the battlements. The guard on watch nodded courteously to her, then passed by on his tour of duty. Melinya peered over the parapet, searching the starlit plains to the north. Although the company was not expected back from their quest yet, she felt concerned for their safety.

'Where are you, my love?' she whispered into the night air. She almost hoped that he would come riding across the plains on Windrider, his dark hair streaming out wildly in the breeze. But the plains remained empty, and her fears uncalmed.

'Guard him, Toroth,' she whispered again. 'Guard them all!'

In another part of the castle, Kess too was restless. He lay on his bed fully dressed, wishing he could sleep, yet at the same time unable to settle. He too was thinking of Elsinoth—but his thoughts were darker than those of Melinya. While she pleaded for help, he struggled with doubt and despair; fought to try and understand. His faith in the Mighty One had always been real—he knew Elsinoth's way, and he had always tried to follow it. Yet never before had his faith been so sorely tested.

Somehow, things had always seemed so straightforward before. Now, everything was so complicated. When he had been younger, and his parents had been so cruelly taken from him, Elsinoth had been like a caring father. Kess had found that he could 'talk' to the Mighty One about all his problems, his fears, his joys. Although there had been no spoken reply, he knew somehow that Elsinoth had heard, and he had felt the inner peace that had carried him through the darkest times. Linnil had felt it as well, and this had strengthened the close bond between the twins still further.

Now that bond had been broken. His sister lay as if in a trance, holding on to life by a slim and fragile thread. Kess still shook with anger at the way Dargan had treated her.

But his thoughts returned to the one question which kept troubling him: where was Elsinoth? Had Kess been fooling himself all the time? Was Whisper right when she was so cynical about the Mighty One? Was Elsinoth just a figment of his own imagination? Deep inside, he knew that wasn't the case, but his frustration needed an outlet; and so he struck out at those things that were closest to his heart.

He missed his friends, particularly Valor and Athennar; he had steadily grown to depend on them, and the unspoken understanding he seemed to share with them. He missed, too, Merric's quiet friendship; Gatera's down-to-earth qualities; and Rrum's steady strength. And now he missed Meltizoc's wisdom too, even though he had recently felt slighted by the wise man's suspicions about Whisper.

Grunting, he levered himself from the bed. At least he could go and see if Meltizoc was making any progress! Slipping silently out of his room, he wandered down the interconnecting corridors that led to the wise man's chamber.

Hearing conversation inside, he stopped, then tapped on the door. Tolledon's voice bade him enter. As he opened the door, the bright light of a blazing lamp made him blink for a moment. Entering the room, he was delighted to see the portly Meltizoc sitting propped up in his bed.

'Good meeting!' Kess said in surprise. 'It's good to
see that you've recovered!'

The wise man chuckled. 'There is much strength
left yet in this rotund frame,' he said, patting his
stomach. 'I still feel a little ragged, but I will soon be
plaguing you all once more! And how are you, my
young friend?'

'I'm well . . .' started Kess, but then he blurted out,
'but I don't understand what's happening! Why is
everything taking so long? Why does Dargan seem to
be winning? And where is Elsinoth? I'm beginning to
doubt that he even exists!'

'These are troubled times, and there are no easy
answers,' interrupted Tolledon. 'I, too, have struggled
with such questions of faith in the past. Indeed, even
this day messengers came to report a blight that has
fallen upon my beloved Hallion.' He told Kess about
the message from Athennar—that the land around
Hallion was beginning to fade.

'So perhaps Elsinoth *doesn't* exist after all!' said Kess
bitterly. 'If he did, surely he wouldn't allow such
things?'

'He allows us to follow our own choices,' said
Meltizoc quietly. 'Dargan chose to follow evil, and we
are suffering the effects of that choice. But do not
question Elsinoth's ways—they are very different from
ours. He sees what we may never see; but his help is
always there for those who seek it. It may come in a
different form or at a different time from that which
we expect. His will is his own: he will work with us,
but he is not a toy, to be manipulated by our wishes!'

'Then perhaps I should have chosen not to believe
in him, if his way is so difficult!' muttered Kess.

The wise man smiled, then gently beckoned Kess
to sit on his bed. 'And how would that have helped
you, my friend? Truth is truth—you can't change that,

whatever you choose to believe. Elsinoth exists. You may decide not to believe or to ignore that, but it does not change the truth: he still exists. I have seen many a person fall from Elsinoth's ways because they cannot understand them. They fail to see that the alternative is to rely solely on their own strengths—and in doing so, they will always eventually fail. Others rely on their friends—but they, too, have their weaknesses and will fail them. Elsinoth alone will never let you down. Yes, Elsinoth's ways may appear difficult at times—but in the end, they are the only safe route, and may not prove to be as difficult as you think. Trust him! After all, isn't it better to try and follow the right path, even though it may lead through difficult ground?'

Kess shrugged. 'I don't know any more. All I know is that I want Linnil to recover. Then perhaps I will believe you.'

Meltizoc nodded his understanding. 'It has been a difficult time for you—more difficult, perhaps, than for any of us. But don't set conditions on your faith—just trust. True faith struggles on through the dark—it doesn't give up. I think you know that Elsinoth is -with you if you take time to think. Search your heart, and you will find him.'

'Perhaps,' muttered Kess.

Tolledon came over and gripped his shoulder. 'Until now, your faith has been like a light, shining through these times of trouble. My son has spoken long to me about the new strength and trust that has been rekindled in his own heart. We have all grown complacent in the past; it is easy to believe when things go well. However, faith will eventually be tested by the problems of life. Hold on to the peace inside you—it is more valuable than many a precious gem.'

Perplexed, Kess stared at the Guardian. How did

he know about such things? He had never heard him speak of them before!

'Meanwhile,' continued Meltizoc, 'you can best help your friends by praying that they find the Globe and return here safely.'

'But what if it is Elsinoth's will that they should fail?' asked Kess, still dazed and confused.

'Then at least they will have failed while trying to do what is right. Surely that is better than failing because they gave up or decided not to fight because they thought that evil was stronger?'

'I suppose so,' conceded Kess. 'But sometimes it's so hard to keep on fighting!'

'Indeed,' replied Meltizoc, the old twinkle returning to his eyes. 'But while we still breathe, we *must* fight. Dargan may seem invincible, but his power is puny in comparison to Elsinoth's.'

'Then why doesn't Elsinoth just attack him and defeat him?' asked Kess.

'Because that is not his way. He chooses to fight evil through those of us who follow him—when we let him.' The wise man eased his neck from side to side, and flinched at some hidden pain.

'Enough talk!' said Tolledon. 'Sometimes your wisdom does not extend to your own health, old friend!'

Meltizoc nodded, but looked at Kess with a question in his eyes.

Kess forced a smile. 'It's good to see you looking better,' he said. 'I'll think about what you've said. At the moment, I feel as if I'm walking aimlessly through a fog—a bit like my time in the Whistling Waters.' He shuddered as he remembered the experience. 'Please pray for me, that I may have the strength to fight my way through.'

Meltizoc nodded. 'It is a strong man indeed who

can face up to his own weaknesses. One last thought before you go: perhaps Elsinoth believes in you more than you believe in him!'

Kess looked startled, then smiled—this time, a real smile. 'I'd never thought of it that way!' he said. Shaking the wise man's hand, he left the room with a slight spring in his steps. He had much to think about, but once more the hope in his heart had been rekindled.

11

Fire Fight

The figure of the Flame Master walked slowly across the floor of the cavern.

'What are you all doing up there?' it asked.

Athennar was puzzled. What was the creature talking about? He shook his head to clear his vision. Like Merric, he had been sleeping until he was disturbed by Valor's call. Then he realised there was something familiar about the Flame Master's voice . . .

As he focused on the creature, he gave a joyful shout of recognition. 'Fashag! You came!'

The gnome grinned and waved a welcome. It was hardly surprising that they had mistaken him for the Flame Master in the dim red light of the cavern—his whole body was wreathed in small dancing flames.

Valor moved over to join Athennar by the bars of the cage. 'How did you escape your fire-shadow?' he called. 'And what about the Flame Master?'

'Who?' asked Fashag.

He was answered by a hissing noise from the crack in the cavern wall. The hunched shape of the Flame Master emerged, bathed in crimson fire. 'Who are you—and how did you passss my guardians—ssss?' it demanded, circling Fashag warily.

'Your guardians? Oh, you mean this thing! I think it likes me—look, it's wrapped itself around me!' replied Fashag, undeterred.

Now Athennar understood. In some way, the fire-shadow and Fashag had become as one—which explained the flames licking around the peace gnome's body!

The Flame Master, both confused and enraged, continued circling Fashag, and hissed almost uncontrollably. 'You will pay for thisss—no one defeatsss my ssservantss and lives—ssss!'

'Oh no?' said Fashag, peering at the creature as if examining a prize specimen. Then grumpily he added, 'Stay still, will you! Let me have a proper look at you!'

In a raging fury, the Flame Master gave an enormous hiss and lunged at him. Fashag, taken by surprise, was knocked to the floor. Seeing its chance, the creature leaped on him. All the watching prisoners could see was a burning mass of flame; mingling, changing: first dark red, then yellow, then orange. Bright flashes filled the room. They were accompanied by angry hisses and muttered curses.

Suddenly there was an arc of crimson fire. The Flame Master shot through the air and straight into the fiery pit. A gurgled, hissing scream filled the cave, and a huge dark red flame scorched the bottom of the stone cage. Athennar shielded his eyes. Then the fires died down once more.

When he looked again, Athennar saw the gnome lying on the floor of the cavern, immobile. 'Fashag!' he called desperately.

For a moment, nothing happened. Then the Animal

Crafter sighed with relief as Fashag stirred and struggled slowly to his feet.

'Yes, what is it now?' he asked crossly.

'You're all right!' gasped Valor.

'Well, of course I am. I'm a Fire Crafter, aren't I? You don't think a simple creature like that would be able to get the better of me, do you?'

'Will the Flame Master return?' Athennar asked.

'Probably. It'll be licking its wounds for a while yet, though, I suspect—and it won't want to show its face again while I'm still here.'

'Can you get us out of here?' asked Valor.

'Give me time!' grumbled the gnome. 'People are always in such a rush these days!' Wandering over to the curtain of flame at the foot of the steps, he walked straight into it, then began to turn round and round. The fire wrapped itself around him. Then, when he was totally engulfed in it, Fashag ran his hands down the sides of his body. The flames died down, leaving the now instantly recognisable yellow figure of the gnome.

Fashag then pulled a lever he had spotted near the bottom of the steps, and the bars of the cage lifted up. Meanwhile, Athennar and Valor were attending their friends. Gatera had slept through all the excitement, and it took some time to waken him. Eventually, however, he staggered to his feet. Rrum had been watching quietly, and now trundled over to help his friend.

Merric had watched Fashag's appearance with some bemusement, wondering if he was suffering hallucinations. When he realised they had really been rescued, he tried to stand. But his feet were too weak, and he sank back on to the floor. Valor and Athennar, having woken Gatera, now came over and helped the minstrel to his feet. They had to take virtually all of his weight as they half-carried him down the steps. Gatera and Rrum stumbled down behind them.

Fashag looked at the troubadour, and then grunted, 'He'll live! He's a strong 'un—just caught a bit of fire-scorch, that's all. He needs some water.'

'Can we go back through the cave of the fire-shadows?' asked Athennar.

'I wouldn't recommend it. I would be safe, but I think you would all still be at risk. If there are more of those things, I might not be able to protect you all.'

'There's only one alternative, then,' Athennar replied. Signalling Valor, they carried Merric towards the other exit. The rest of the company followed wearily.

Some way along the tunnel, a small stream cut across the passage. Gratefully, Athennar and Valor propped Merric against the passage wall. The minstrel groaned and winced.

Dousing a cloth in the stream, Athennar bathed Merric's face with water, while Valor filled all the flasks. After distributing these among the company, he gently pressed one to the minstrel's lips. A small trickle slipped down Merric's throat, and he coughed. Giving a weak smile to Valor, he nodded to signal he could drink more.

Once Merric had drunk, Valor left him to recover and joined the others, who were also sitting with their backs against the rough stone wall.

The cold water was very refreshing, and soon the friends were feeling stronger. Merric was still pale, but assured them that he would be able to continue after a little more rest.

'I feel as though my life-force had almost drained away,' he croaked.

Fashag nodded. 'Fire can be very dangerous if you

don't understand its ways!' The troubadour managed another weak smile in reply.

'But how did you get here?' asked Valor. 'How did you know we were in trouble?'

Fashag nodded towards Athennar. 'You can thank your friend here,' he said.

Valor looked at the Animal Crafter. 'I don't understand—'

'When I left Hallion, I took the precaution of sending Sash ahead to find Fashag,' explained Athennar. 'I remembered that Hesteron had spoken about burning lakes, and I thought we might be able to use his talents if you had been unsuccessful. Little did I know that he would be needed to save our lives!'

'That leopard of yours gave me the shock of my life!' grumbled Fashag. 'I was fast asleep, and awoke to find her breathing down my neck! How she got past my guard fires, I'll never know! I was about to singe her to a frazzle when I saw the pendant hanging from her neck. I remembered you telling me about her when we travelled back from the Ice Kingdom, and realised that you were probably in trouble—again! So I just followed her here, though at times I wished I hadn't—she's led me at a fair pace for the last two days!'

'But how did you get through the cavern of winds and the burning lake?' asked Valor.

Fashag pulled a long coil of rope from his backpack. Tied to one end was a twisted metal hook. 'Something I made in my forge when I was younger,' he explained, looking at it proudly. 'I used to use it for scaling walls. It came in handy in the windy cave. I slung it ahead of me, and once it had caught on one of those rock pillars, I could haul myself along fairly easily.'

'But what about the burning lake?' asked Valor. 'Surely you're too short to leap from stone to stone?'

'You cheeky young whippersnapper! It wasn't the lake that was the problem—it was that underground river! I hate getting wet—and the current nearly swept me away!'

'But—' persisted Valor.

'But when I reached the burning lake as you call it, I just waded through it. It was a marvellous experience! It wasn't deep—it only just came up to my waist. It was a bit thick to walk through, and took a while, but my fire-crafting knowledge helped and protected me. Those strange steps were a bit confusing at first, but I soon got used to them.'

Gatera chortled, and Athennar raised an eyebrow. 'You are full of surprises, my friend,' he said. 'But what of Sash?'

'She struggled as far as the burning lake, but couldn't go any further. I sent her back. She seemed to understand.'

'Good,' replied Athennar, a look of relief spreading over his face. 'Now, if we are all rested, we must proceed. We're not out of danger yet—and we still haven't found the Globe!'

The others looked at him in surprise—they'd almost forgotten the reason for coming to the caves.

Quickly, Athennar explained the nature of their quest to Fashag, who muttered for a while but finally nodded in agreement. Then, with Gatera supporting the weakened Merric, they trudged across the little stream and on down the tunnel. They had relit their torches, as only a faint glow filtered into the tunnel now from the fire caves.

The tunnel wound its way on, the rough-hewn walls glistening with damp. It began to slope upwards slightly, and they struggled on, all except Fashag still feeling the strain of their recent imprisonment.

Soon they reached another cave. Daylight filtered

into it from a hole in the roof in one corner. The walls
of the cave were damp, and covered with a blanket
of moss. In another corner was a small, dark opening.
Bending down, they crept through cautiously.

The passage was short and led to a smaller, mossy
cave. There was no exit—just a roughly hewn rock
throne against the far wall, with what appeared to be
a misshapen log lying untidily across its seat.

'We're trapped!' groaned Gatera. 'There's no way
out!'

Rrum ambled over towards the throne. Suddenly
he stopped. The log of wood moved, uncurling itself
slowly.

'Who are you?' asked a deep, resonant voice.

'It's alive!' gasped Valor. 'What is it?'

'Itt is a Moor Man,' grated Rrum.

'Ah, one of my distant Rrokki cousins, I presume!'
intoned the Moor Man. Its voice seemed ill-fitted to
such a spindly frame. The knobbly figure was covered
in fine green tufts: it looked as if an ancient tree was
coming to life. Stretching its arms, the creature
yawned.

'Look!' said Athennar. The others followed his
pointing finger. Cradled in the lap of the Moor Man
was a beautiful glowing green sphere.

'What is it?' asked Valor.

Merric, who had been holding on to Gatera
unsteadily, looked at it in awe. 'The Globe of Truth!'
he whispered.

12

The Keeper of the Globe

'Stay back!' commanded the Moor Man as the friends advanced towards him. Despite his frail features, there was great strength in his voice.

The friends hesitated a moment, then Athennar spe e. 'We have travelled long distances to find the Globe; the safety of the Realm depends upon the help it can give us.'

'The Globe of Truth is in my care; I will not release it,' the Moor Man said.

'We could take it by force,' muttered Valor.

Athennar looked at him sharply. 'That is not our way,' he reminded him. The Mountain Guard grimaced and fell silent.

'If you should try such a foolish act, then I would destroy the Globe,' the Moor Man replied.

'No—you can trust us,' Athennar said. 'I am the son of Tolledon, Guardian of the Realm. A great evil is spreading throughout the land—and the Globe is our only hope of challenging it.' He recounted some of Dargan's evil activities.

The Moor Man shrugged. 'This is of little concern

to me. I live only to safeguard the Globe. Countless years have I dwelt here, keeping it in my care, guarded by the Flame Master and his helpers. How you passed them, I do not know. But I do know that the Globe stays with me.'

Rrum shuffled forward slightly. 'Our peopple are distantt cousins,' he said in his peculiar grinding tones. 'My friendds tell the truth. Whatt use is itt to prottect the Globe if all else falls aroundd itt?'

The Moor Man crossed his spindly legs and thought for a moment. 'I am old; all I know is my duty,' he said. 'That duty is to guard the Globe with all my life.'

Merric, whose strength was now beginning to return, spoke quietly. 'The Globe was crafted by Toroth—the mighty Elsinoth as you would call him. I believe it was formed as a symbol of his truth.'

The Moor Man nodded.

'It was placed in your trust to protect it from those who would seek to use it for evil.'

Another nod.

'It is now such evil men who threaten our world. Would Elsinoth wish it to be hidden away, when it could reveal a truth that is sorely needed in these troubled times? Was it not created to help us in our time of need? Such a time has now arrived!'

The Moor Man gazed at him doubtfully, his tufty eyebrows wavering as he pondered these new thoughts. 'I fail to see how the Globe would help you,' he said gruffly.

Athennar quickly explained Linnil's illness, and their hopes of finding Dargan's new lair if they could get her to face the truth.

'And how do I know that you are not servants of the very evil you claim to want to destroy?' the Moor Man asked, still unconvinced.

The friends looked at one another, each trying to

think of an argument that would convince him. Merric began to smile. 'You are the Keeper of the Globe,' he replied. 'Seek, then, the truth within its depths. It will confirm all that we have said: the peril faced by the Realm, and our own search for the Globe.'

The Moor Man pondered for a moment, passing a knobbly hand across his mossy brow. 'Very well,' he said at last. 'But I warn you—should any of you seek to take the Globe while I search out the truth, your quest will come to a sudden and fruitless end.'

'We understand,' Athennar replied, glancing at Valor.

The Moor Man beckoned Athennar forward. 'Come and place your hand on the Globe and repeat all that you have told me,' he instructed him. He raised the Globe, though it remained nestled in his hands.

Athennar stepped forward and rested one large hand on the top of the Globe. He then repeated the account of their conflict with Dargan, and of the danger to the Realm. Between his fingers, he could see swirls of pale green moving gently within the globe. As he spoke, a pulsating glow also came from the sphere.

When he had finished, an expectant silence filled the room. Athennar stepped back to await the verdict. Eventually, the Moor Man looked up, his craggy face looking unaccountably weary. 'You have spoken the truth,' he said, shaking his head. 'It is I who have been unwise. You may take the Globe. Use it well. Guard it with your lives.'

'Perhaps we could return it here once our quest is accomplished,' suggested Athennar.

'Or you could come with us!' boomed Gatera.

'No,' the Moor Man said sadly. 'My time is at an end. I have grown very weary, and must pass on my duties to others. Now you must keep the Globe.

When the time comes, you will know what must happen to it.'

'But how do we use it?' asked Valor.

The wrinkled features of the Moor Man relaxed slightly, and a sparkle came back to his old brown eyes. 'With great care! The Globe shows what is true: merely that. It will not—nor should it—reveal your destinies; those are in the hands of Elsinoth alone. Nor will it say what has passed; it merely confirms what is. Do not use it lightly, however—merely its existence is a celebration of truth, and it was crafted to give aid in moments such as now and to remind the Realm of the truth of Elsinoth.'

He paused and then continued, the strong voice now sounding aged and weary. 'To find the truth, speak out what you see to be the truth. If you are deceived, the Globe will reveal this. For those who lie, they may be forced to face the truth: the answer of the Globe cannot be denied. But it will only tell you if something is true or false; whether a motive, or a statement. For instance, it confirmed that you spoke truly about the evil of Dargan, but it cannot tell where he will be found—for that would interfere too greatly with your own fate. I repeat: use it wisely, and Elsinoth will guide you through the truth. But be prepared! The truth is sometimes difficult to face!'

He eased himself from the throne, cradling the Globe carefully in his hands. He was taller than they had expected, and once erect looked even more like an old, withered, moss-covered tree. With great dignity, he walked slowly over to Athennar. 'Son of the Guardian, it is apt that I should place this in your trust.' He bowed slightly and offered the Globe to the Animal Crafter.

Fashag, standing nearby, muttered something about pomp and ceremony, but Athennar ignored him. 'Do not worry,' he said to the Moor Man. 'We will take great care of the Globe.' He looked at the small sphere now resting in his palm. There was no movement within it now. It felt surprisingly light. Gazing into it, he could see pale green streaks—yet it seemed as if they were at great depths, yards or perhaps miles inside it. Disturbed by the sight, he looked up at the Moor Man once more.

'Thank you,' he said. 'You have fulfilled your duties well, Ancient One.'

'Alas, I have failed,' replied the Moor Man sadly. 'My pride almost stopped me from giving you the Globe. I would have kept it here while all around me the Realm fell into desolation.'

'You have not failed—were you not protecting the Globe?' Merric said.

However, the Moor Man shook his head. He was inconsolable.

Before anyone could stop him, Valor, who had moved forward to get a closer look at the sphere, grabbed it from Athennar's hand. Athennar reached out to stop the Mountain Guard, but Valor shook his head. 'Remember the last line of Meltizoc's rhyme!' he said. He placed the Globe carefully back into the Moor Man's hand. 'See for yourself,' he said gently. 'Ask the Globe whether or not you have fulfilled your task.'

The Moor Man looked at him in astonishment, then nodded. He whispered to the Globe for a while, then closed his eyes. When he reopened them, they were moist with tears. Passing the Globe back to Athennar, he looked at Valor. 'Thank you, young man,' he said in a barely audible voice. 'Again, you spoke the truth. Now I can rest peacefully.' He smiled, nodded, and walked back to the throne.

Once seated, he looked upwards. 'My thanks,

Mighty One!' Then he gave a long sigh, and his head drooped on to his chest.

Rrum rushed over to help him. He examined the Moor Man, and then stepped back respectfully.

'Is he—' faltered Valor.

'Yes. His taskk is accomplishedd,' the Rrokki replied quietly.

Merric whispered, 'Truly he was a faithful servant of Toroth.'

'He must have lived here for years—centuries even,' said Gatera, overawed by all that had happened.

The minstrel nodded. 'A life of complete service.'

'Well, let's try and find a way out of here!' grumbled Fashag, disturbing the solemn atmosphere.

Athennar nodded. 'You're right, my friend! Unfortunately, that could prove difficult!' Untying his backpack, he carefully rolled the Globe of Truth inside a blanket before putting it in the pack.

Fashag, meanwhile, had a thoughtful frown on his face. Then he shrugged, and scratched his ear. 'I think I can find a way out,' he said.

'Not through the fire again!' groaned Gatera.

'No.' The gnome beckoned them to follow him, and led them out of the cave and back into the next chamber. Pointing at the hole in the roof of the cave, he said, 'That's our exit!'

'And how are we going to get up there—fly?' demanded Valor.

'No,' said Fashag again. Removing his backpack, he pulled out the long coil of rope and the hook he had used in the cavern of winds.

'Stand clear!' he warned. The friends backed away.

Whirling the rope round and round, Fashag suddenly let go. The hooked end shot upwards through the hole, some ten feet above their heads. Fashag tugged on the rope, and the hook came crashing down into the cave. 'Why doesn't it ever work properly the first time?' he grumbled. He tried twice more before the hook lodged firmly in something out of view.

'This hook was only built to take my weight,' he said, looking Gatera up and down. 'Give me one of your stronger ropes, and I will take it up with me and tie it around a rock.'

Valor unslung a rope from his shoulder. The little gnome took it and then shinned neatly up his own line. Within moments his yellow face was peering down over the edge of the hole.

'I've secured this end!' he shouted, dropping the thicker rope down, and pulling his own up.

It was a struggle to get out of the cave, but eventually they managed it. Gatera almost became wedged in the hole, but managed to hoist himself through, gaining a few scrapes on his arms as he went. Rrum was unable to grip the rope easily, so Athennar tied it around his body, and Gatera pulled him up from above. Merric was similarly helped up, as he still felt too weak to climb. Valor, after an argument with Athennar, insisted on being the last to climb the rope.

Soon they were all standing beside the hole. Breathing in the fresh air, they looked around. They were perched on a rocky ledge that was virtually inaccessible from above or below. In the distance, they could see the horses waiting patiently near the entrance to the Black Caves.

After tying two ropes together, they either climbed or were lowered down the rough cliff face. When they reached the bottom, Merric heaved a sigh of relief. 'The fresh air is a balm to my aching body!' he said.

The others nodded their agreement. All felt relieved to have escaped the dark tunnels. A black shape bounded over to greet them.

'Sash, you old rascal,' said Athennar, fondly stroking the leopard's head. 'My thanks for your help in saving us!' Sash nuzzled him in response, and gave a satisfied snort.

With renewed energy, the company walked back towards the horses. As the light was beginning to fade, they decided to make camp for the night, giving them more chance to regain their strength before the long journey southwards. Fashag, however, decided to start off straight away for his home. The others tried to dissuade him, but when they realised that he wouldn't change his mind, they thanked him profusely for rescuing them.

'Thank the leopard, not me!' grumbled Fashag. 'I wouldn't have come, but I've been wanting to explore the caves for some time—I kept hearing rumours of fires here. I might come back one day when the Flame Master has recovered, and see if I can talk some sense into him!'

Athennar smiled, and said, 'Nevertheless, we are truly grateful for all your help. You must visit us in Hallion when our task is completed.'

Nodding awkwardly, Fashag turned and trotted off into the darkness. Once he had gone, Athennar and Gatera prepared a meal, while Valor bravely re-entered the cave system to retrieve Merric's lute. Soon they were eating and singing, accompanied by the minstrel, who had recovered sufficiently to strike up some lively tunes as he sat with his back to a tree.

Athennar smiled to himself. Tonight they could afford to relax. They would find out soon enough whether their quest for the Globe would have the desired result—or whether it had all been just a costly waste of time.

13

The Power of Truth

It was nearly a week later when the friends finally arrived back at the fortress. On the return journey they visited Hallion. Riding across the plains near the waterfall was a disheartening experience. They could all clearly see the limp and yellow appearance of the grass. Then when Athennar saw the falls, he gave a gasp of dismay. The once proud and gleaming curtain of water had slowed to a weak cascade, tumbling uncertainly from the lip of the lake above.

Inside the vale the situation was little better. Around the glade where Dargan had landed, several of the trees were fading. The blight seemed to be spreading outwards, creeping through the woods and across the valley.

The visit to Hallion had taken the edge off their excitement at finding the Globe. However, their hearts began to lift again as soon as they sighted the Fortress of Fear. It was strange that such a grim structure could now cause their hopes to rise.

As they approached, they could just make out the tiny figures of the guards walking along the battlements. Soon the great wooden gates of the fortress opened wide in greeting. Coaxing the horses into a trot, they rode into the courtyard.

Tolledon and Kess were awaiting them, their faces mirroring the mixture of anxiety and anticipation they felt.

'Did you find the Globe?' Kess asked eagerly.

Athennar, dismounting and clasping his father's outstretched hand, nodded and smiled at the eager young man. 'Yes, after a long struggle!' he replied.

'Can we take it to Linnil?' asked Kess.

'Patience, my young friend,' counselled Tolledon. 'Our colleagues are tired and hungry—and we need to hear their news first, so we know how best to use the Globe.'

Kess' face fell, but Valor joined him and gave him a hearty slap on the back. Kess winced and coughed. 'Don't worry—it won't be long now!' said Valor.

At that moment, Vallel and Hesteron appeared. Soon all the friends were talking excitedly as they walked towards the main dining hall. Only Kess remained silent, frustrated by this further delay.

After dinner, the whole company crammed into Linnil's room. Even Meltizoc, still weakened from his enforced time in bed, had managed to trudge along the corridor from his own room.

When everyone was assembled, Athennar reverently drew the Globe out of his backpack. He glanced at Kess and Merric, standing either side of Linnil's bed, ready to help her should she need it. 'You must be prepared for the fact that this may not work,' he cautioned them. 'Or if it does, the strain of being forced to recognise the truth may harm Linnil.'

The two nodded, and Merric replied, 'If we were to do nothing, then Linnil's fate would be certain: she still fades. Although the Globe may harm her, we have little choice but to try it.'

He glanced at Kess, who nodded and added, 'We have *no* choice—we have to use the Globe!'

Athennar sat on the bed and looked at Linnil. Her eyes were open, but there was no sign that she was aware of anyone else in the room. Taking her hand, he said, 'Linnil, I don't know if you can hear me. We want to help you—to show you the truth and to try and bring you back to us. We all care for you—hold on to that! Now may Elsinoth protect and strengthen you!'

Gently, he placed the sphere in the palm of her hand. Then, pulling her other hand over the top of the Globe, he held it there.

'Linnil,' he began, 'you have been deceived. Your mind has been bound by cords of darkness . . . .' Linnil groaned, but said nothing.

Athennar continued, 'You are under the power of Dargan's will. You—'

'Dargan!' called Linnil. 'Dargan, I love—Dargan, I love—Dargan?' She trembled violently and tossed her head from side to side.

Athennar kept her hands clasped tightly around the Globe of Truth. Green shapes swirled in its depths.

'Dargan!' she screamed. Her friends watched helplessly as she struggled with a turmoil of thoughts.

'Dargan is a deceiver. You don't love him!' called Athennar. 'He has tricked you!'

'Dargan—where are you?' shrieked Linnil. Beads of perspiration glistened on her forehead. 'You told me—no—I don't understand!' She heaved convulsively. 'Dargan!'

'You don't love him, and he doesn't love you,' Athennar said forcefully. 'This is the truth. You must face it! Come back to us, Linnil!'

'Dargan?' she groaned in bewilderment.

'Dargan isn't here,' persisted Athennar. 'And he doesn't love you!'

'Dargan—I—you—we—you tricked me!' she cried. 'I don't love—I don't love you! Or do I?' Her frail body arched, and it was all Athennar could do to keep her hands on the Globe.

'No. No love. Trapped. Let me out! I must fight. Dargan! You deceived me!' Linnil sat bolt upright for a moment, a look of fear and madness in her eyes. Then it faded, and she groaned and collapsed back on the pillow, and closed her eyes.

Carefully, Athennar let her limp hands fall from the Globe. 'We must let her sleep for a while,' he said.

'Is she cured?' asked Kess, unable to keep the note of desperation from his voice.

'I don't know,' Athennar answered wearily. 'The Globe may help to bring her back to full awareness. Unfortunately, it can't cure her faded body. Hopefully, once her mind is released, the fading process will halt. How we can reverse it, however, I have no idea. We will have to pray that as she begins to eat more, her body grows stronger. For now, she needs rest. If we have succeeded, she will let us know when she is ready to talk—I hope. Will either you or Merric stay with her, Kess?'

'We will both stay,' interrupted Merric. Kess smiled gratefully at him.

'Good! Let us know as soon as she awakes.'

The company filed slowly out of the room, leaving Merric and Kess with Linnil, each of them holding one of her hands.

Some two hours later, Kess felt Linnil's hand twitch slightly. Her eyes opened slowly. At first, it seemed as if she didn't recognise him. Then she croaked, 'Kess?'

'I'm here, sis,' he whispered, stroking her forehead with his free hand, as his eyes filled with tears of relief. 'It's all right—everything's going to be all right.'

Linnil sighed and closed her eyes again for a moment.

'I will call the others,' Merric said to Kess.

Linnil's eyelids fluttered open again. 'Merric? Oh, Merric!'

The troubadour leaned forward and kissed her forehead. 'Good meeting!' he said, in a husky voice. He managed a smile as Linnil squeezed his hand.

Linnil smiled weakly in return. 'I've had such a dream,' she whispered, 'such a terrible dream . . . '

'You're safe now,' Kess said. 'Do you feel like talking?'

'Give me a few moments. I still feel so confused.'

'Merric will go and find the rest of our friends. You rest again now, for a while. I love you, sis—welcome back!'

'I love you too,' she whispered, then smiled again before closing her eyes. 'Both of you.'

Merric kissed her forehead again, and reluctantly left the room to find the rest of the company.

Within half an hour, the group was once more assembled in Linnil's room. Linnil was now sitting up, though still looking frail and tired.

'How are you feeling?' asked Tolledon.

'Confused,' she replied in a soft voice. 'I'm not even sure where I am, or how I came to be here.'

'You're at the Fortress of Fear,' Tolledon replied. 'You were brought here by a Tark, from Dargan's new hiding place.'

'A Tark? Dargan?' Her brow furrowed, and she groaned. 'Then it wasn't a dream—it was true!' She frowned again. 'The last thing I remember was being taken to a strange room. Dargan had the Sceptre. He started talking to me, and I tried to fight. I tried, but—' She began to weep.

'Slowly, my love, slowly,' warned Merric.

Kess stroked his sister's hand, calming her. 'You're safe now. There's nothing to worry about. Dargan can't reach you here.'

'But he made me say I loved him, and I don't!' she blurted out, sitting upright. 'But he kept telling me I did until I couldn't think of anything else. Then I don't remember any more until I heard a voice. The voice told me that it was all a lie—I didn't love Dargan. I knew the voice was speaking the truth—I don't know how, but I just knew. But all the time, I felt a battle going on inside me—Dargan's will against the voice. It was a terrible struggle, but the voice won!'

Kess nodded. 'That was Athennar. He used the Globe of Truth to help you face up to Dargan's lies.'

'The Globe of Truth?' she repeated stupidly.

Athennar showed her the Globe, and then she nodded. 'I remember now—wisps of green floated all around me, forcing me to listen to you—to listen to the truth.' She sighed and sat back. 'It hurt, though— I thought I was going to be pulled apart!'

'Linnil, there's something we desperately need to know.' Meltizoc smiled kindly at her, then said, 'We have to find Dargan. Can you remember anything about the place where you were held captive?'

She shook her head for a moment, then paused. 'Yes—I do remember now: it's gradually returning. After Dargan captured me, the Tark took us to a castle of some kind. I don't remember too clearly—I was dazed during the flight. At the castle, I was taken down a hole. I remember seeing a chest or something similar next to it. Then there were endless horrible passages, and an underground lake.'

'Can you tell us any more about the place, or about the castle?' Meltizoc persisted.

Linnil shook her head again. 'It's all too much of a blur at the moment, I'm afraid. Wait! There is something! I remember: Dargan told me the name of the place. Now, what was it? Ah, that's right—the Tower of Braggad!' she said triumphantly.

Meltizoc looked at Tolledon. The Guardian commented, 'I have heard of Braggad, but I don't know anything about a tower.'

'I will see if it is mentioned in the Tome of Neldra, or on the map that Kess and Whisper brought back,' the wise man said.

'Whisper?' said Linnil.

Whisper was hiding in the background, behind Gatera and Hesteron.

'I'll explain later,' Kess said.

'The two Zorgs may have heard of the tower,' mused Tolledon. 'I think I'll have another talk to them!' Looking at Linnil, he said, 'Thank you, Linnil. You have done very well. Now you must rest and regain your strength.' He turned to face the rest of the assembled crowd. 'We have work ahead of us, my friends! Prepare yourselves—in the next day or two another journey will begin—the journey to find Dargan and the Sceptre!'

14

Back to the Southlands

'No, Father, you must stay here!' Athennar was resolute.

Tolledon shook his head. 'I am the Guardian of the Realm, and as such, ought to lead the company in our search for Dargan.'

'No. You are needed here—and in Hallion. The people need your support and guidance. And if anything happens to us, there must be someone to act as a focal point of resistance to Dargan.'

'If you fail, there is little we will be able to do!'

'Perhaps. But as Guardian, your strength will serve the Realm best here. Besides,' Athennar's eyes twinkled, 'you might hold us up!'

Tolledon looked sharply at his son, then chuckled. 'Perhaps you're right. I'm not as young as I used to be. But at least take Hinno and Callenor with you. They won't hold you back, and you may benefit from their skills and wisdom. They will also help to keep the two Zorgs in line.'

'Agreed.' Athennar took his father's hand in a warm grasp. 'Never fear, Father. We will defeat Dargan—we must!'

It had been a busy day. Meltizoc had found a vague reference to the Tower of Braggad in the Tome of Neldra, but its exact location was unclear. Tolledon had then paid a visit to Gur'brak and Bar'drash to see if they could help. The Zorgs were astonished to hear the Guardian's request.

'The Tower of Braggad? Yeah, we know it,' said Gur'brak. 'We worked there for a brief spell, so to speak. Ha! It's way down south, beyond the Wailing Hills. It's a gloomy place, though.'

'Do you think you could lead us there?' asked Tolledon.

'Nah,' said Bar'drash. He was rewarded by a kick from Gur'brak.

'P'raps. What's in it for us?' the Zorg captain asked.

'Who knows? Possibly your freedom, if you serve us well.'

'Why should we trust you?'

'We are people of our word. Those who follow Elsinoth believe in honesty. But we can't prove that— it's a risk you'd have to take.'

'And why should you trust us?'

'We don't. But we will treat you fairly as long as you behave. But I warn you: any sign of betrayal, and it might mean your death.'

Gur'brak thought for a moment, and then shrugged. 'All right.'

'What?' complained Bar'drash. 'Don't I get a chance to say something?'

'No!' replied Gur'brak.

The next morning, the company assembled in the courtyard, having said their farewells to Linnil. She was still far too weak to travel.

'I suspect she will not fully recover until Dargan is defeated,' said Meltizoc.

Kess had wanted to remain with his sister, but she had insisted that both he and Merric should be part of the company. 'You were chosen for this quest from the beginning,' she told him. 'You must see it through to the end, and ensure that Dargan doesn't succeed!'

Eventually, Kess had succumbed. He now stood talking to Merric and Valor. Hesteron and Vallel were nearby, chatting to Gatera and Rrum. They were relieved to be leaving the grim fortress for a while.

Tolledon, meanwhile, was giving final instructions to Athennar, Callenor and Hinno. Callenor was charged with guarding the two Zorgs. Gur'brak and Bar'drash, after some initial loud protests, had finally agreed to travel on horseback—one in front of Callenor, the other in front of Hinno. The Zorgs hated the idea of riding, but Gur'brak eventually decided that anything was preferable to being cooped up in their cell any longer.

Meanwhile, Meltizoc spoke quietly with Melinya, who was also one of the travellers. Although Athennar had tried to dissuade her, she was determined not to be parted from him again.

As the company began to mount their steeds, a figure dressed in grey strode across the courtyard, leading a horse.

'Whisper!' groaned Kess.

She smiled at him. 'I think I owe you this much,' she said. 'Besides, it will be good to be on the move again!'

Kess looked doubtful, but said nothing.

'Prepare to leave!' called Athennar. When they were all ready, he addressed them once more. 'The Tower of Braggad lies far to the south-east. To reach it, we will have to cross the Long Ravine. There is only one bridge, and that has apparently been destroyed recently—possibly even by Dargan. Meltizoc therefore recommends that we cross it at its very beginning, at the edge of the Fetid Marshes. We will travel via the Withered Wood . . . .'

Vallel shivered. 'I don't like the sound of that!' she whispered to Hesteron.

'Shhh!' he said.

' . . . We will then cross another ravine and follow the coast as far as the Wailing Hills. Beyond the hills, we should find the Tower. I caution you to be on your guard at all times. Although Dargan will not be expecting us, there will doubtless be other dangers to face before we reach his hiding place! Our Zorg friends here—' he coughed and looked sideways at Gur'brak and Bar'drash, who shuffled uncomfortably on their horses '—know the Southlands better than any of us, and will help us to find the best routes. If they betray us . . .' He left the sentence unfinished, and the Zorgs looked nervously at each other. They grew even more nervous when they noticed Gatera fingering his double-headed axe. The Land Crafter had fashioned a new handle for the weapon during his stay at the fortress.

'Now let us start our journey,' said Athennar. 'Forward, friends, to find Dargan and the Sceptre!' The rest of the company gave a ragged cheer as Windrider led the procession out of the gates of the fortress.

Two days later, they reached the start of the Long Ravine. It was little more than a deep gulley at this point, ending abruptly at the Fetid Marshes. Narrow animal tracks criss-crossed their way down to its floor. The travellers negotiated the tracks with some difficulty, leading the horses and slipping and sliding precariously on some of the narrowest sections. Soon, however, they were all gathered at the bottom of the gulley.

Athennar scanned the opposite bank. Its paths looked even more dangerous than the ones they had followed downwards. For a moment, he wondered whether to follow the gulley for some way to see if there was an easier exit at a later stage.

'The ravine becomes much steeper just around that bend,' said Hinno, who had scouted this area during the long search for Linnil.

'Then we have little option but to climb!' Athennar said.

Sash, who had joined them for the journey from the fortress, padded past him and began to lope up one of the tracks.

'Good girl!' called Athennar. 'I think you've chosen the best route!' He started leading Windrider carefully up the trail. Fortunately, the path wasn't quite as narrow as it had at first appeared. Puffing and panting, the company struggled upwards. At one point, Whisper's horse started to slide backwards on some loose gravel. Whisper slipped as well, but hung on grimly while the horse regained its footing. Then, with a tug on the reins, she coaxed it upwards once more.

Kess watched with a grim expression on his face. He still hadn't really forgiven Whisper for drinking the fluid that might have helped Linnil. The resentment gnawed away inside him like a persistent ache.

Finally, the whole group reached the top and looked around. This area was separated naturally from the rest of the Southlands, and was less harsh and barren than the region around Dargan's old stronghold. Several low hills undulated away from them, covered in a dark green, coarse grass. Occasional solitary pine trees broke the scene.

'This place looks so lonely!' Vallel said. There were

no streams or rivers in sight, just the grass and the trees.

Hesteron smiled and slipped his hand inside hers. 'At least there's fresh air!' he replied, a little breeze teasing its way through his hair. 'And if the landscape's lonely, then we will have to provide it with some company!'

Vallel giggled and gave him a hug.

Gur'brak was squatting nearby, and overheard their conversation. 'Pah!' he said to Bar'drash. 'Remind me never to fall in love!' Despite his apparent surliness, the Zorg, like Hesteron, was relieved to be in the open air. During the past two days, he had been observing his travelling companions carefully. He had an unexpected urge to discover why they often seemed so cheerful, even though their quest sounded hopeless—what little he had heard of it. He had even listened carefully the previous night when Merric had sung a few carefree tunes around the campfire. However, the crafty Zorg had made sure that Bar'drash was asleep first—he had enough troubles without being laughed at by his companion.

Once the company was rested, Athennar signalled them to remount. Callenor prodded the two Zorgs into action, and they grumpily climbed back on to their horses, with a little difficulty. Gur'brak had decided that Zorgs were definitely not built for riding!

'Where are we going now?' grumbled Bar'drash.

Athennar, passing by, overheard the question. 'Our next destination is the Withered Wood,' he replied.

'What?' huffed Gur'brak. 'I thought you were joking when you said we were going there! We—we can't!'

Surprised by the Zorg's alarmed tone, Athennar reined in. 'Why? Is there a problem?'

'Yeah! The Withered Wood—that's the problem! It's an 'orrible place!'

'Horrible?' queried Athennar. 'Why?'

'I don't know,' Gur'brak replied in a grumpy voice. 'I've just heard tales. Some of my lads were scared silly when they went near it once—and Zorgs don't scare easily!'

Athennar tried hard to suppress a smile. 'Why?' he repeated.

'They didn't say exactly. Something about strange 'owling noises.'

Athennar looked at him hard for a moment, trying to see if the Zorg was telling the truth. Finally he said, 'Well, it's our shortest route. If your friends survived to tell the tale, I'm sure we will!' He urged Windrider on to join Melinya.

'Nobody ever listens!' grumbled Gur'brak. 'Well, don't say I didn't warn you!'

'We heard you!' said Callenor. 'We'll just have to be more careful when we get near to the woods, or we might all be howled to death!' He chuckled and coaxed the horse to follow Windrider.

The next two days were uneventful. The company saw no one, and there was very little sign of either birds or animals. As they reached the top of yet another small hill, Hinno called out, 'That must be the Withered Wood!'

They all followed the direction of his pointing finger. Some distance ahead of them was a dark blur on the landscape. As they drew closer, the blur resolved itself into a mass of twisted, crooked trees. The wood looked as if it had once been tall and strong. Now, however, the tops of the trees were all bent over; the branches crooked and interlocking. None of the trees had any leaves, but it was difficult to look into the heart of the forest. The dense tangle of branches made it seem dark and unwelcoming.

Athennar turned to address the company. 'We will avoid the Wood. Don't ride too close to the trees. Our Zorg friends say that there are strange tales about this forest, and I'm inclined to believe them. Keep your eyes open and your senses alert!'

The words had hardly left his mouth when several of the horses started snickering nervously.

'What's the matter with the horses?' called Valor, patting Sundust, who was also shifting uneasily. Kess, meanwhile, was trying to calm Blazer, who was snorting heavily.

Before Athennar could answer, the reply came floating on the wind: a long, drawn-out howling.

'Oh, no!' rumbled Gatera. 'What now?'

15

Attack of the Grey Runners

'We'll all be killed!' wailed Bar'drash.

'Stop gibbering!' muttered Gur'brak nervously. 'That howling noise is bad enough without you adding to it!'

The eerie call from the Withered Wood stopped, and the riders urged their horses onwards. The ground was becoming uneven and rocky, so they were unable to travel as quickly as they would have liked.

A sudden cry came from Hesteron. 'Look!' The others turned to look at the Withered Wood. Some distant shapes had started racing towards them.

Kess could just pick them out—silver wolf-like animals loping alongside strange, grey-clothed figures.

'Grey Runners!' breathed Athennar.

'What?' asked Melinya.

'Grey Runners—creatures I have only heard of in rumours. I never realised they could actually exist. I remember little about them.'

'I believe they are said to hunt in packs, and

116

will kill and eat almost any living being,' said Merric.

Kess shivered. He didn't like the sound of this at all!

Spurring Windrider forwards, Athennar called, 'Faster, everyone! We must try to outrun them!'

The company sped onwards, the horses somehow managing to thread their way through the scattered rocks without faltering. Gatera and Rrum raced alongside. Looking back, the Land Crafter shouted, 'They're gaining on us!'

Kess risked a glance over his shoulder as Blazer galloped over the rough ground. Gatera was right—the grey figures and the wolves were definitely closing.

'Over there!' shouted Athennar, pointing to a particularly rocky area. In the middle of the rocks was a wide patch of grass.

Reining in Windrider, he sprang from the saddle. 'Leave your horses here, and form a semi-circle in front of them!' he urged. He then snorted at Windrider and spoke softly to Sash before leaping onto a rock, his sword drawn. Melinya jumped up on the next rock, despite his protests. She drew her own slim sword.

Valor, Vallel, Hesteron and Hinno rushed to other rocks, fitting arrows to their bows. Gatera stood in a wide gap between two boulders, his axe ready. Rrum waited patiently beside him. Merric, Whisper and Kess took up positions towards one end of the line.

Callenor, meanwhile, was arguing with Gur'brak and Bar'drash.

'Give us some weapons!' complained Gur'brak. 'You can't expect us to defend ourselves if we're unarmed!'

'You'll have to make use of some rocks or something—I can't risk giving you swords. You might just decide to use them on us! Stay near me, where I can keep an eye on you!'

'Aw, that's not fair!'

'We won't attack you—honest!'

Callenor gave the two Zorgs a rough push forward. 'If you can't do anything useful, stay behind this rock!' he growled. He leaped onto the boulder, knowing he must give his attention to the forthcoming fight. The Zorgs would have to look after themselves.

The grey figures and wolves were now much nearer. Kess counted over twenty of each. The company was badly outnumbered. Their opponents travelled in pairs: each Grey Runner had a silver wolf running alongside. Some hundred yards away, they all stopped. Then the wolves lifted their heads and let out a haunting howl. Before the sound had died away, the Grey Runners also lifted their heads and gave a similar wail; the chill and deathly tones echoing around the company.

The friends all grimaced, and Gur'brak and Bar'drash covered their ears. All felt the same—the noise seemed to slice through them, wrenching at their very souls.

Then, with the howl still floating in the air, the attack began. Both Runners and wolves sprang forward and began running at a steady pace, their eyes fixed on their intended victims. The wolves drew back their lips, revealing rows of vicious fangs.

Athennar stood on one of the foremost rocks at the centre of the semi-circle, his hand raised. 'Archers, prepare!' he called.

When the creatures were well within range, he dropped his hand and shouted, 'Now!'

Each of the arrows found its mark: three wolves and a Grey Runner fell to the ground. To the archers' surprise, the other partners in each pair—three Runners and a wolf—also collapsed as if they, too, had been hit.

The archers quickly notched new arrows on to their

bowstrings. This time, there were three direct hits: two runners and a wolf fell, accompanied by their partners. One pair lay twitching in agony. The fourth arrow had hit a wolf in the back leg, but it continued running forward with a limp, its Grey Runner also limping, as if in sympathy.

'When you are attacked, concentrate your efforts on either the wolf or its Grey Runner!' shouted Athennar. 'Hurt one, and the other will be hurt, too!'

'That should even up the numbers a little!' boomed Gatera.

But there was no more time left for talking. The enemy was only yards away. Before the archers had time to fire again, the Grey Runners had vaulted on to the back of their wolves, urging them forward. Together, they leaped at the waiting company—a snarling mass of grey and silver.

Gatera found himself facing one of the largest wolves. Combined with its Grey Runner, it was a formidable opponent. It seemed as if hands and claws, legs and jaws all stretched out to grab him. Steeling himself, he swung his axe with all of his might. The wolf dodged, and the axe spun out of his hands. The Land Crafter grabbed his staff and swung it as the animal again attacked. This time, it landed with a crack on the head of the wolf. Both animal and Runner crashed to the ground, senseless.

Rrum, meanwhile, latched his own strong jaws on to another wolf's leg. His opponents screamed and writhed in agony, but he hung on until the wolf collapsed, then dispatched its Rider with a quick blow before either could regain their balance.

Another wolf had bounded on to the rock on which Athennar was standing. It lunged at the Animal Crafter, but he leaped nimbly aside. Briefly he considered trying to communicate with it, but its eyes were too full of hate to expect any response. Growling, the wolf and its rider turned. Athennar slashed at them with his sword, but this time the wolf dodged. It crouched, then charged. Athennar swiftly side-stepped and sliced his sword deep into the creature's side. The animal and its Grey Runner toppled from the rock to lay struggling on the ground. Athennar leaped down, and finished them with another sword thrust. He then looked around, and was relieved to see that Melinya had also managed to overcome a pair of attackers. Despite her gentle ways, she was well versed in the skills of hand-to-hand fighting.

Athennar then noticed two wolves that had slipped through the semi-circle and were running towards the frightened horses, several of which were beginning to shy away. The Animal Crafter whistled urgently. A black shape slinked out of the rocks and started racing to intercept the wolves. Sash had heard his call! She leaped at the nearest creature, and it tumbled over, spilling its rider on to the ground.

The Grey Runner regained his feet and, as Sash attacked the wolf, threw himself at the leopard. Sash was bowled over, and the Runner's wolf was upon her instantly, tearing at her flesh. Letting out a howl of victory, the wolf turned slightly to sink its teeth into Sash's throat. The next moment it collapsed as Athennar's blade ran through its partner's heart.

Sash lay motionless. Athennar stood shocked for a moment, but was forced to turn his attention back to the battle.

The second wolf that had broken through the defence had come face to face with Windrider. The brave white horse stood its ground valiantly, then reared up as the wolf sprang, knocking it and its rider to the ground. Before the wolf could recover,

Windrider turned and broke its skull with a well-aimed
kick of his hooves.

Fierce fighting was still taking place all around
the rocky enclosure. One wolf had bowled down
Hesteron, and its Grey Runner had leaped on top of
the winded Air Crafter. Screaming, Vallel jumped
from her rock. She drew her slim elven blade and
plunged it into the Grey Runner. The wolf grabbed
at her, tearing her jerkin with its teeth. She stabbed
again, and both Runner and wolf fell still.

Relieved, she helped Hesteron to his feet. The next
moment, both were attacked and sent flying by yet
another snarling partnership. They would have
suffered badly if Merric hadn't spotted their plight.
The minstrel dived at the Grey Runner. The two of
them tumbled over and over. First one was on top,
then the other. Vallel and Hesteron were meanwhile
trying to struggle to their feet while the wolf snarled
and lunged at them.

Suddenly, the Grey Runner was on top of Merric
once more. The minstrel felt his breath being crushed
out of him. Desperately, he lunged with his sword.
The blade slipped beneath the Runner's guard and
into his side. He collapsed with a sigh, and Merric
pushed him away.

Meanwhile, Kess was faring poorly. He had been
sent flying by a wolf, and the creature and its rider
now sprang on top of him. Desperately, Kess grabbed
at the wolf's throat, trying to keep the savage jaws
away. The creature was incredibly strong. The Quiet
One knew he was just seconds away from death. The
wolf shook its head free from his grasp. Kess rolled
quickly to one side. Expecting to feel its jaws close
around his neck, he put up his hands protectively.
Instead, he heard a strange wail, and turned to look.
The heads of both the wolf and its rider were enclosed
in a thick grey mist.

'Kill it!' yelled Whisper, who was still weaving her hands in the air. Kess lay still, momentarily transfixed. Muttering, Whisper drew her own sword and stabbed the Grey Runner. The wolf turned and lashed blindly at her, its cruel claws raking her face. Whisper screamed, and stabbed the Grey Runner again. Wolf and rider crumpled as Whisper clutched the side of her face, moaning in agony.

Callenor meanwhile had dispatched one wolf and was looking to see where he could help when he heard a strangled scream from below. A silver shape was advancing slowly on the terrified Bar'drash and Gur'brak. Callenor jumped from the rock between the creature and the Zorgs. His sword stroke pierced the Grey Runner's side, but the force of the impact knocked the weapon from his hand. The wolf staggered, but recovered and fastened its jaws on his leg. Callenor yelled as the teeth crunched through to the bone, which snapped under the pressure.

Gur'brak, surprised that Callenor should try and protect them, sprang into action, released from his trance of fear. Grabbing the fallen sword, he hacked at the Runner, time and again, even after the bloodied figure had collapsed, its life gone. Then the Zorg prised the dead wolf's fangs apart, freeing Callenor's leg.

The Hallion man had turned deathly pale, but nodded gratefully at the Zorg. 'My thanks,' he whispered hoarsely.

'Just repaying you!' said the Zorg gruffly. 'You saved us first! Besides which, if that slobbering beast had killed you, it would've been us next!' He looked around for his companion. Bar'drash was nowhere in sight.

Valor stood nearby, a look of cold determination on his face as he finished off one of the remaining wolves. He wiped his blade absentmindedly on his cloak.

Hinno, meanwhile, had faced the leader of the pack, a huge and wizened wolf. The creature had the cunning gained from many years of battle. It approached the elf warily, circling him, keeping out of reach of the flashing sword. Then, seeing an opening, it sprang. Hinno had been waiting for the attack, but its speed still surprised him. He was bowled off his feet and crashed against a rock. His sword fell from his hand. Rolling to one side, he tried to find the weapon. As he reached out, his hand was clamped by that of the Grey Runner. The Runner's grip was cold and clammy, but very firm. Twisting Hinno's arm, he pulled the elf's head back. Hinno looked into the deep, soulless pits that were the Runner's eyes. He noticed the man's sharp, pointed teeth, the long, dog-like nose. Then the Runner's face drew away and was replaced by that of the wolf—startlingly similar in many ways. The wolf's jaws fastened on Hinno's throat. For some reason, a picture of his friend Tolledon—proud, handsome, strong—flickered unexpectedly into Hinno's mind. It was his last thought.

16

The Newcomer

The leader of the wolf pack and his Grey Runner let out a long, drawn-out howl. Realising that most of the pack had been killed, the pair turned and led the two remaining wolves away, retreating back to the distant shelter of the Withered Woods.

The company breathed sighs of relief as the wolves sloped away. Bodies lay strewn all around the rocks: the broken corpses of the Grey Runners lying next to their silver-furred partners.

As the wolves left, there was the sound of a horn blast, and a brightly coloured figure came riding towards the company. Sliding from his horse, he said, 'Ah! Good meeting, friends. I see I arrived just in time to scare off those vermin! Allow me to introduce myself—my name is Falron.' He flicked a speck of dust from his red and yellow shirt.

Athennar frowned. Being sociable was the last thing he felt like doing at the present. Ignoring the man's first comments he replied, 'Good meeting. Excuse us if we do not extend a very hearty welcome. We have had a hard battle.'

'Indeed, indeed! I am only sorry I could not have arrived earlier! I would soon have dealt with those oversized puppies!'

'If you will excuse us, we have some injuries to attend.'

'Certainly! Please forgive my intrusion!'

Athennar turned wearily and hauled the heavy, bleeding body of Sash into his arms. He called the rest of the battered and exhausted company together at the heart of the grassy circle.

Gatera walked over solemnly, carrying the torn body of Hinno. Kess tended Whisper, while Callenor hopped forward, one hand on Gur'brak's shoulder. The Zorg felt sure that this was as much to restrain him from running off to join Bar'drash—wherever he might be—as for support. However, Callenor was still obviously in much pain from his broken leg.

As they gathered together, Athennar lowered Sash to the ground very slowly; then trudged over to join Gatera, who had lain Hinno on the grass. Hesteron was examining the elf, but shook his head as Athennar approached. The Animal Crafter knelt and bowed his head in grief. Hinno had been a lifelong and valued friend. Melinya knelt beside him, taking his hand in hers.

The rest of the company stood in silence, each nurturing his or her own memories of the brave elf leader.

Athennar finally stood and whispered, 'Love light; know peace; follow truth; live free.' Vallel gulped back the tears as she heard the words her sister had also uttered as she lay dying.

After pausing for a while, Athennar turned. Asking Merric and Valor to bury the elf's body beneath a cairn of stones, he motioned Hesteron to join him.

First, he bade Callenor to sit down on a nearby

rock while Hesteron examined his leg. The Air Crafter did what he could, strapping the limb with lengths of cloth, and applying herbs to the wound. Then, leaving Callenor in Melinya's tender care, Athennar and Hesteron turned their attention to Whisper. She was moaning quietly, still clutching Kess with one hand and her face with the other.

Hesteron pulled out the pouch of healing lotions and herbs that he always carried. 'This should ease the pain,' he said, dabbing some salve on the gouge marks. 'But you must return to the fortress with Callenor. Tolledon will treat the wounds with some ointment that should help them to heal completely.'

Whisper started to protest, but Kess quietened her. 'You must go back,' he insisted, 'or you may be scarred for life.'

At first she shook her head. Then, gritting her teeth, she nodded. 'I'm sorry I can't help you any longer,' she said. 'I hope I've at least made some amends for my selfishness.'

Kess looked at her gratefully. 'You saved my life— what more could a man ask? I'm sorry I've been so angry with you lately—I was upset about Linnil. Perhaps I can ask one thing—go back and look after her for me, would you?'

Whisper smiled, even though the action brought a wince of pain. 'Of course,' she replied.

'Is anybody else hurt?' asked Athennar. The others shook their heads. Then the Animal Crafter led Hesteron over to the prostrate body of Sash. 'Can you help her?' he asked hoarsely, a mixture of fear and hope in his eyes.

Hesteron ran his skilled fingers over the form of the black leopard. 'Her breathing is shallow, but I think I can do something to help her,' he said. Rubbing some of the salve into Sash's wounds, he added, 'The wounds are quite deep, but I don't think they've done any permanent damage.' Then he searched through his backpack and produced a small bag filled with red flower heads. Spitting on them, he crushed the petals between his fingers, then waved them under Sash's nose.

The leopard stirred, whined slightly, and opened her eyes to look up imploringly at Athennar. The Animal Crafter stroked her head gently. 'It's good to have you back with us,' he whispered. A pink tongue rasped at his hand, and he managed a small smile.

'Will she be able to travel with us?' asked Valor. The young Mountain Guard had become very fond of Sash.

Athennar nodded. 'I think so. She is very strong; she just needs some rest for an hour or two.' Turning to Callenor, he said, 'It is best if you and Whisper start the journey back to the fortress now. Merric, if you, Gatera, Rrum and Valor can accompany them past the Withered Woods, that should be sufficient to deter any further attack from the three remaining wolves.'

The small group was soon ready to leave, Callenor having had some assistance to mount his horse. Although riding was very painful with his broken leg, it was the only feasible way to travel back to the fortress.

Athennar shook Callenor's hand. 'Tell my father about the battle and about ... Hinno.' Callenor nodded his understanding.

Whisper looked down at Kess from her horse with a wistful expression on her face. 'Farewell,' she said, pursing her lips.

Kess took her hand and held it briefly. 'Farewell— and thank you,' he replied.

'Do not fear,' Whisper added, 'I will tend Linnil as if she were my own sister.'

Kess tried to smile, but he knew he would miss the silver-eyed woman. The resentment that had been eating at him had drained away, and had left his heart feeling lighter than it had for some time. However, he was now taunted by frustration—just as he had begun to grow closer to Whisper again, she was having to leave.

Once the group had departed, Athennar turned his attention to the new arrival. Falron had been sitting quietly on a rock, watching the events with mild interest.

'Forgive us our discourtesy,' Athennar said. 'As you can see, the battle has caused us some difficulties. We will have a meal as soon as the others return. Will you join us?'

'By all means!' replied Falron.

Athennar introduced the remaining members of the company. Falron raised his eyebrows when Gur'brak's name was given. 'A Zorg! I wondered what he was doing here!'

Gur'brak shifted uncomfortably, but said nothing.

'He is helping to guide us to our destination,' Athennar explained, 'along with his companion, Bar'drash, who appears to have taken advantage of the distractions of the battle to disappear. You don't know where he went, do you, Gur'brak?'

The Zorg captain shrugged. 'Wherever he's gone, he won't last long out there without my help. One good howl from the wolves and he'll soon come scuttling back!' He cleared his throat. 'You—er—you don't think we should be moving on, do you? I mean, the wolves might come back again at any time!'

'They might, but I doubt it,' replied Athennar. 'I for one am not moving until our friends return and until Sash has recovered sufficiently to travel.'

'Huh!' snorted the Zorg. 'Why can't we leave the

wretched cat to look after itself?' Seeing a warning glint in Athennar's eyes, he fell silent.

Within an hour, Merric, Valor, Gatera and Rrum returned. They had seen no further signs of any wolves or Grey Runners, although they had heard a distant howl from the Withered Wood.

Hesteron and Vallel had prepared some bowls of stew, which were heating over a makeshift fire. The Air Crafter had added some herbs that would help the company to relax, and would also provide some strength for the next stage of their journey. The pleasant smell wafted on the breeze.

Merric's keen ears picked up a grunt from behind a nearby rock. Tiptoeing stealthily over, he dashed behind the rock and emerged again leading Bar'drash by the ear.

'Ow! Leggo! That 'urts!'

'I told you he'd be back!' muttered Gur'brak. 'I might've known he couldn't resist the smell of food!'

Merric pushed Bar'drash over towards his companion, and the Zorg collapsed in a heap, sulking and nursing his bruised ear.

Gur'brak sighed. 'You never could get anything right, could you, hog's breath? Now I've got to put up with your moaning all over again.'

'Aw, c'mon, boss,' Bar'drash replied. 'I only came back to see if you were all right.'

'Yeah, that's about as likely as a Tark kissing a Zorg to sleep,' scoffed Gur'brak. 'You only came back for one thing—to feed that fat belly of yours!'

Merric grinned, and left the Zorgs to their bickering.

Everyone settled down to eat, the troubadour perching on a small rock next to the newcomer. 'Why is it that you are travelling in these parts, Falron?' he asked.

Falron pointed at Merric's lute, propped up beside the minstrel. 'Like you, I am a follower of the gentle arts,' he replied. 'Not a musician, oh no, but a writer of poems and stories. My home is in Lanwick, where I owned a boat—a small but sturdy craft. One day, I set sail from the Northlands for the Isle of Mindrod. Alas, a heavy storm blew up, and my craft was blown southwards. Eventually it splintered against some rocks on the east coast. I was fortunate indeed to escape with my life and my belongings.' He patted his battered backpack and the huge hunting horn that was strapped around his shoulder.

Pausing for breath and for a gulp of the steaming stew, he continued: 'When I realised I was in the Southlands, I decided to explore. I thought the area might be the source of new inspiration for my poems. Indeed, your little fray today has already given me some ideas:

The wolves came racing o'er the land,
The Grey Ones too were—'

Athennar, who had been listening to the conversation, held up his hand. 'Enough time for poetry later,' he said.

Falron smiled, giving a little shrug.

Merric watched, unimpressed. He was not convinced by the poet's story. Still, the man seemed amiable enough.

'Where did you find your horse?' asked Valor suddenly.

Falron paused before answering. 'I met him as I was wandering through a secluded valley. I have no idea where he came from. I suspect he is fairly old, and may have been in the Southlands for many years. As you may have noticed, I ride bareback. I made the bridle and reins myself—my abilities are quite wide-ranging, if I may say so.'

The others looked at the horse. It had no saddle, just a tattered blanket thrown across its back. The bridle was crudely fashioned from leather, and the reins were no more than loosely twined pieces of fraying rope.

'May I travel with you?' Falron asked suddenly. 'I sense that you are on some kind of quest yourselves—otherwise you would hardly be travelling together in such numbers in these lands. I feel you could prove to be the source of many tales and poems!'

Athennar laughed. 'I don't know about that, my friend. Where we are going is highly dangerous—as you can see, we have already lost one of our number, and two more have had to withdraw.'

'All the more reason why I should accompany you!' exclaimed the other. 'I am no mean swordsman, and would not be a burden.'

Athennar shrugged and looked at the others. 'Any objections?' he asked. They all either shook their heads or grunted their agreement. Only Merric stayed silent.

'Very well,' Athennar said, nodding to Falron. 'You are indeed welcome. But may I suggest you cover your clothes with something a little, um, less colourful?'

Falron laughed, and produced a brown cloak from his backpack. 'Agreed!' he said. 'My clothes mirror my character; but I admit that they tend to make me somewhat conspicuous.'

Athennar was about to reply when a large dark shape sidled up to him and nuzzled against his knee. 'Sash, my faithful friend! How are you, girl?' He spoke in soft purring tones to the leopard. She snorted back at him.

Hesteron bent over Sash to check her wounds, then nodded to Athennar. 'She will be sore for some while, but she will be able to accompany us.'

'Good!' replied Athennar. 'We will travel slowly this afternoon—we all need to recover our strength after the battle with the Grey Runners. We have a long way to go, and who knows what dangers may yet await us?'

Merric pursed his lips. Like the others in the company, he knew that the worst was yet to come. They still had to find Dargan—and his powers were far stronger than those of the wolves or the Grey Runners!

17

The Search for Water

Two days later, the company reached the edge of a steep cliff. Far below, a river wound its way lazily towards the High East Seas. A long, old wooden bridge stretched across the chasm that separated them from the far cliff.

Kess looked at the structure apprehensively. He wondered who had made the bridge, and why. Each side of it was formed from the trunk of what must have once been a very tall, slim tree. Between the two sides was a walkway of short weathered planks. The whole bridge looked as if it had perched there for years, even centuries. Kess hoped that it hadn't rotted during that time.

Bar'drash was more outspoken about his doubts. 'Aw, I'm not going across there!' he said. 'Last time I tried to cross one of these things, I nearly fell over the side!'

'In that case, p'raps we should just push you over the edge now, to save time,' muttered Gur'brak.

'Aw, c'mon, boss . . . .'

Athennar gingerly tested the bridge. It was surprisingly firm despite its old, slightly battered appearance.

He had to tread carefully, as in one or two places a plank was missing. However, he slowly worked his way across to the other side. Then he returned, stepping more quickly now that he was sure it was safe.

'Why did you come back?' asked Valor.

'The horses will need to be reassured before they will cross the bridge,' the Animal Crafter replied. 'Will you help me?'

At the fortress, Athennar had spent several hours explaining some of the basic skills of Animal Crafting to Valor. Together they now calmed the horses, and soon they were ready to cross.

'I'm not going!' complained Bar'drash, as Merric tried to prod him into action. A moment later he was swept off his feet by Gatera, who clutched him under one great arm.

'Ow! Leggo!' yelled the enraged Zorg, kicking and screaming.

'If you do much more of that, I'll drop you!' warned Gatera.

Bar'drash stopped kicking, but his complaints could be heard all the way across the bridge. 'Oh no! I'm gonna die! You can't do this to me! Stop 'im, boss!'

Gur'brak, however, was too concerned about his own safety to worry about Bar'drash. He wished he had asked Gatera to carry him across as well. As it was, he edged his way on to the bridge behind Vallel, Hesteron and Melinya.

'Get a move on!' said Valor, nudging him from behind. The Zorg stumbled, and broke out in a cold sweat. What if he fell over the side?

The next moment, he felt a gentle hand grasp his. Climbing to his feet, he looked straight into eyes of pale sapphire.

'Come, walk with me,' said Melinya, still holding his hand. Gur'brak reluctantly walked a step behind, clutching her hand nervously. He only hoped that Bar'drash was still occupied by his own fears, otherwise he would never be able to live this down. Being led meekly across the bridge by a woman, indeed! Still, she was a very beautiful woman—even he could see that— and her hand was comforting, her voice reassuring.

Meanwhile, the others trooped across the bridge behind him in slow procession. Falron's horse remained a little nervy, but after further soothing words from Athennar followed the poet across.

Finally, they all reached the other side, Sash being the last to make the journey. She padded confidently across the bridge, as sure-footed as ever.

Bar'drash lay in a heap, his one eye closed. 'Never again!' he muttered. 'Never again!'

'What are you making such a fuss for?' grumbled Gur'brak, having recovered quickly from the ordeal. He looked around to make sure no one else was listening, then added, 'It wasn't that bad.'

Bar'drash growled and scratched his deformed ear. 'Never again!' he said.

After a hasty meal of bread, cheese and fruit, they were on their way once more. The landscape became increasingly rocky as they progressed. The sparse trees were bent over like hunched figures; the result of the wind's buffeting over many years. Even the coarse, spikey grass leaned over in a permanent, submissive bow to the south.

Heavy clouds darkened the sky, adding to the air of defeat and gloom. Their progress grew frustratingly slow. At times, sudden outcrops of rock would bar their way, forcing a detour, and the terrain gradually became more hilly.

By late afternoon, the travellers were very weary. Reaching the top of a small rise, they looked down on a cluster of ruined buildings standing next to a large

copse of gnarled trees. Athennar sent Merric ahead
to scout for any sign of danger. The minstrel soon
signalled the company to join him by the collapsed
stone huts.

The nearest building was the largest, so they
decided to make camp within its walls, out of reach
of the constant bite of the wind.

'Our water supplies are getting low,' Hesteron
informed Athennar.

'And there have been no signs of any streams or
rivers since we crossed the bridge,' added Vallel.

'Aye, and all this healthy walking brings on a
thirst!' boomed Gatera, licking his lips.

Athennar pondered for a moment. 'We must search
the surrounding area carefully. As there must once
have been a community here—though by the Realm,
I don't know why anyone would want to live in a place
like this—there should be some water nearby. Vallel,
your talents will be especially helpful. If you, Gatera,
Hesteron and Rrum could scout around, the rest of
us will gather wood and prepare a meal while you are
gone. Let me know as soon as you are successful.'

The four friends dutifully set off to check the copse
and the hills. 'First, we should search through the
wood,' suggested Hesteron. 'With all these trees, it
seems the most likely place for water. If we spread
out, we can keep sight of each other as we walk
through it.'

They started slowly, with Gatera on the extreme
left, Hesteron to the right, and Rrum and Vallel in
the middle. Walking was easy; the ground was covered
with layers of leaf mould, and there was very little
undergrowth. They were only yards within the fringe
of the copse when Vallel shouted, 'Over here!'

The others ran to join her. She was standing in a
clearing beside a small, round well. 'There seems to

be water in here, yet something troubles me,' she said, sniffing the air. She shrugged. 'Perhaps it's just my imagination.' Finding a small stone, she dropped it into the well to see how far down the water was. The stone disappeared into the water without making a single sound, and without causing any ripples.

'Nott goodd water,' said Rrum, shaking his head.

Nodding thoughtfully, Vallel said, 'I tend to agree with you, Rrum.'

Hesteron said, 'Well, we could try drawing some— that might help us to decide. I'll go and find a bowl. I'll fetch Athennar as well—I think he'll want to see this.'

He was soon back, accompanied by the rest of the company, who were all curious to see the well. The only other one Kess had seen before was at the Fortress of Fear—in his Valley home, all the folks drew their water from the river or the numerous streams.

Vallel repeated her trick with the stone. Then Athennar handed her a deep wooden bowl tied to a length of thin rope. 'Try lowering this down,' he suggested.

She lowered the bowl slowly down to the water. It disappeared beneath the surface. When she started to draw it up again, she gave a gasp of dismay. The rope came up, but the bowl had completely vanished!

Merric examined the end of the rope. 'Passing strange! It is almost as if it had been cut with a knife!' he exclaimed.

'Well, this water definitely isn't safe to drink—even if we could reach it,' said Hesteron. 'No wonder no one lives here any more!'

'We must search further, in case there is another source of water nearby,' said Athennar. 'I will join you, along with Melinya and Merric. Valor, can you and Rrum keep an eye on the Zorgs, and collect some wood for the fire? We won't be very long.'

The Mountain Guard smiled. 'No problem,' he said.

'Meanwhile, Kess,' continued Athennar, 'perhaps you and Falron could start to prepare the food.'

Kess nodded, and Falron gave a little salute. 'At your service, sire,' he said. Merric watched the two as they walked back towards the hut. He couldn't decide whether the poet was being sarcastic or just good-humoured. However, this was no time to ponder such things. He joined Hesteron and Vallel, and the three of them started to search the copse for any further sign of water. Meanwhile, Athennar, Melinya and Gatera set off to check the rocky slopes beyond the ruined buildings.

Valor and Rrum were left alone in the little clearing with the two Zorgs. 'Right, pick up any loose branches you can find, and we'll take them back to the hut,' instructed Valor.

Grumbling to themselves, the Zorgs sauntered over to the edge of the clearing to find some sticks. Bar'drash nudged Gur'brak and hissed, 'Here's our chance!'

'What are you talking about, frog's brain?' replied Gur'brak.

'Our chance! To escape! Look, they're picking up wood as well! No one's watching us! Let's go!' Not waiting to hear his captain's reply, he dropped the few sticks he had collected and started running through the trees.

'Stop!' called an angry voice. Valor rushed after him, brandishing his sword. Bar'drash turned to his right, desperately looking for some thicker under-growth that would slow his opponent down. He knew that the Mountain Guard was much faster than he was, but if he could find somewhere where his stocky build would be to an advantage . . . .

Looking back, he caught sight of what seemed to be a rolling boulder. Then he was sent flying, and landed with a grunt on a pile of leaves. Rrum straightened himself up as Valor reached the prostrate Zorg.

Holding the tip of his sword against the Zorg's neck, the Guardsman growled, 'One more trick like that and it will be your last! Rrum, can you go and check that the other one hasn't escaped?' He yanked Bar'drash to his feet, then pushed him ahead as they followed the little Rrokki back to the clearing.

Much to Bar'drash's surprise, Gur'brak was still there. 'Why didn't you run?' he hissed.

'Because I've got more sense, stench-bag,' his companion replied.

'Pah!'

Valor gave the Zorg another encouraging push, and told him to start collecting firewood again. Bar'drash reluctantly obeyed, muttering to himself all the time.

Meanwhile, Athennar, Melinya and Gatera were making their way slowly up a steep hill, some twenty yards apart. Rocks jutted out of the slope like shoulder blades thrusting through the matted grass. The three friends struggled upwards until Gatera called, 'I've found some water!'

Athennar and Melinya scrambled over to join the Land Crafter. A stream of water—so clean and clear that it was barely visible—tumbled down between some rocks. Then, after a few yards, it mysteriously disappeared into the solid ground.

Gatera picked a long blade of grass and dipped its tip into the water. The end of the leaf disappeared.

'It's the same as the water in the well!' he breathed. 'What can have happened to it?'

Sighing, Athennar replied, 'Who knows? Perhaps Dargan found out that people used to live here, and decided to make sure that they wouldn't be able to do so again. Anyway, it doesn't look like we'll find any water that's drinkable. Come on, let's go back and join the others!'

They were just turning round when Melinya caught sight of something moving. The water, as if sensing them, had changed its course, and was now flowing straight towards them.

'Look out!' she called. Gatera and Athennar dodged to one side and she started to follow, but tripped. The water surged forward thirstily as she lay on the grass, winded. Dazed, she saw that it had already reached the edge of her travelling cloak. She tried to roll out of the way, but was blocked by a large boulder. Alarmed, she realised that there was no time left— she couldn't escape the deadly liquid.

18

Dark Plans

Tolledon paced up and down the empty courtyard. His heart was heavy. He was worried about the fate of the company; about Hallion; and most of all, he mourned the loss of Hinno.

Whisper and Callenor had arrived at the fortress the previous day, Whisper guiding the horse towards one of the southern gates with difficulty. Callenor had fainted from the pain of his broken leg, and was slumped over the horse's neck. Somehow, despite her own pain, Whisper had managed to keep him from falling off while she steered the animal towards the fortress.

Fortunately, the alert elves on the battlements had seen the riders approaching, and three horsemen were dispatched to help them into the fortress. On arrival Whisper, too, had collapsed.

Tolledon then faced a harrowing period of time: ministering to the two wounded travellers without being able to find out what had happened to the rest of the company. Whisper's wounds were bathed and treated and Callenor's broken leg was carefully reset.

Callenor soon revived, aided by his strength and fitness, and was able to tell Tolledon about the battle with the Grey Runners, and of Hinno's death. The Guardian wept unashamedly. Hinno had been a close and trusted friend for many decades.

Now, as he paced, he pondered his next move. There was little he could do to help the company, except pray for them. For a flickering moment, he felt totally inadequate—the fate of the Realm had, in a way, passed from his hands.

'What's troubling you, my friend?'

Tolledon looked up as Meltizoc came wheezing across the courtyard. He gave a heavy sigh in reply.

'Try not to worry. You have done all you can,' the wise man reassured him.

'Yes, but I feel so helpless. As you know, I am a man of action. I find it very difficult just to sit and wait.'

'I know. So I suggest that we do something: tomorrow we should travel to Hallion together. Hinno's friends need to know of his untimely death.'

Tolledon stopped pacing. 'You are right as usual, my friend. A journey to Hallion is just what I need, though it will be hard to carry such news. However, I will also be able to see for myself the damage that Dargan has inflicted upon my beloved valley. We will start in the morning. The change of air and scenery will do us both good. I tire of these stone walls and floors!'

'Then that is settled!' smiled Meltizoc. Inwardly, he breathed a sigh of relief. He was concerned to see his friend so troubled. The trip to Hallion might lighten his spirits. Pursing his lips, he followed his friend back into the fortress.

Dargan chuckled to himself. He was making faster progress than he had expected. Every time he used the Sceptre, he could feel a surge of triumph as he fed off its power, twisting it to his own ends. And each time he used it, he found new outlets for the power.

First, it had been his small experiments on the potted plants—pathetic though those tests now seemed, they had been minor victories at the time. Then it had been the insects, and then—he chuckled once more—the girl. He wondered whether or not she had faded into oblivion yet. It was a fate she deserved for having dared to try and thwart his plans!

Following that, there had been the shrubs and rocks in the area outside the Tower of Braggad, and then the most pleasing conquest of all—his masterful plot against Hallion. He had succeeded in attacking the very heart of the Realm. Soon the rest of the Realm would be trembling in fear at his awesome power!

Most recently, he had experimented on the elf captured at the Fortress of Fear. As he thought about it, Dargan's expression turned into a sneer. The pitiful creature! Although it had tried to resist his will, its puny struggles had only served to urge him into greater efforts.

When he realised how easily he could control the elf—and how rapidly he could cause the feeble creature to fade, Dargan had given a snort of pleasure. Then he had tossed the elf aside, like a discarded toy, leaving him in a crumpled heap in the castle courtyard, ready for Targul.

Surprisingly, the Tark had not enjoyed its 'meal'. Fixing Dargan with its venomous green eye slits, it communicated its displeasure. *The elf was 'stale', and of little nutritional value. You completely drained it of its mental energies!*

Secretly, this pleased Dargan as it confirmed the success of his powers. However, he needed to keep the Tark happy.

'Take your pick of my slaves,' he said. 'While they will not be as, um, tender as the elf, they should provide you with sufficient nourishment.'

Targul had withdrawn, apparently satisfied for the moment, enabling the Dark Master to turn his mind to more important issues.

The following day, out of sheer curiosity, he had returned to the scene of his early experiments on the cliff face outside the tower. To his astonishment and delight, there was not a single tree or shrub in sight! Although he had originally only tested his powers on a few bushes and trees in the area nearest to the tower, all the other plants along the entire length of the cliff face had now vanished as well! Equally, some of the larger rocks that used to jut out across the path to the tower had also started to fade.

Now, as he thought about these new surprises, a crooked smile once more worked its way across Dargan's face. His control of the Realm was going to be even easier than he had anticipated! All he had to do was visit an area, twist the Sceptre's power until it strengthened his own will, focus it in a concentrated attack on a few plants and shrubs, and then leave the area and await the results. The fading process, once started, would spread out, just like the ripples from a pebble thrown into a pond. How fast and far it would spread, he didn't yet know. However, that would become clear in time.

Meanwhile, he could start the process by visiting some more areas in the Northlands, and then he could sit back and await the results. He felt sure that it wouldn't take long for the whole Realm to become a cold and barren place.

Before he began to put the final stages for his plans into action, however, there was one problem left to solve. Clearing the Realm of all but essential vegetation was one thing; conquering the minds of its peoples was another, far more difficult task.

The gloating smile left his face for a moment. He needed to delve deeper into his books, to see if there were any clues that might help him. Then he would need some more subjects for his experiments. Powerful as he was, he couldn't risk another raid on the fortress—they would be ready for him now. No, perhaps he could persuade Targul to find one or two of the other Tarks. The creatures could then scour the Northlands for any signs of humans. They might be able to find a small group of travellers, or perhaps some bandits. Either would suit his purposes.

The smile returned to his face, and he rubbed his hands in eager anticipation of the battles ahead. He had no fear of them, for of one thing he was sure—he would be victorious! No one could foil his plans. The Realm would soon be completely under his control!

Tolledon cradled his head in his hands, and half-wished he hadn't agreed to come on this trip to Hallion. The task of telling Hinno's family and friends of his death was hard enough. Harder still was the discovery of the extent of the changes in his homeland.

Reaching the once grassy plains that led to the Falls of Hallion, he had almost fallen from his horse with shock and dismay. 'The grass!' he whispered in a hoarse voice. 'It's gone!' Bare earth stretched away before him, broken only by occasional clumps of yellowing grass. The clumps served as painful reminders of the past beauty of the area.

The small party made its way in silence towards the falls. Then Tolledon reined in his horse, suddenly realising that something else was wrong. 'The falls!'

he cried. 'They've stopped! Where has all the water gone?'

'Dargan's work, curse him!' muttered Meltizoc. The news that had filtered through to the fortress had led them to expect some changes, but this was far worse than either of them had imagined.

Tolledon just sat and shook his head in sheer disbelief. Instead of the joyful, white cascade he loved, just a solitary trickle of water wound its way down the rock face.

A young female rider approached, her horse's hooves thundering over the hard ground. The Guardian winced at the sound.

'Good meeting, sire. I'm pleased to see you. We've missed you sorely in Hallion.'

Tolledon shook his head once more, this time to clear his thoughts. 'I've been away too long,' he replied. 'The fading—has it affected Hallion?'

'It spreads, sire, ever outward. The people are afraid —they don't know what to do. It's like a deadly disease.'

'A disease that will not be halted until Đargan himself is defeated!' A determined, steely tone had returned to Tolledon's voice. 'And defeated he will be! He must be!'

They followed the woman slowly up the passage behind the falls—or what remained of them. When they reached the open air once more at the top, Tolledon gave a small sigh of relief. As he looked around, everything seemed as he had left it: the green pasture; the merry chuckling streams; the strong trees moving softly to the tune of a light breeze.

Then he realised that there was a difference—not in the landscape, but in the people. They were no longer the happy, contented folk he had left behind. Even the children played quietly, with few signs of boisterousness or laughter.

Some of the older folk came to greet him, respectful but solemn. He could sense the anxiety; see the fear that lay behind their eyes. Then it was as if a gate had burst open, and all their questions came tumbling out. What was happening to their beloved vale? How could they stop it? Where was Dargan? Had he been caught? Would he be caught?

Tolledon and Meltizoc answered their questions as best they could, and then proceeded to a hut beside the Great Cabin. A hot meal was awaiting them—along with more people, and more questions.

After dinner, they accompanied some of the leading men, women and elves through the woods to the glade where Dargan's evil had been unleashed against the vale.

The Guardian was alarmed to see how much the fading had spread. The clearing where Dargan had landed was, like the plain beyond the falls, just bare earth now. It was also a much wider area than before, several of the trees around its edge having disappeared completely. Dozens of the trees beyond, deep into the wood, were also showing symptoms of the blight. It was a strange, sad sight—some were almost transparent, others were showing the early signs of losing their colour and vigour.

Gritting his teeth, Tolledon took a deep breath. He couldn't afford to let his friends see how shaken he felt. Inside his mind, however, the questions raged incessantly. How much further would the fading spread? How much stronger had Dargan grown by now? He had already underestimated the Dark Master's strength. The Sceptre had obviously enabled him to increase his powers enormously. Would the company be able to find Dargan in time, before his power became too great to resist? For Hallion, it appeared as if it might already be too late.

19

The Wailing Hills

Strong arms plucked Melinya out of the path of the water. She gasped in relief as Athennar carried her safely out of the stream's reach. Once they were some distance away, he lowered her gently on to a large rock.

'Did the water touch you?' he asked.

She shook her head. 'I don't think so.' Looking down, she checked to make sure. One edge of her travelling cloak had disappeared, as if something had taken a large bite out of it.

'The water has returned to its original course!' called Gatera, who had been keeping watch.

'Good!' replied Athennar, partly in acknowledgement of the Land Crafter's words, partly in relief that Melinya was unhurt. He then helped Melinya to her feet, and the three friends trudged back down the uneven slope.

Kess and Falron were sitting outside the stone hut tending some rabbits, which were sizzling on a long spit over a blazing fire. Gur'brak and Bar'drash were huddled against the hut wall, both of them apparently asleep.

'Any sign of water?' asked Kess as the three friends approached.

'No,' replied Athennar. 'And we're unlikely to find any!' He briefly explained their discovery of the small stream.

Valor, crouching nearby, groaned. 'Well, we'll have to eat some fruit with the meal tonight. What water we have left should be given to the horses.'

Athennar nodded in agreement.

Within minutes, Hesteron, Vallel and Merric returned, also having had no success in their quest. The company sat down to their meal that evening in a quiet and sombre frame of mind.

The next day dawned grey and chill. Hesteron, who had been for another brief scout around, said, 'There's plenty of cloud overhead, but little likelihood of rain, I fear.'

Vallel sniffed the air and held her hand up to test it, then sighed, 'I'm afraid you're right.'

'Never mind,' replied Athennar. 'At least it's not hot! We must make good progress today, and yet keep careful watch for any signs of a stream or river.'

Soon they were all ready to set off on the next stage of their journey. Gur'brak rode on Blazer with Kess. The Valley man tried to ignore the stale smell of the Zorg, but it was virtually impossible. After a couple of hours, Kess developed an annoying itch that seemed to move rapidly around his body.

Bar'drash meanwhile perched on Sundust with Valor. However, the Mountain Guard was becoming increasingly impatient with the Zorg's constant grumblings, and several times had to restrain himself from pushing Bar'drash off the horse.

The only lively member of the company was Falron,

who rode along singing a merry song in a curiously tuneless voice.

The clouds continued to thicken, and a heavy breeze plucked at their clothing. After a little while the rough terrain again flattened out, much to the travellers' relief. Far in the distance across the plains, perhaps two or three days' ride ahead, they could just make out a range of low, dark mountains.

'The Wailing Hills,' Gur'brak explained to Kess. 'The Tower of Braggad is beyond them.'

Kess shivered. He didn't like the look—or the sound—of the distant hills, any more than he liked the look of the bleak landscape all around them.

They travelled steadily onwards, with still no sign of any water. By the time they camped that night in the shelter of a cluster of tall rocks they were all feeling both weary and thirsty. Fortunately, there was still plenty of fresh fruit available.

Athennar was most concerned about the horses and Sash. 'We must find drink for them tomorrow,' he said. 'It is unfair to keep pushing them over such rough terrain without any water.'

Melinya gave him a little hug. 'We must trust in Elsinoth, my love. He will provide.' She ignored the rude snort that this remark drew from Bar'drash.

After their meal, most of the company fell silent, engrossed in their own thoughts. Many thought of Hinno; and of Linnil, still weak and ill. To relieve the atmosphere of gloom, Merric produced his flute and played a gentle but familiar melody. Melinya started to sing, her crystal voice immediately lightening their hearts. One by one, the travellers joined in. Soon the music was floating around the campsite, and for a while they all forgot their troubles.

Gatera, who was on watch in the rocks, also began to relax. At first he had been concerned about the volume of sound, but then smiled to himself. He realised that this was just what the company needed— a brief time of enjoyment in the midst of their relentless pursuit of Dargan and the Sceptre.

The following day brought another long trek across the parched and forbidding landscape. The journey became a continuous slog through rocks, dust, and coarse yellow grass. The weather showed no sign of changing; the drab greyness of the clouds mirroring the dismal nature of the barren countryside.

By the afternoon, a series of low hills had broken the monotony of the plain. To spare the horses, the company had all dismounted, and now struggled dispiritedly from slope to slope. Vallel, lost in thoughts of her home in Tarrelford, stumbled over a rock, and fell heavily to the ground. Hesteron rushed to her aid, but was surprised when she waved him back.

'Ssshh!' she urged, then shouted, 'Can everyone stand still for a moment, please?'

Puzzled, the rest of the company came to a halt as Vallel pressed her ear to the ground. 'I thought so!' she said triumphantly. 'Water! It's somewhere nearby!'

Gatera stepped over to a clear patch of ground and wiggled his toes. 'She's right!' he boomed.

Working together, the Water Crafter and Land Crafter pinpointed the direction of the sound, and then led the company across the hillside. Hesteron, sensing the air currents, also gave a slight smile of satisfaction.

Passing over the brow of the hill, they came to a craggy dell. Nestled among the rocks was a large pool of clear water.

'At last!' said Valor, about to rush forward.

Athennar held him back. 'Let's make absolutely sure

that it's safe first,' he warned. Picking up a stone, he
threw it into the pool. There was a pleasing 'plop'.
Just to make sure, the Animal Crafter knelt down
beside the pool and lowered a stalk of grass into the
water. To everyone's relief, it was still intact when he
pulled it out again. Then, motioning to Vallel, he
asked her to give them her opinion of the water.

Letting some run between her fingers, she gave a
grunt of pleasure, then took a cautious sip. 'It's
lovely,' she said.

'Good!' breathed Athennar in relief.

'Thank you, Elsinoth,' whispered Melinya.

Athennar continued, 'I suggest that first we fill all
our canteens, let the horses drink, and then bathe our
tired bodies. Women first, men later.'

Valor groaned good-naturedly, and Kess grinned
at his friend. 'Don't worry—it'll soon be our turn. I
think I'll make sure I get in there before Gur'brak
and Bar'drash, though—the water will be unfit for
anything after they've been in it!'

It transpired that the Zorgs weren't too keen on
the idea of bathing in the water. When their turn
came, they resisted strongly. In the end, Athennar
and Valor picked up Bar'drash and Gatera grabbed
hold of Gur'brak. Standing on a rock beside the
pool, they threw the fully-clothed Zorgs into the water.
They disappeared momentarily in the wake of the
splash, then rose spluttering to the surface, having
found that they could just stand upright without
drowning.

'Yow! It's cold! Aw, no, I'm soaked!'

'What d'you expect, cloth-brain?'

'I'm getting out!'

'Oh no you're not!' roared Gatera, watching from
the bank. 'Not until you've washed yourselves
thoroughly!'

The Zorgs groaned as they moved to a shallower area and made a feeble pretence at washing.

'Ow! I've stubbed my toe!' yelled Bar'drash, falling over and splashing Gur'brak in the process. Gur'brak in turn started to splash his companion, and soon they were engaged in a full water fight.

'They seem to be enjoying it after all,' Kess whispered to Valor.

'Yes, and perhaps we'll all benefit from it, if it removes some of that awful smell!' The Mountain Guard wrinkled his nose in an expression of distaste, and Kess laughed.

The water served to refresh all the company, lifting their spirits once more. They resumed their journey with a new hope in their hearts. As if in encouragement, the sun shouldered its way out from the heavy clouds in a seeming act of defiance. Although its brightness could do little to cheer the dull landscape, its warmth lent strength to the travellers' weary limbs. Now the horses had been watered and had rested for a while, the company was able to mount up and travel at a greater speed.

The slopes once more gave way to an arid plain. In the distance lurked the ominous presence of the Wailing Hills, drawing ever nearer with each step.

By the late morning of the following day, they had reached the foothills that preceded the main mountain range. For indeed, the hills were actually low, rounded mountains, sitting uncomfortably in the middle of the plains.

'Which way now?' Athennar demanded of Gur'brak.

'There are only two passes through the Wailing Hills,' the Zorg replied. 'Um, we always use the Long Pass—it's difficult and narrow in places, but it's not too bad.'

'Good.'

'Er, d'you need us any more?' Gur'brak asked, casting a sideways glance at Bar'drash.

'Of course,' replied Athennar. 'Why do you ask?'

'It's just that—well, Dargan might not like us helping you.'

'Precious help you've been so far,' muttered Valor. Gur'brak scowled.

'You seem to forget that you are our prisoners,' Athennar reminded him. 'And we have no guarantee that you're telling the truth. You could still be in league with Dargan. At least if we keep you with us, I can deal with you if I find out that you've betrayed us!'

'Oh no,' groaned Bar'drash. 'We just can't win!'

'Perhaps not,' replied Athennar. 'But if we all come out of this alive, you will be granted your freedom.'

Gur'brak didn't reply. He wasn't really sure what he would do with his 'freedom' now. With most of the Zorg army disbanded, he wasn't sure where he would go or what he would do.

For the moment, he pointed the company in the general direction of the Long Pass. There would be time enough to worry about his future when this was all over—if he was still alive!

Two hours later, they reached the pass. It was as if a knife had sliced a section out of the mountain: steep cliff walls rose on either side of a deep cleft, which formed a winding alleyway. Dismounting, the company led the horses slowly forward. As soon as they rounded the first bend, the wailing began. The Zorgs, who had used the pass several times before, were undisturbed. However, the rest of the company found it very unnerving.

'It sounds like the moaning of a lost soul,' muttered Gatera. The noise also brought back memories of the howling sounds in the Black Caves—and of the Grey Runners.

'Press onwards!' called Athennar as one or two of the group hesitated.

'It's eerie,' grumbled Valor. 'I don't like it!'

'At least it isn't dangerous,' Bar'drash replied. 'Not like those 'orrible wolves.'

Athennar pursed his lips. He hoped the Zorg was right.

The wailing grew louder and more troubled. Athennar, in the lead, tried hard to ignore it. If the Zorgs had come this way before, it must surely be safe—unless they had been deceiving him! Rounding a bend, he gave a gasp of annoyance.

Gur'brak, trudging along beside Kess, said, 'That wasn't there last time!' A section of the mountain had broken away, and completely blocked their route. It looked as if the fall was very recent.

A rumbling sound came from high above, and Athennar wheeled Windrider around to face the others. 'Back!' he shouted above the wails and the grumbling noise. 'Or we could be buried under another landslide!'

The company hurriedly tried to turn. For a moment, there was confusion, with horses and men getting in each other's way. Then, as rapidly as they could, they made their way back to the entrance of the pass.

When they had recovered their breath, Athennar approached Gur'brak. 'Now what?' he asked. 'You said there were two passes.'

'Er—yeah, but the other one hasn't been used for years.'

'Perhaps not, but we have little choice but to try it.'

'But we can't—I mean, it's dangerous. People die in there!'

'Why?' asked Athennar suspiciously.

Gur'brak shrugged. 'I dunno,' he replied in sullen tones. 'I've never been that way, and I don't know anybody who has. I've just heard the rumours—and I don't like it!'

'Rumours!' snorted Valor.

'Do not scoff too readily, my friend,' Merric advised him. 'Do you not remember the rumours of the Withered Wood? They seemed strange, yet were only too true.'

Athennar paced up and down for a while, then said, 'Unfortunately, we have no choice. There is no way round. We will have to try the other pass. Show us the way, Gur'brak!'

The Zorg looked surly, but pointed his finger eastwards. 'It's about a two-hour walk—perhaps one hour's ride—in that direction,' he said. 'But don't say I didn't warn you!'

'Yes, you tell 'em, boss,' chipped in Bar'drash. 'It's an 'orrible place, 'orrible. Even its name is 'orrible.'

'Why?' said Kess.

'They call it the Valley of Darkness,' replied Gur'brak. 'And believe me, it's said to live up to its name.'

20

Attacked!

By mid-afternoon, the travellers had reached the entrance to the Valley of Darkness—a narrow, almost indiscernible trail that led up through an area of scrub to another gap between two of the mountains. There were still several hours of light left, so Athennar decided to proceed. He was getting increasingly anxious to find Dargan before the Dark Master became too powerful for them.

The track snaked upwards at first, then passed through a long, level stretch of woodland. Breaking out into the open space once more it came to a sudden stop.

'Oh no!' groaned Valor. They were standing on the lip of a small cliff. Below was a wide valley, with a well-defined path running through it. However, the only way down was a steep trail that wound across the face of the cliff.

'The horses won't make it down there,' muttered Gatera, echoing Valor's thoughts.

Reluctantly agreeing, Athennar decided to camp for the night before tackling the cliff. Openly relieved, the others unsaddled their horses and began to relax.

Early the next morning, Athennar instructed the
company to gather all their weapons and essential
provisions, and to leave anything else behind. Before
setting off, the Animal Crafter spoke softly to each of
the horses. He bade them await the travellers' return—
and to make their own way back to the fortress should
the company not come back.

The friends then scrambled down the narrow track,
only Sash and the elves making light work of the task.

Hesteron was in the lead when they reached the
valley floor. He stopped and sniffed. He could sense
some strange undercurrents in the air. Turning to
Athennar, he started to speak. To his dismay,
although he knew he was talking, he could hear
nothing. Urgently, he tapped the Animal Crafter on
the shoulder, mouthing his alarm.

The rest of the group realised the problem as soon
as they tried to ask what was happening. None of them
could hear.

Another of Dargan's warped ideas! thought Hesteron,
cursing the Dark Master for his evil.

Meanwhile Athennar waved his arms to attract
everyone's attention. By a series of gestures, he
signalled that they should continue their journey,
keeping a close watch for any sign of danger. Then
he led the way forward, the faithful black shape of
Sash at his left side, Melinya at his right.

After an hour's travel, the floor of the valley dipped
slightly. Ahead of them were the remains of what
must have once been a thriving township. Clusters
of battered wooden huts stood between widely
spaced trees, with well-worn roads running off in all
directions.

Hesteron wondered if the deserted feel of the place
was also a result of Dargan's activities. However, it
seemed as if this 'wooden city' had lain forgotten for

a long time, possibly centuries. Many of the buildings had collapsed; others were covered in lichen and ivy.

Vallel drew his attention to a bright green, mossy plant at the base of a large, spreading tree. The plant was covered in tiny droplets of water. Then Hesteron pointed out a delicate fern which seemed to move as if teased by a gentle breeze, even though the air was still and heavy.

They were so distracted by these new discoveries that they didn't notice they were being left behind. Hesteron looked up just in time to notice Merric's back disappearing around a bend in the main track.

He tugged at Vallel's sleeve, and motioned her to follow him. Thinking she was just behind him, he set off, marvelling at the new sights all around. Then something disturbed him: a change in the air currents. He switched his attention to it, analysed it. It came again. It was as if someone was screaming.

Looking around, he was alarmed to see Vallel under attack. A filthy white, hairy arm had reached out of the tree and grabbed hold of her jerkin by the neck, pulling her off the ground. Her mouth opened in another silent cry for help as Hesteron rushed towards her. Slashing at the white arm, he caught a brief glimpse of a vicious face and sickly yellow eyes. He missed, and the creature continued to draw Vallel up into the tree.

Desperately, Hesteron grabbed hold of her legs and pulled. Vallel tumbled downwards, collapsing on top of him. The next moment, two of the white creatures jumped down from the tree, and leaped on top of the elves before they could get up.

Flexing the long claws at the end of its strange fingers, one of the creatures forced Hesteron's head backwards, exposing his neck. As it leaned forward, its lips drew back to reveal a double row of sharp white teeth.

The Air Crafter struggled and kicked. Out of the corner of his eye, he could see Vallel struggling as well. Desperately, he renewed his efforts. He was unsuccessful. The creature seemed to smile as it opened its jaws wide to bite him.

The smile froze on its face. It slumped forward, and Hesteron quickly pushed it off. The creature that had attacked Vallel was already scuttling back to the safety of the tree, one of Valor's arrows protruding from its back. Hesteron looked at the creature that had attacked him. Merric stood beside it, pulling his sword from its side.

The minstrel helped Hesteron to his feet. He had fortunately noticed that the two Crafters were missing, and had returned with the Mountain Guard just in time.

The Air Crafter smiled his thanks. He was unhurt. Vallel, similarly, had survived almost unscathed, thanks to Valor's quick actions. She had just one or two scratches on her wrists, and her jerkin—already ripped from the earlier attack of the wolves—was badly torn.

Within moments, the rest of the company had arrived, having been alerted by Kess who had seen Valor and Merric run back. They gathered around the dead creature. It had a long, thin body, covered in dirty white hair, and ending in an even thinner tail. Its wiry arms stretched almost as far as the bottom of its hind legs which, like the arms, ended in clawed hands.

Athennar studied the creature's face. Its long, pointed jaws—with the lips still pulled back, displaying the cruel rows of teeth—reminded him of the tadrats they had seen in the tunnels leading to Dargan's stronghold. However, this face was even more vicious and primitive, with the two yellow eyes sunk into deep caverns either side of the nose. Behind the eyes were two small, rounded ears, which seemed out of character with the creature's harsh, angular features.

Athennar ensured that no one had sustained any bad injuries, and then signalled the group to move on, this time motioning them to keep close together.

The path led them through the centre of the wooden city. Although overgrown, the track was wide and had once obviously been well used. It twisted in between the huts and the trees, with several sharp changes of direction. The company had just passed around one such corner when the attack began. The white creatures dropped like falling leaves from the trees. From behind and in front they came, shuffling along awkwardly on their hind legs, waving their arms in the air.

The travellers were badly outnumbered. 'Form a circle!' Athennar tried to shout, then had to push his friends into position when he realised they would be unable to hear him. He signalled Melinya to stay in the centre of the circle with the two Zorgs. Despite her frail appearance, he was sure she would be able to foil any escape attempt. She would also be safer there. Bar'drash happily hid behind her, peeking out occasionally to see what was happening. Gur'brak meanwhile stayed close by her side.

Several of the travellers drew their swords: Gatera stood ready with his double-headed axe, and those with bows fitted arrows to the strings. As the creatures came closer, gathering speed, the archers fired. Three or four of the beasts fell, causing the others to hesitate. Then on they came again. The brief pause had allowed the archers to string new arrows to their bows and fire, and again more of the creatures fell to the ground.

This time, however, the others kept coming. From

now on, it would be hand-to-hand fighting. The creatures pressed forward, slashing at the travellers with their long claws. The friends parried with their swords and counter-attacked. As their assailants tried to back away, they crashed into more of their kind, still pushing forward.

For a moment, there was chaos. The creatures—apparently unused to walking on the ground for long periods—tripped over each other and themselves. This enabled the company to go on the offensive. But their opponents soon recovered, and again attacked the travellers.

Hesteron frowned. Although the creatures were clumsy, they could easily win by sheer weight of numbers.

The company fought back, but the mass of white continued to surge forward. Kess fell, followed by Vallel. Hesteron quickly helped her up. He was then knocked down himself. A creature jumped on top of him. *Not again!* he thought. However, a sword thrust from Merric finished the beast. Kess, meanwhile, had been rescued by Gatera.

Hesteron clambered to his feet. Next to him stood Falron, waving his sword around dangerously, and nearly hitting Hesteron in the process. *A fine help he's turned out to be!* thought the Air Crafter sourly. Then he caught sight of the hunting horn slung across the poet's shoulder. Even as he fought off a particularly large creature, a thought was forming in his mind. It was perhaps hopeless, but worth a try.

Meanwhile, two of the creatures had leaped on to Gatera. Rrum immediately fastened his jaws on one of them, and it soon let go. It fell to the ground, writhing in agony. With what would have been a roar, Gatera slung the other one back into a mass of its fellows. Then bravely he pushed forward himself, swinging his axe with all his might.

The creatures scattered as he cut a path through them. However, they soon re-formed behind the Land Crafter. Too late, he realised the folly of his actions. He was cut off from his friends!

Several of the creatures jumped on him at once. He staggered and collapsed, their combined weight driving him to the ground. Athennar and Valor, seeing him fall, fought furiously to reach him, but could make no progress.

Then Sash leaped forward, snapping at one creature, tossing another aside. Others started to back away from her, alarmed by the ferociousness of her attack. Athennar and Valor hurtled through the remaining creatures surrounding Gatera, followed by Rrum. The Land Crafter threw off the two or three beasts that still clung to him, and regained his feet. The four friends then fought their way back to their companions.

Another group of creatures was attacking Merric. Melinya left the two Zorgs to help him, her slim blade darting here and there. One large creature charged at her, but she was surprised to see it knocked out of the way by Gur'brak.

Still the creatures pressed forward. The company was weakening. Hesteron managed to grab hold of Falron, and signalled to him desperately. Before the poet could respond, Hesteron was engulfed by a tide of white. Melinya fell as well, and Athennar was unable to reach her. 'No!' he screamed, but no one could hear him.

21

Into the Darkness

The next moment, as quickly as they had come, the creatures turned and fled, scuttling back to their trees. Many held their hands to their ears, and looks of anguish twisted their faces.

Falron stood proudly, the hunting horn still pressed to his lips. Hesteron, struggling to his feet once more, gave a weary smile. He was glad the poet had understood his signal. Some distant memory—or perhaps even a prompting from Toroth himself—had made him think that sound might be the way to fight the creatures. After all, they had probably spent most or all of their lives in a silent world. Although Falron's horn hadn't made any noise that the company could hear, it had caused a great vibration in the air—Hesteron had clearly sensed it. It had obviously upset the creatures. The Air Crafter wondered if they hunted by sensing the tiny vibrations caused by movement. If so, the disturbance produced by the blast from the hunting horn would be more than their delicate ears could stand.

Athennar clapped Falron on the back and smiled

his thanks to Hesteron. Meanwhile Gatera, scratched and bruised, returned to the company after dusting himself down. Rrum held the Land Crafter's huge hand and looked up at him, reassured that the giant had not suffered any worse harm. Kess, Melinya and Valor were all scratched, too, but they were mainly superficial wounds.

The friends now moved rapidly through the city, Falron fingering the hunting horn and his eyes flicking from side to side. Gatera and Valor formed the rearguard, vigilant for any signs of attack.

Soon they reached the outskirts of the city, having encountered no further opposition. Hesteron breathed a sigh of relief. They had been fortunate indeed to pass through virtually unscathed. That was in part due to the creatures' clumsiness on the ground. They had constantly got in each other's way, leaving little room to wield their claws. Some had even ended up wounding others of their own race by mistake.

Looking back at the wooden city, the Air Crafter sighed once more. He was aware that other dangers probably awaited them before they reached the end of the pass. He squeezed Vallel's hand. For now they were alive—and he intended to ensure that they remained so.

The road slipped around a bend, and the city disappeared from sight. As the small group of travellers trudged onwards through the silence, the steep mountain sides frowned down upon them in disapproval.

A little while later, the valley widened once more, the road becoming little more than a track winding through its centre. Kess noticed a mountain stream off to one side. It was strange to see the water flowing between the mossy banks, yet not be able to hear it.

A sudden movement caught his eye. Athennar was

waving at the company. A short distance ahead was a disturbing sight: the valley disappeared completely. It was as if the world came to an end at an impenetrable wall of black 'fog'. And yet it wasn't exactly fog. Although they couldn't see into it, there was nothing misty about it; it was just totally black.

The company began to move forward, but Athennar held up a restraining hand. Tying a rope around his waist, he gave the other end to Gatera. Then, again signalling the company to wait, he crept forwards to the edge of the blackness. One more step and he disappeared.

Kess noticed Melinya flinch. For a second he wondered if Athennar could have fallen over a precipice, or if he had dissolved completely. Memories of the Mistress of the Mist came flooding back. Then, to his relief, he noticed that the rope still hung from the edge of the fog at waist level.

Gatera was busy paying out the rope. After a while, he stopped. Little jerks came from the line, then, to everyone's joy, Athennar burst back into their view, materialising out of the blackness as suddenly as he had disappeared.

The Animal Crafter shrugged his uncertainty of how thick the darkness was; and covered his eyes to show that he had been unable to see anything. Then he waved Gatera and Rrum off to the left, and Falron and Kess to the right, signalling them to repeat his investigations in another section of the fog. He indicated that he wanted to know if it was any thinner at either edge.

While the scouts set off on their tasks, Athennar motioned the others to sit down and take a rest. Beckoning to Hesteron, he drew the Air Crafter off to one side. The two of them then began to discuss, with many signs and much arm waving, the best way to proceed through the wall of black.

Over at the right side of the valley, close to the little stream, Kess began to sidle nervously towards the edge of the blackness. Falron was holding the other end of the rope, and gave him an encouraging wave. The Quiet One gulped and then stepped bravely forward.

It was a strange, frightening sensation. He was abruptly cut off from everything he had ever known. He could see nothing, hear nothing. Even when he waved his hand an inch in front of his face, he was unable to see it. Fearing that he would lose his grip on reality, he clutched tightly to the rope tied around his waist. It was a solid and real reminder that he was not alone.

Cautiously he continued, fearful in case he should fall into some deep chasm. The ground remained firm beneath his feet. He took another step forward, and another, and another. He tried to think of his friends, his sister; of Hallion, even of the Fortress. No images came to his mind, just blackness.

Meanwhile, Valor and Merric had wandered over to the edge of the fog, curious to see if they could find out more about it. Valor stretched out his arm, and his hand and wrist disappeared as soon as they passed into the veil of black.

They were both standing so close to it that neither of them had time to react when the blackness suddenly seeped forwards and surrounded them. Within a second they were cut off completely from their friends.

The unexpected surge—almost a rhythmic pulse— in the blackness had also engulfed the two scouting parties. Rrum, like Kess, had already entered the fog, tied securely to a rope held by Gatera. Now the Land Crafter was also swallowed up before he could move. He tried to turn around and walk back, but it seemed as if he had lost all sense of direction. After ten steps, he knew that he was lost.

Slowly he began reeling in the rope. He felt reassured as it grew tighter; at least he would have Rrum's company in here! He kept a slight strain on the rope and walked forward until his leg hit something. Rrum!

Gatera pursed his lips in the darkness. He realised that the poor little fellow would be confused—Rrum would have no idea why Gatera had also entered the blackness. Reaching down, he picked up the little Rrokki, and gave him what he hoped was a reassuring pat on the head.

Over on the opposite side of the valley Falron, too, had been taken unawares. He had been daydreaming when the black fog had surged forward. Taken by surprise and disorientated, he had frozen, then turned in all directions trying to see a way out.

Trapped! he thought. *Will all my plans be for nothing?* Calming himself, he stood still and tried to think. If he stepped in the opposite direction from the rope that connected him with Kess, paying it out as he went, he should be able to get back into the open air again.

He tried, but failed. It seemed as if he was shut off from the world. *What now?* he thought, biting his fingers. The action at least served to reassure him that he was still alive.

Feeling a sudden tug on the rope, he panicked. He was being drawn further into the blackness! Dropping the rope, he took a step backwards. It was only then that he realised what he had done. In a moment of madness, he had lost the only link left with anyone else within this dark void! Getting to his hands and knees, he searched around in desperation for the end of the rope. It would at least lead him to Kess—and the two of them together might have a better chance of staying sane while they tried to find a way out of here!

The rope was nowhere to be found. Huddled alone in the darkness, he shook with fear.

Deciding that he had gone forward far enough, Kess turned to go back. He pulled on the rope to let Falron know he was returning. The next moment, the rope fell slack. Kess' mind raced. What had happened? Had Falron payed out some more rope, thinking that Kess wanted to go further?

Frantically Kess grabbed the rope and kept pulling, pulling . . . until he reached the loose end. His heart sank. What had happened to Falron? Why had he left him alone here in this darkness? Had Falron and his other friends been attacked?

Steadying himself, the Quiet One drew a few deep breaths. He was alone. His only hope now was that somehow Elsinoth would guide him through this mess. What was it Meltizoc had said? Elsinoth alone will never let you down? Kess struggled hard to believe in that, despite his past disappointments. Saying a mental prayer for help, he started to walk forward. Anything was better than just standing still. Somehow he had to get out of this blackness!

The next moment he bumped into something— something soft and yielding. Whatever it was hit out at his legs, and he was sent sprawling to the ground. Dazed, he wondered what had attacked him. Was it some hideous monster of the dark, preparing to kill him? Or was it just his imagination? Perhaps he had bumped into a mossy bank with rocks jutting out!

If only he could shout out! If only he could hear! If only he could see!

22

Lost in the Dark

Athennar watched in alarm as the blackness seeped forward, and his friends disappeared. He raced towards the dark curtain, but was too late. Realising the danger of being trapped himself, he skidded to a halt. Then he ran back to the others and motioned them to their feet. Taking one of the longest ropes, he tied it around his waist and then passed it on to Melinya. She did likewise, and then gave it to Gur'brak and Bar'drash. The Zorgs looked at it sullenly and waved their arms in protest. However, Athennar indicated that they could either obey or be left alone to face either the blackness ahead or the white creatures of the wooden city behind. Reluctantly, they tied the rope around themselves.

All six of the remaining travellers were soon linked together in a long line, with Athennar in the lead and Hesteron at the rear. The Animal Crafter made a short leash for Sash, too, to ensure that she wouldn't wander off into the blackness by herself.

He then pulled two torches from his backpack. Handing one over to Hesteron, he kept the other for himself. He wasn't sure whether the torches would be effective within the black fog—hence his precaution of tying everyone together. Once they were all ready, he walked steadily forward and through the black barrier.

Valor rested his hand on the pommel of his sword. The blackness was unnerving—much more so than anything else he had experienced. It was something he couldn't fight, couldn't resist, couldn't even see. He felt totally cut off from his friends—even more than he had in the mists by the Whistling Waters. However, his Mountain Guard training took over. Underneath his impulsive exterior there remained the same steely determination that had first led him on this long quest. It seemed a long, long time since he had set off in pursuit of Carnak, his father's murderer. He knew that he would now need all his strength and courage if he was to make his way safely through this expanse of nothingness.

He drew his sword. He could at least use it to feel for any large obstacles ahead of him. Deciding one direction was as good as another, he gritted his teeth and started to work his way forward.

Merric, meanwhile, was also walking slowly through the blackness. It didn't disturb him as much as the others. His philosophical elven nature could cope with the darkness, even though he didn't like it. However, what did trouble him was finding a way out. He was only too aware of the danger of falling over the edge of a cliff, or of breaking a leg. No one would ever find him in here. In his mind he hummed a light tune of hope to himself, and prayed that Toroth might guide his feet.

I need to see! Kess screamed again to himself. He wished he had a torch in his backpack, but he had left his behind with the horses—only Athennar and Hesteron now carried a supply. A thought touched the edges of his mind. A distant voice echoed in his memory; something long forgotten. ' . . . *In this pouch are the petals of a rare flower. Should you ever be in need of light, crush them and they will give a bright glow for a short time . . .* ' Of course! Tolledon's gift, given so long ago, right at the start of this long and arduous quest!

Taking off his backpack, he fumbled inside it. He remembered seeing the pouch when he had lightened his load before leaving the horses. For some reason— probably because it was so small—he had left it in the backpack.

Ah, there it was! His anxious fingers pulled out the pouch and felt inside. Grasping one or two of the petals, he crushed them between his finger and thumb.

A pure bright light shone out. Despite its intensity, it didn't hurt his eyes. He breathed a sigh of relief and picked up his backpack. Keeping the little pouch in one hand, he held up the other, which glowed with the light from the crushed petals. He could see for about ten yards in all directions.

As he twisted round, he gave a gasp of horror. A dark figure was rising from the ground just behind him. Then he breathed a sigh of relief as he realised that it was Falron. The poet must have been the object he had bumped into a few moments earlier. But why was Falron here?

The next moment, the poet was slapping him on the back, a great smile spreading across his face. Kess returned the smile. It was good to see a familiar face. Now they would have to find a way out of the blackness before the light faded from the crushed petals.

As he gazed around, a slight sparkle caught his eyes. Water! Of course—the mountain stream! Grabbing Falron's arm, he pointed eagerly to the stream. They

could follow it—it would lead them out of the darkness
and back to their friends.

Falron, obviously worried about the possibility of
being left alone once more, grabbed hold of the loose
end of the rope. He looped it round and round his
waist, then tied it so that he and Kess could walk
comfortably a few yards apart.

The two men then worked their way across to the
stream. When Kess began to follow it back upstream,
he felt a tug on the rope. Falron signalled that they
should go downstream. Kess stopped for a moment.
He knew the company had to pass this blackness
somehow. Perhaps Athennar had told Falron that the
fog was only a few yards thick. Turning, he moved
past the poet and led the way downstream.

They had been travelling for some distance when
the light from the petals began to fade. Kess was
becoming increasingly alarmed—surely they should
have reached the other side of the black fog by now?
Opening his small pouch, he tipped the last few petals
into his hand. He crushed them, and once again a
bright white light shone out.

Again they pressed forward. After making good
progress, the light again began to fade. Kess urgently
rubbed his fingers in the few flaking remains of the
flower. The light brightened slightly, but he realised
they had little time left. Motioning to Falron, he
climbed the mossy bank next to the stream, and
stepped into its shallow waters. At least if the light
gave way, they could continue to follow the water!

Falron followed him, having realised the reasons
behind his actions. They continued to plod forward,
more slowly now as the light began to fade.

A few minutes later, it flickered and died. Once
again they were surrounded by complete blackness.
Kess felt a slight tug on the rope, and gave an

answering tug to Falron. Then they made their way carefully forward, with the Quiet One leading the way.

They struggled on, time having little meaning in this dark and empty world. Then, without any warning, Kess walked into a dazzling light. He closed his eyes—it was too bright. Then he felt Falron bump into him, and heard a gasp as the poet also encountered the light.

Shielding his eyes with his hand, Kess opened them slowly. It wasn't a light he had walked into at all—it was the open air! They had reached the opposite side of the blackness! The daylight wasn't even bright once his eyes had grown accustomed to it, but rather cloudy and grey.

He turned around. Yes, there behind them was a great curtain of black. In front and off to their left, a path led from the centre of the valley into a rocky gulley.

Stepping out of the stream, which trickled away among the rocks, he stopped in surprise. He could hear the water!

'I can hear again!' he shouted.

Falron put his hands to his ears. 'There's no need to deafen me!' he said. But his voice, too, sounded unusually loud after the long silence.

The two travellers sat down on a flat rock to recover their composure.

'What happened back there?' asked Kess. 'Why were you in the fog, and why had you let go of the rope?'

'Oh, I dropped it when you tugged it,' replied the poet. 'Then I—er—realised you wouldn't be able to find your way out of there. I thought I might be able to catch you and pull you back.'

Kess was surprised that the poet should have risked his life on his behalf. 'Thanks,' he said. 'But why did you insist we carry on rather than go back?'

'Oh, when I saw you had a light, I thought it would make more sense if we could find out how thick the darkness was.'

Kess was unconvinced, but let the matter pass.

'I think we should go and scout the land down below,' suggested Falron, 'so that we can report to the others if—or should I say when—they get through the darkness.'

'You go,' said Kess. 'I'll wait here. Then, if any of them have followed us, they'll know we're safe.'

'No, come with me,' insisted Falron. 'It won't take us long!'

'I'm not coming!' Kess snapped. Then, apologetically, he added, 'I need a little rest. You go.' He yawned and closed his eyes for a moment.

There was a sudden movement behind him—a quiet rustling noise. As he turned to see what was happening, he felt a heavy blow on the back of his head. Falling off the rock, he slipped into a different kind of darkness.

Gatera trundled barefoot across the uneven ground. He had no fear of stumbling—his Land Crafter's instincts warned him of any rocks or holes nearby. Rrum perched on his shoulders, his hands clutching Gatera's head. The Land Crafter steadied him with one hand, while with his other he used his staff to test the ground ahead. It was a slow process, but they made their way gradually down to what seemed like the floor of the valley. Gatera then tested the ground again. He could just sense the mountain stream, running far off to his left. Assuming that it was the same stream he had noticed earlier, he realised he was facing the wrong direction if he wanted to come out at the far side of the blackness. There was little point in going back to his friends without finding out how thick the fog was.

A part of him, however, squirmed at the thought. What if there was no 'far' side? What if it continued like this for ever? He put the thought to the back of his mind. The feel of the stream and the ground were real enough—he knew that they were still in the valley, and that therefore there should be a way out.

Valor continued to probe his way forward across the mountain slope. After a while, he became totally disorientated. His mind was not only confused about direction—he may even have been travelling in circles—but also about the ground itself. He could no longer tell whether it was sloping up or down.

Resolutely, he closed his mind to all such thoughts, and hung on grimly to his one purpose: to get out of this darkness. Minutes seemed to stretch into hours and, as far as he knew, even into days—nothing made sense any more. He trudged on and on, occasionally tripping, but always forcing himself to get up and continue.

Like Kess, he was shocked when he suddenly broke out into the light once more. It seemed as if by pure chance he had made it to the other side! He stumbled and collapsed, then fell fast asleep, totally exhausted.

He awoke an hour or two later to the sound of a chilling cry. It pierced his dreams, calling him urgently back to consciousness.

'Tarkkk! Tarkkk!'

Rubbing the drowsiness from his eyes, he looked around. He was still surprised to think he had made it through the black fog—he knew he could have been staggering around inside it until he died.

Then his memory dredged up the call that had woken him from his sleep. The cry of a Tark!

He looked up, and could see its grim silhouette a little way above. It was flying southwards. Then it saw him. It spiralled down from the sky with amazing speed. The Mountain Guard stood his ground. He knew there was little point in running, and he had already discarded the option of fleeing back into the darkness—there was no way he was going back in there again! No, he would fight—and show this overgrown green bird that he was not a man to be trifled with.

He pulled out his sword and waited. The Tark hesitated—it had expected the man to run. Then it swooped.

Shouting the battle cry of the Mountain Guards, Valor slashed at the creature. His blade bounced off its leathery wings. He slashed again as it flapped above him. This time, the sword bit into the side of one fleshy foot, and green fluid spurted out. The creature gave a shriek of annoyance and attacked.

It knocked Valor to the ground, smothering him with its wings. The Mountain Guard's sword flew from his hand and landed some feet away.

The Tark had landed astride him, and grasped his left arm with one of its spikes. Drawing back his fist, Valor punched the creature in the side of its face. His fist met hard bone.

The Tark barely flinched. This time, Valor hit it in the stomach, though he could get little power behind the punch. The creature was waiting, and grabbed his wrist with its other spike. Valor squirmed and struggled, but could not get free. Slowly, almost hypnotically, the Tark lowered its head, the hooked bill drawing ever closer to his face. Valor tried not to look at the green eyes, but he was caught in their glare. Then he felt a sharp, stabbing pain in his mind.

23
Betrayed!

Athennar paced slowly forwards through the gloom. In the yellow torchlight, he could only see a few yards ahead. Although he could see the flame of Hesteron's torch when he looked back, he could barely make out the Air Crafter's figure.

As he walked, his mind searched for ways of finding a route through the darkness all around. While the torchlight was a reassurance, and helped them to avoid any large rocks, it gave no clue to the direction they should take. He had started by following the narrow track that ran along the valley floor—but once they had entered the black fog, it became impossible to distinguish it from the rest of the ground.

He wished he could communicate with Sash. Perhaps the leopard would know which way to lead them. As it was, she had no way of knowing that they needed to reach the other side of the darkness—for her, it was just another adventure. He fondled her head as she padded alongside, and a rasping tongue shot out in response and licked his hand.

Perhaps he should let her lead anyway. She was

unlikely to travel around in circles. Twitching her leash, he pointed for her to walk ahead. The leopard seemed to understand, and obligingly moved in front. The line of travellers fell in behind her, and stumbled on through the gloom.

Suddenly, a strange shape loomed out of the darkness ahead. It was moving straight towards them. Athennar drew his sword, then breathed a sigh of relief. Merric!

The minstrel danced forward to greet his friends. He had been wandering hopelessly through the blackness when he had noticed a hint of grey. Rubbing his eyes—he had forgotten that they were still open—he had strained to keep sight of it. At first he thought it was an illusion, then he had wondered if it was a glimpse of daylight beyond the dark. Whichever it was, he decided to walk towards it, hoping it might be the way out of this blackness. His disappointment when he realised it was the light from a torch was soon replaced with joy at seeing his companions.

After many hands had welcomed him, he tied himself to the end of the rope behind Hesteron. The small procession, still led by Sash, continued on its way.

After some time, the ground became more uneven, with an increasing number of rocks scattered carelessly around. Athennar sighed inwardly. He hoped that Sash had led them in the right direction! At that moment, the leopard climbed up onto a mossy bank, strewn with boulders. Puzzled, Athennar followed. He wondered where Sash was going.

Soon he realised why the leopard had brought them here—she wanted a drink! They had come to the mountain stream. Sash lapped up the water and looked back at Athennar as if expecting a word of thanks.

Athennar gave a silent groan. All the time he had

thought they were travelling forward, when actually they had been moving across the valley to the right hand side. Then the realisation dawned upon him, as it had on Kess some hours before—they could follow the stream downwards.

He signalled the others to join him on the bank. They would have a drink and a rest here, and then continue their journey.

Kess awoke with a dull pain in his stomach, and to a strange lurching sensation. Opening his eyes, he could vaguely see the ground moving beneath him. As his dulled senses cleared, he realised that he was being carried over someone's shoulder. He struggled to get free, then felt his hands tied behind his back.

'Well, well! So you've awoken, have you?' The lurching stopped, and he was lowered onto a large mound.

'Falron!'

'Very perceptive, my young friend.'

'You won't get away with this!'

'Oh, won't I?' The poet laughed. 'It seems that I already have! Your friends are far behind—probably still lost in the Valley of Darkness. Before you think of shouting for help, or trying to escape, I should warn you that we're in a very dangerous area.' The poet swept his arm in an extravagant gesture to indicate the surrounding landscape.

Kess looked all around. The area was one of mottled brown sand, flecked with occasional shrubs and large fleshy plants armed with spines. It didn't look particularly dangerous.

'Quicksand,' Falron explained. 'It's all around. Fortunately I've been this way many times before, and know the safe route through. However, should your friends come rushing after you, or should you try to escape, you are unlikely to survive for long.'

Kess glared at him. 'Where are you taking me? I'm of no value to you!'

'Oh, but you're wrong, so wrong. Dargan will pay a pretty price for you!'

'Dargan!'

'Who else? I have helped him for many years, since he first lived in the Tower of Braggad. I act as his ears and eyes—if I let him know of any unfriendly activity, he rewards me well.'

'So you're a spy!' Kess hissed.

'That is one word for it. However, about two years ago I, er, freed myself from Dargan's service and decided to explore more of the Realm—mainly so I could spend some of my well-earned wealth. I spent some time in the Northlands, but found it an unfriendly place—too many people. I also ran out of money. So I came back, and fooled those stupid Zorgs at the fortress into believing that Dargan had given me special permission to bring a horse into the Southlands. A horse is a powerful advantage in a land where most other creatures travel by foot. However, I was aware that I was unlikely to be popular with Dargan. For weeks I have been trying to think of a way by which I might regain his favour.

'When I met up with you and your friends, I saw my chance. By capturing someone, I could prove my loyalty to Dargan. He would also be likely to pay me well for my trouble. My main problem was how to separate one of you from the others. Perhaps by knocking out whoever was on guard in the middle of the night? Possible, but rather risky. Fortunately, the Valley of Darkness did my work for me!'

'You—you—traitor! You coward!' spluttered Kess.

Falron sniggered. 'I have been called many things

in my time,' he replied. 'People think me a fool or a weakling. That's why I wear bright clothes—so that people believe that I am harmless. To be underestimated gives me an advantage.'

'And what about me? What will happen to me when you hand me over to Dargan?' asked Kess.

Falron shrugged. 'I care little what happens to you. You will have served your purpose.'

Kess fell silent. He could see that there was no way of reasoning with the 'poet'.

'Now, I grow tired of this conversation,' continued Falron. 'On your feet—you can walk the rest of the way! I was growing rather weary of carrying you!'

Kess struggled to his feet, then suddenly turned and sprinted away across the sand. Falron made no attempt to stop him.

Within a few yards, Kess plunged straight into a large patch of quicksand, and began sinking. 'Help!' he shouted. 'Get me out of here!' He strove to break free, but his hands were still tied behind his back and he was unable to reach out for firm ground.

Falron sauntered over, grinning at the sight of the floundering figure. 'If you weren't so valuable to me at the moment, I wouldn't bother!' he said. He unslung his spare rope and formed a loop in one end, which he tossed over Kess' shoulders. Straining and heaving, he managed to drag the Quiet One back to solid ground.

'I hope that's taught you not to try any more tricks!' the poet warned.

Kess lay exhausted and bedraggled, saying nothing. Relenting a little, Falron untied his wrists and propped him up against a rock while he recovered.

Kess immediately felt for his sword. It was gone. Falron, noticing the movement, pulled back his own cloak and revealed the hilt of an extra sword. 'Is this what you were looking for?' he asked. Drawing the sword, the poet held it close to Kess' neck.

'Now it's time to be going,' he hissed. 'You walk ahead—and don't forget that I'm the one with the weapons!'

Kess struggled to his feet, still dripping with wet sand.

'Now, shall we go?' asked Falron.

Two hours later they reached the edge of a long ridge of rock. The top of the ridge was a few feet above them. Falron tied Kess' hands behind his back again, leaving a short length of rope with which to guide him.

'Now that we've reached the end of the quicksand, I don't want you trying to escape again,' he said. 'Not that there's anywhere much you could go, except to the Tower!' He pushed Kess up the steep slope that led to the top of the ridge. Beyond was a short stretch of open sand, leading to a rocky escarpment. There, perched halfway up the cliff, was a sinister castle.

'The Tower of Braggad!' Falron proclaimed triumphantly.

Kess stared at the structure. It was grim and forbidding—a stark warning of the evil that dwelt within.

Scrambling down the other side of the ridge, they made their way onto the sand. Falron stopped and removed his brown cloak, revealing his bright red and yellow shirt. Then he blew a loud, ringing note on his hunting horn.

'They'll know who I am, and won't fire on us,' he explained; somewhat nervously, Kess thought.

They could see a lone Zorg parading up and down the battlements next to the main tower. On hearing the horn, the creature scuttled off somewhere.

By the time they reached the castle door, four Zorgs

were awaiting them. Ignoring Falron's protests, they marched the two newcomers into the castle courtyard.

Kess gazed around as he stood waiting. The castle seemed in a poor state of repair. Loose bricks had fallen from the walls and lay scattered on the courtyard floor. The floor itself was marked by tufts of dark grass which had forced their way up through the gaps between the stones. Many of the flagstones were cracked and broken. The main tower, perched in one corner, was intact; but even so, it looked battered and worn.

He glanced at Falron. The poet seemed on edge, and was fidgeting with the strap that held his horn.

A few more minutes passed, then a familiar figure appeared, striding confidently across the courtyard, his cloak billowing out behind him in the cold breeze. Dargan!

A chill swept over Kess as he remembered that first meeting in the Dark Master's stronghold. It seemed a long time ago.

'Ah, visitors!' Dargan's voice was soft but mocking. 'Welcome to my simple home!'

Falron bowed nervously and cleared his throat. 'Sire, I found this man and his friends wandering around in the Southlands beyond the Wailing Hills. When I had the chance, I captured him and brought him here!'

'Indeed! What happened to the others?'

'Lost, sire, in the Valley of Darkness. It is unlikely that they have survived.'

'Very good. You have done well, Falron. Tell me, where have you been these past two years?'

The poet shuffled his feet and stared at the ground. 'I—er—found nothing of interest to report to you, sire.'

The Dark Master nodded, and Falron breathed an audible sigh of relief.

Dargan turned to Kess. 'Welcome,' he said again, his teeth gleaming in a hard smile. 'I presume you are a friend of the girl—Linnil?'

'Her brother,' rasped Kess. 'And I promise that you will suffer for the evil you have done to her!'

'Tut, tut!' said Dargan. 'What kind of remark is that to make to your host?' He turned back to Falron.

'I expect you would like your payment now?' Dargan asked him.

'That is very generous, sire. Most kind.'

The Dark Master stepped towards him with the same fixed smile, and offered a small pouch that jingled with coins. As the poet reached for it, Dargan plunged his other hand forward. Falron collapsed, clutching the slim white dagger that now protruded from his stomach. He gasped once, then lay still.

'No one betrays me and lives!' hissed Dargan, retrieving his dagger. He wiped it on Falron's shirt. Glaring at Kess, he said, 'As for you, you will provide another interesting specimen for my studies. If by chance any of your friends have survived, I will have a welcome awaiting them.'

He motioned to the Zorgs. They grabbed the rope that was still tied to Kess' wrists and started to bundle him across the courtyard towards the tower.

'No!' said Kess, struggling to break free. He was rewarded by a vicious kick from one of the Zorgs.

'As I was saying, welcome to the Tower of Braggad,' said Dargan. 'Enjoy this view of the outside world. It will be your last!' Chuckling to himself, he strode past the prisoner without sparing him another glance.

24

The Journey to the Tower

The pain stopped as abruptly as it had begun.
Struggling to regain his thoughts, Valor gazed
upward. He felt as if he was in a living dream—or
more, a nightmare. A cold, vile face of green leered
down at him. It had a long brown neck.

The brown resolved itself into fingers that pulled
the head backwards. There was a sudden snap, and
Valor felt as if a heavy weight had been dragged off
his body. He closed his eyes again. It had all been too
much . . . too much.

Gatera gazed down at the pale form of the young
Mountain Guard.

'Is he all rightt?' asked Rrum.

The Land Crafter knelt and checked for signs of
life. 'I don't know,' he replied. 'I can't tell what damage
that creature has done.' He nodded at the twisted body
of the Tark, lying a few feet away.

The two friends had burst out of the blackness just
in time, a little way below the point where Valor was
battling with the Tark. Despite being partly dazzled
by the light, Gatera had soon realised what was

happening. Lowering Rrum to the ground, he had come to the Mountain Guard's aid just as Valor had succumbed to the mental powers of the Tark. Grabbing the creature's head from behind, he had heaved backwards with all his strength until its neck had snapped.

Bending down, Gatera gently lifted Valor from the floor. 'There's a stream nearby,' he explained to Rrum. 'Perhaps the water will help to revive him.'

'I hope so. He is a brave youngg man. He foughtt hardd againstt the Tarkk.'

The two friends then set off down the hill and across the valley. Reaching the stream, Gatera propped Valor against the mossy bank. He splashed some water over the Mountain Guard's face, and waited hopefully for signs of revival. There were none. Valor was still breathing, but it was as if he was either unconscious or in a deep sleep from which he could not be woken.

Gatera paced up and down, wondering what else he could do.

'Perhapps Hestteron couldd helpp,' suggested Rrum.

'You may be right,' Gatera replied. 'I will go back and fetch him—the others will be wondering where we are. Will you—'

He was interrupted by a black shape that seemed to burst out of the mist.

'Sash! And Athennar! It's good to see you! Is Hesteron with you?'

Athennar, still blinking from the sudden light, pointed back into the blackness. One by one, a series of figures emerged.

'Daylight!'

'I can 'ear again, boss!'

'Stop shouting, you stupid lump of lifeless fat!'

'Oh, to hear the sound of water again!'

'And to feel the breeze at last!'

'Ah, the poetry of light!'

As the confused travellers regained their senses and untied themselves from the rope, Gatera explained how he had found Valor fighting the Tark.

Hesteron knelt down beside the Mountain Guard and examined him closely. 'There is little we can do,' he said after a while. 'The Tark seems to have numbed his mind.'

'Will he recover?' Merric asked, looking in concern at his young friend's pale features; almost willing him to return to consciousness.

'It is difficult to say. Who knows what the Tark has done to him?'

'I have never heard of anyone who has been attacked in this way and lived,' added Athennar. 'The simple fact that Valor has survived so far—thanks to Gatera's prompt action—is perhaps a sign of hope.'

'What do we do now?' asked Melinya. 'It seems unlikely that he will recover soon, yet for the sake of the Realm we must continue to seek Dargan.'

'If he cannot walk, I will carry him,' Gatera replied firmly. 'We cannot leave him alone in such hostile country.'

Athennar nodded his agreement, then turned to survey the group. 'The only ones missing are Kess and Falron,' he said. 'They must still be wandering around within the blackness. If they have not returned soon, we must go in search of them. They may have found their way back to the other side of this accursed fog.'

'Not so!' called Merric. He had wandered a little way from the rest of the company, lost in thought as he pondered the Tark's attack on Valor. Now, he stood up and waved a small pouch. 'This is the pouch that Tolledon presented to Kess when first we left Hallion!'

'Then where is Kess?' growled Gatera.

The minstrel examined the soft moss for any signs of Kess or Falron. Then he gave a grunt of recognition. 'Something heavy fell here,' he said. 'I would suggest that it was Kess; that he was attacked and fell, dropping his pouch.'

'But who would attack him?' asked Vallel. 'Was it the Tark? Are there any signs of any creatures having been here?'

'No,' the minstrel replied, looking puzzled. 'The only footprints I can see are those of Kess and Falron. And I can find only one set of prints leading down towards the path out of the valley.'

'Strange,' said Athennar. 'If indeed they have come this way, where are they now? Surely they would have waited for us?' He shook his head. 'We have little choice: we must continue our journey now—we may yet catch up with them.' Giving a smile of encouragement, he added, 'Is everyone rested? Good!'

Having filled their flasks with water, the company left the little stream and headed towards the rocky mountain path. The track wound down a deep gully in the mountainside, then spilled out on to a sandy plain. The land ahead looked parched; drained of its soul. A sharp, cold breeze plucked at their clothes, adding to the sense of desolation.

As they reached the plain, a familiar haunting sound wafted through the air. It seemed to come from beyond a long ridge, some distance ahead.

'Falron's hunting horn! They must be in trouble,' said Athennar. 'We must help them!' He broke into a run, followed closely by Melinya and Hesteron. Within moments, all three were floundering in a sea of sand. They sank to their waists with alarming rapidity.

'Quicksand!' muttered Gatera, who had lowered Valor to the floor. 'Stay as still as possible!' he shouted. Then he, Vallel and Merric threw ropes to their struggling friends.

Bar'drash meanwhile nudged Gur'brak.

'Don't even think about it, shrivel-head!' growled the Zorg captain before his companion could speak. 'I'm not escaping just to get stuck in this lot! And I'm certainly not going back up that mountain!'

Athennar, Melinya and Hesteron were soon back on dry land, looking a little bedraggled and sheepish.

'My apologies,' Athennar said. 'That was very careless.'

'You weren't to know it was quicksand,' rumbled Gatera.

'How can we get through it? Can we follow Kess or Falron's footprints?'

Merric scanned the sand carefully. 'No. The wind has already blown loose sand over most of the prints. Although there are a few signs left, there are not enough to follow. Perhaps the Zorgs can be of help?'

Gur'brak shook his head. 'Nah—we always came through here with other Zorgs who knew the way.'

Athennar scratched his head, but Gatera smiled. 'I think my craft may prove useful here. I didn't have time to warn you before you rushed off, but I could sense that the ground was unstable. I should be able to guide you through safely, though it may take a little time.'

'I hope it won't be too late for us to help Kess and Falron,' said Hesteron.

Vallel knelt on the ground and pressed her hand against it. Then she straightened. 'I have never encountered quicksand before, Gatera. It's strange— I can sense the water in it. It's yet another example of how two of our crafts are intertwined!'

The Land Crafter gave a booming laugh. 'Quite so, lass! I must say, though, that I prefer solid ground to this watery, shifting stuff!' Bending to pick up Valor, he started to thread his way through the maze of quicksand patches, followed by his friends.

It was a slow process, and it was nearly two hours before they finally reached the long ridge. Athennar and Merric scrambled up to peer over the top. The first thing they saw was the Tower of Braggad, perched squat and ugly against a rocky mountainside. There was no sign of Kess or Falron. A solitary Zorg plodded back and forth along the battlements of the tower. After a few more minutes, the two friends climbed back down to rejoin the company.

'What news?' asked Hesteron, who had again been tending the unconscious Valor.

'The Tower is within reach,' Athennar said. 'However, it won't be easy. There is a Zorg on duty on the battlements.'

'Only one?' grunted Gatera. 'Dargan must be getting careless.'

'One is all that is needed,' Merric replied. 'He would see us as soon as we started to cross the sand.'

'Perhaps we should wait for nightfall,' Melinya suggested.

Athennar shook his head. 'No, the guard would still be likely to see us. And we can't afford to wait. If Dargan has captured Kess and Falron, they need our help now. Unfortunately, he will probably be expecting us.'

'But we can't just walk across there in broad daylight!' exploded Hesteron.

'I have an idea!' said Merric. 'Have you noticed these plants?' He pointed to the fat, prickly plants that were dotted between the patches of quicksand. 'If one is cut in half, you will find that it is filled with a thick, sticky liquid.'

'I don't understand,' said Athennar, puzzled.

The minstrel didn't answer him at first. 'Who still carries a blanket?' he asked.

'I left mine with the horses, to lighten the load,' replied Hesteron.

'I have mine,' Melinya said. Athennar and Vallel also indicated that they each had one.

'With mine, that is a total of four,' said Merric. 'If we smear the outside of the blankets with the juice from the plants and then cover them with sand, it may prove an adequate camouflage. We may escape notice—Zorgs are not the most keen-sighted creatures!'

'What d'you mean?' snarled Bar'drash, rubbing his empty eye-socket. He was rewarded by a cuff from Gur'brak. 'Quiet, bread brain!' growled the Zorg captain.

'It may just work!' said Athennar.

Merric unstrapped his leather blanket from the top of his backpack. Then he and Athennar moved across to the nearest large plant. While the minstrel supported it—taking care not to get stabbed by the huge spines—Athennar sliced the top off with his sword. Inside the bottom half was a pool of thick yellow liquid. Cutting the plant at the base, they carried it gingerly to the blanket, and tipped out some of the fluid. Then they spread it over the leather surface.

'Now to see how effective it will be,' muttered Athennar. They turned the blanket over and wiped the sticky side in the sand. When they turned it back again, Athennar looked at it with a critical eye. 'Hmm, not bad,' he said. 'From a distance, it should blend in moderately well with the sand.'

They soon had all four blankets covered. Melinya, Vallel and Merric would use one, Athennar and Gur'brak the second, and Hesteron and Bar'drash the third.

'What about Valor?' asked Hesteron.

Athennar grimaced. 'I have been wondering about him. It is not safe to leave him here—for one thing, if he regains consciousness, he may go wandering off into the quicksands. The best I can suggest is that you continue to carry him, Gatera, and wrap the blanket around yourself like a cape. If we tie a short piece of rope around it at your neck, it should form a hood. It's a slim hope, but perhaps the Zorg guard won't notice you.'

Merric had again been to the top of the ridge, and he now joined them. 'If we move forward when the guard walks from left to right along the battlements, we may be able to escape detection. During that time, his back is turned slightly, and it is doubtful that he can see this part of the plain without looking over his shoulder.'

'Yes—I could easily walk a few yards then crouch down with my head covered,' suggested Gatera. 'I can also peek out and tell everyone when to move forward again.'

'Very well,' sighed Athennar. 'We have little alternative. I suggest we all travel across at the same time. Sash will have to cross by herself. She can travel faster than any of us, and hopefully the guard will not notice her.' He spoke softly to the black leopard.

'What about my little pal here?' asked Gatera suddenly. They had forgotten Rrum, who had just returned from a foray for some 'food'.

'There is no need to worry. There are many small rocks in the sand. One more will not be noticed!'

'I hope you're right,' his huge friend said.

The company made its way to the top of the ridge and crouched there, blankets at the ready, waiting for the Zorg guard to complete his walk along the battlements. Once he had turned to go back, they dashed down to the plain below. Then they started half crawling, half scrambling across the sand, partly covered by the blankets.

'Now!' hissed Gatera, and they all hid beneath their blankets. The Land Crafter bent down and disguised himself and Valor as well as possible. He waited until the Zorg had completed his walk and then whispered for them all to move forwards once more. Hesteron had to prod Bar'drash into action, poking him in the side when he started to complain. 'Quiet!' he hissed.

So they crawled forward across the sand, Rrum somersaulting alongside. Although there was not far to go, time seemed to have stopped.

Up on the battlements, the weary Zorg continued to plod backwards and forwards, thinking of his sore feet; of the two prisoners who had recently been captured; and of how much he would enjoy a jug of ale. Suddenly he awoke from his daydreams. Out of one corner of his eye, he thought he saw movement out on the plain.

He turned and gazed at the stretch of sand. He could have sworn he had seen a rock moving! Then he was again distracted—he thought he glimpsed a wild animal disappearing behind the side of the mountain—but he wasn't sure. He rubbed his tired eyes. There was nothing else in sight, just the same expanse of sand and boulders. Grunting to himself, he resumed his march.

'That was close!' whispered Hesteron, his eyes peering out from beneath his blanket. Gatera nodded as he led them forward once more. Within minutes they reached a rough path, hidden from the battlements by a rocky spur jutting from the mountain.

Tossing his blanket aside, Athennar looked around. It was a grim place—devoid of any plants, except one or two almost transparent shrubs. The Animal Crafter pursed his lips as he recognised Dargan's handiwork. He then drew the company together. 'Well done!' he whispered. 'We made it!'

'Aye,' rumbled Gatera. 'But how do we get into the castle without being seen? This path leads straight to the main doors—and our blankets won't be able to hide us from the Zorg any more!'

Athennar sighed. He had anticipated this problem earlier, but had forgotten it on their journey across the sand. Now they had come this far, was it all in vain? He wanted to reach the tower unannounced, so that Dargan had little time to prepare any opposition. It now seemed likely that they would be deprived of even that small element of surprise.

25

Fading Hopes

Meltizoc sat on the edge of Linnil's bed, pondering over the problems facing the Realm. Everything seemed to be happening too quickly, and he felt a sudden pang of helplessness. He was particularly concerned for Tolledon—he seemed to have aged since their visit to Hallion. The Guardian was struggling with so many concerns: the continuous fading of his beloved valley; the grief he still bore over Hinno's death; the worry about the progress of the small company in the Southlands, led by his son; and his fear for the very future of the Realm. Yet still he worked feverishly, encouraging his troops; planning new strategies; listening to the problems of others. Meltizoc prayed that Elsinoth would continue to give Tolledon the strength he so clearly needed.

The wise man gazed once more at Linnil. She was sleeping at the moment. He had hoped that the Globe would stop the fading. It hadn't. Her hands and arms were steadily growing paler. A frown furrowed Meltizoc's brow. He wished there was something he could do to help the Valley girl.

A light knock came at the door, and he rose to answer it. It was Whisper, now almost fully recovered from the battle with the Grey Runners.

'How is Linnil?' she asked.

'Asleep,' he whispered.

'Awake,' came a weak voice from behind him. The wise man chuckled and opened the door fully so that Whisper could enter.

Turning to Linnil, he took her frail hand in his. 'How are you feeling?' he asked.

'Weak, but alive.' She managed a faint smile. 'Is there any news of Kess and Merric and the others?'

The wise man shook his head. 'Not yet. I suspect that it will be some days before we know whether or not they have been successful.'

'And if they have failed?'

'Then we shall know all too soon, I fear. Have courage, Linnil. Elsinoth is with them!'

To his surprise, Whisper nodded her agreement. 'I have seen your brother's strength. It comes from a well deep within; and yet from something—or some-one—far stronger than just himself.' She blushed. 'I can't really explain it, but I'm sure Meltizoc must be right.'

Linnil gave another small smile. 'And how is Callenor—and Tolledon?'

'Callenor is recovering well. As for Tolledon, well, he is never still. When not helping or organising others, he paces up and down thinking of new ideas, new hopes for the future.'

'Is there really any hope?' whispered Linnil.

'Of course. There is always hope. It is strange: when all seems hopeless, that is when hope is most often sought—and found. For those who trust Elsinoth, hope is a way of life. Hold on, Linnil.'

'I am trying,' she said, closing her eyes. 'I am trying.'

Meltizoc motioned to Whisper and they tiptoed away, leaving her to sleep.

Dargan's eyes were closed but he was wide awake, his mind probing recent events; deciding on the best course of action. Falron's arrival had come as something of a shock. It was not so much the return of the poet that had startled Dargan—the Dark Master had dismissed the man as a cringing fool some time ago. Indeed, the man's usefulness had begun to wane before he had disappeared two years previously.

No, it was the sight of Falron's prisoner that had come as a surprise to Dargan. Perhaps he had underestimated his enemies. He had never expected any of the girl's friends to reach the tower. He had thought they would have been too dismayed by his show of strength in subduing Linnil's will; had half expected that they would have spent all their energies in a useless search for a cure for the girl.

He should have known that Tolledon would not have been deflected from his purposes by such an event. Although he hated the Guardian—who stood for everything that the Dark Master opposed—he also held a grudging respect for the man. He had learned much about him from Zendos. Tolledon had power, an attribute Dargan admired—even though the Guardian was too stupid to use his strength to control his subjects.

Opening his eyes, Dargan gazed into space, unaware of the dusty objects all around him, cluttering the room. Momentary doubts flickered through his mind. What if the young man's friends had survived the dangers of the Valley of Darkness? If a fool like Falron had passed through unscathed, surely they could have done so?

Then the Dark Master shrugged to himself. It was

of no consequence—they would provide little competition for his formidable powers. He almost welcomed the thought of their arrival: more subjects for his experiments! Earlier in the day he had sent off Targul to find some of the other Tarks, so they could begin their search for humans. That would no longer be necessary if his enemies were coming to his very door! They would hop like innocent rabbits into his snare—and by the time they realised the folly of their actions, it would be too late!

Cackling to himself, he rose from the ancient padded chair. Briefly, he wondered how the Tark was faring. He wished he had sent the green eye with it. He would then have spotted any enemies trying to approach. Since the other eye had been shattered, he had been reluctant to use the remaining one unless absolutely necessary. He had placed it back in its original home, where he had first found it: slotted into the green face carved at the top of the underground throne. The eyes had been made by some hidden art—probably by a previous Dark Master—many centuries ago.

Although he regretted having not sent the eye, all was not lost. Fortunately, during Targul's absence he had had the foresight to put a Zorg guard on the battlements. Although incredibly stupid, even a Zorg could not fail to see people approaching over the sandy wastes that led to the tower. Indeed, the Zorg who had been on guard earlier had acted with surprising speed to warn him of his recent visitors.

His thoughts turned to the prisoner: Kess, brother of Linnil. Dargan remembered him now. He was the person who had rushed forward to try and grab the sceptre from him in his old Throne Room. Somehow the young man and his sister had struggled free from the power of his will. That still puzzled him. However, now he had dealt with the girl, he had little doubt that he would be able to handle her brother. This time, however, he would not be so merciful. After using the young man for more tests of his power, he would let him fade—alone and helpless—in his small underground cell.

Just a few more refinements to his power, a few more tests, and he would be ready. Then the whole of the Realm would tremble! With a grim smile of satisfaction, the Dark Master left the room.

Kess lay on the hard bed, his hands behind his head, staring at the ceiling. He wondered how much longer he would have to wait before Dargan arrived to torment him. Even that might come as a relief, rather than this long wait, not knowing what was in store.

Shaking his head, he rose and tried the door once more. It was more for something to occupy himself rather than from any real hope that it would suddenly prove to be unlocked.

Why had he allowed himself to get into this mess? Why had Elsinoth allowed it? The thoughts taunted him, echoing through his mind time and again.

Why had none of the company realised that Falron was a spy? Probably because there had been little to suggest it—the poet had seemed genuine enough. Distant words echoed in Kess' mind—the warning given by Meltizoc when he had first met the wise man—a warning that he had long since forgotten: 'Be wary of strangers: some may be enemies in disguise.' Why hadn't he remembered? Kess shook his head. Even now, after being betrayed, he couldn't help feeling sorry for Falron, so easily discarded by Dargan when his usefulness had come to an end.

One of Kess' main worries was for his friends. He had little doubt that Falron was wrong when he had said they had probably died in the Valley of Darkness. Perhaps the poet had deliberately lied to Dargan so that he could escape before the rest of the company arrived. No, after surviving the attack of the white creatures, Kess was sure that most, if not all of them, would come safely through the black fog.

But what if they *had* successfully escaped? Were they heading for a still harsher fate at the hands of Dargan? Now that the Dark Master was forewarned, he would no doubt have some unpleasant surprises in store for the company.

Kess banged his fist against the wall. They must not fail now—not after they had come so far! He thought of Linnil, such a long distance away at the Fortress of Fear. He thought of all the places of beauty he had seen—his own valley, now little more than a distant memory; the sheltered vale of Hallion; Rronadd, the home of the Rrokki people; even the dangerous Jewelled Forest. Dargan wanted to turn the Realm into a bleak, unfriendly world, and its people—those who survived—into mindless slaves. He must not be allowed to succeed!

But what could he, Kess, do? He was powerless—just a small, useless object in some great game of life and death. Despondently he sank back on to the bed and stared up at the ceiling once more.

He wondered how Linnil had spent her time when she had been imprisoned here, probably (the suddenness of the thought shocked him) in this very room. From somewhere deep within, he summoned the last dregs of his resolve and determination. He began to pray to Elsinoth, despite his fears, his inner torment, and his feeling of inadequacy. He prayed as he had never prayed before.

Some time later, the door to Kess' cell creaked open. The Quiet One's eyes jerked open in response—he must have fallen asleep. The solitary candle that lit the room had burned low, and huge, menacing shadows filled the cell. He turned and saw Dargan gazing at him with a mocking sneer.

'I trust you have slept well, my honoured young guest?'

Kess looked at the man, and beyond him, to all that he represented: evil; darkness; and a cold and continuing lust for power. Struggling from the bed, he leaped at the Dark Master, his hands reaching for his throat.

Dargan stepped back, momentarily taken aback by the ferocity of the attack. However, the long years of practised self-control enabled him to regain his composure immediately.

'Halt!' The commanding tone rang out, and Kess froze in mid-leap. Losing his balance, he crashed to the floor.

'Young fool!' rasped Dargan. 'Follow me!' Without pausing to glance back, he strode out of the door.

Kess climbed to his feet, his limbs moving against his will. Vainly he tried to stop himself, but Dargan's power was greater. With the voice still ringing in his ears, he meekly followed the Dark Master.

Arriving at Dargan's room, he waited while the cloaked figure opened the door. Then, still under the Dark Master's control, he entered.

'Sit!'

Kess sat. Outside, no emotions showed, but inside his mind was racing.

'You pathetic creature! You dared to attack me? How little you understand my power! You are no match for me. I could break you like that!' Dargan snapped his fingers. 'However, you will prove useful for my experiments. Like your sister, I will change your personality. As you must know by now, I made her love me. She showed a little resistance at first, but it didn't last long. As for you, I was going to test my power a little further and then discard you. Now, however, I have other plans. For the moment, I shall change you so that you will willingly work for me. I will instil within you a sense of hatred for your friends. Should they come looking for you, you will prove a useful extra weapon in my armoury. Perhaps you will even manage to destroy one or two of them before I destroy you.'

Kess felt a hard knot tighten in his heart. No, surely the Dark Master was incapable of such power? How he hated the man! He struggled, summoning all his drained mental reserves to fight against the invisible bonds that held him. It was useless. He was gripped in the control of a power far greater than his own. Outwardly, his face remained calm. Inwardly, however, he wept with fear and frustration.

'Good,' said Dargan, approaching Kess. 'I will tie you to the chair before I release my power. You have already learned that it is useless to resist.'

So saying, he lashed Kess' wrists and ankles tightly to the chair. Grinning, he moved to a corner of the room and picked up a long, slim object. The Sceptre! Losing all hope, Kess withdrew into himself, trying to block out all that was happening; to pretend that he was somewhere else. However, even his eyes refused to close. He could do nothing but watch as the Dark Master strolled towards him.

Towering over him, Dargan's cold gaze held Kess with a will that would not be denied. 'Now,' sneered the Dark Master, 'we will begin the experiment!'

26

Inside the Tower

'I think I can 'elp.'

Athennar looked in surprise at Gur'brak. He had been wondering how they could reach the castle unnoticed. Even if they managed, they still had to open the main doors somehow. Frowning, he said, 'You? How?'

'Give me a sword, and I'll go ahead alone and distract the sentry. I can soon deal with 'im. He won't suspect another Zorg.'

'Why would you do that?' interrupted Gatera.

The Zorg shifted uncomfortably and glanced at Melinya. 'You've—er—been fair to us.' He looked at his companion for support. 'Haven't they, Bar'drash?' The question was accompanied by a gentle kick.

'What? Aw, c'mon, boss.' Bar'drash scratched his ear and looked almost thoughtful. To Gur'brak's surprise, he said, 'I dunno. I suppose so. We're still alive,' he added grudgingly.

'And how do we know we can trust you?' asked Hesteron.

'You don't!' growled Gur'brak. 'But what've you got to lose? Take it or leave it—I'm not going to risk my neck if you don't believe me!'

'I believe you,' Melinya said softly.

Athennar's eyebrows arched. More surprises! He sighed, then nodded. 'If Melinya believes you, I will trust her judgement. Besides, we have little choice.' He pulled Gur'brak's short, thick sword from his backpack. 'Use it well,' he said.

Gur'brak gave a grunt of assent. 'I'll give a wave once I've got rid of the guard,' he said.

'Boss, can't I come with you?'

'No. This is a job for one.'

'May Toroth guide your steps,' Merric said.

'Huh!' muttered Gur'brak. Without saying any more, he trudged off around the corner towards the Tower of Braggad.

As the Zorg captain stomped up the rough mountain path that led to the main gateway of the castle, his mind reeled under a mass of confusing thoughts. Why had he offered to help? Why stick out his own neck, when in all probability it would be chopped off? Even if he managed to fool the guard (which shouldn't be too difficult), Dargan would destroy him if he ever learned of Gur'brak's treachery.

At that point, he almost turned back. Almost, but not quite. For once in his life, he was in a position to help people who had been kind to him. Melinya's face flashed briefly into his mind, and the Zorg gritted his uneven teeth. His resolve hardened, and he plodded up towards the huge wooden doors.

'Oi! What d'you want?' called down the Zorg guard when he was still a little way from the entrance.

'Got a message for Dargan,' bluffed Gur'brak. 'Can you let me in?'

''E didn't say 'e was expectin' you!'

'Well, he is—and if you don't get down 'ere pretty quick, you'll be in plenty of trouble!'

The guard gave a sniff and disappeared from the battlements. A couple of minutes later, one of the doors creaked open and the Zorg's face peeked out. 'You'd better come in!' he said crossly. 'And don't take all day about it—I've got to get back on duty!'

He let Gur'brak through the door and started to close it. Gur'brak readied himself to draw his sword. He was going to stab the guard, but again Melinya's face flickered in his mind: a kind, gentle face. He left the sword sheathed, picked up a large rock instead, and brought it crashing down on the guard's head. The Zorg crumpled to the ground, unconscious. Gur'brak dragged him to one corner of the room and tied his hands and legs.

Panting from his exertions, he then peeked through the door that led into the castle courtyard. In the centre of the yard lay a brightly clothed figure. Keeping a nervous look out for any other guards, Gur'brak shuffled over towards it. As he had thought, it was Falron. The poet was dead.

Retreating back to the shelter of the entrance room, he slipped out of the huge doors and on to the mountain path. Trotting a little way along it, he waved his hands.

The rest of the company had been keeping a careful watch on the gates from behind a rock. They soon joined the Zorg, and Gatera gave him a congratulatory slap on the back, nearly sending him sprawling. Gur'brak scowled, but then Melinya took his hand and patted it.

'Thank you,' she said. 'That was very brave.'

The Zorg coughed and looked away. This woman had an unnerving effect on him! To hide his confusion, he grabbed hold of Bar'drash, who was sitting against a rock, watching.

'C'mon fleabag,' he said. 'It looks like we're in this to the end!'

'Aw, boss, can't I just stay here and have a snooze?'

He was rewarded by a well-aimed kick on the ankle. 'No! Now get moving!'

Once inside the castle, Athennar and Hesteron left the company in the entrance room while they went to check Falron. They soon returned, looking very solemn.

'He's dead, as Gur'brak reported,' Athennar said. 'Killed by a sword or dagger, I think.'

'Is there any sign of Kess?' asked Merric.

Athennar shook his head. 'Assuming he came this far, he must have been captured.' Turning to Gur'brak, he asked, 'Where can we find Dargan?'

The Zorg moved over to the chest in the corner of the room, and yanked it away from the wall, revealing the trapdoor. 'Down there,' he said. 'There's an underground cave system. I've only been down there once. It was 'orrible—very spooky.'

'Thank you,' Athennar said, adding unexpectedly, 'You are free to go. You've served us well. This is our fight now.'

The Zorg looked surprised, then shook his head. 'No. We'll come with you. There's nowhere else for us to go—and I want to see what 'appens.'

'Aw, boss—'

'You can stay here if you want,' Gur'brak said to Bar'drash. 'I don't fancy it myself. Besides, a Tark might arrive, and I'd rather face Dargan than one of them!'

'Then you don't know him very well,' Athennar said. 'You are both welcome to join us—but keep in the background, out of the way.'

'Don't worry—we will!'

Athennar reached into his backpack and handed Bar'drash his sword. 'You may need this,' he said.

'And no tricks!' growled Gatera.

Unbolting the trapdoor, Athennar heaved it back. Then, lighting three torches, he passed two to Hesteron and scrambled down the hole. Sash, who had been padding back and forth across the room, immediately leaped down to join him. One by one, the others followed, the senseless Valor being passed down to Gatera once more. Despite the dangers ahead, none of them wanted to leave the Mountain Guard behind.

When they had all climbed down to the rough floor below, Athennar looked around. A wide passage led away from the trapdoor. A little distance ahead, it ended at a great stone door. Motioning the others to follow, he moved quickly along until he reached it. The door's large iron bolts were already drawn, but when he pulled on the handle, the door wouldn't open.

'Rrum!' he called, pointing at the lock. 'Can you help us?'

'Itt will be a pleasure!' grated the little Rrokki. He immediately set to work grinding the stone away with his tough jaws.

Some time later, just as everyone was beginning to get restless, Rrum turned around. 'Itt is done,' he said.

'Thank you,' replied Athennar. Putting his shoulder to the door, he pushed. It swung open easily, and a slight draught came from beyond, causing the torches to flicker.

'Onwards, my friends,' said Athennar in a soft voice. 'We must be getting near our destination. Keep alert, and as quiet as possible.'

The light shone on the expectant faces of his friends. *We must not fail,* he thought, while giving them an encouraging smile.

The passage twisted and turned for a little way, then split unexpectedly into three.

'Merric, you and I will take the left-hand fork. Hesteron, you and Vallel check the centre path. Valor and Melinya, please stay here with the Zorgs, while Gatera takes Rrum and explores the tunnel to the right.' Pulling another torch from his backpack, he lit it and gave it to the Land Crafter.

Merric joined Athennar, and the two friends set off down the left passage. The tunnel wound its way slowly into the mountain, and they were soon out of sight of the company.

After some time, the rough stone walls disappeared beneath a covering of dull green moss. Merric reached out to touch it. It stuck to his fingers, and he had to prise them away.

'Keep your distance from the walls!' he hissed to Athennar.

The Animal Crafter nodded. He too had noticed the moss. As he took another look at it, he had to blink his eyes. The wall seemed to move—as if a very slow ripple was working its way along it.

'Did you see that?' he whispered.

Merric nodded. 'I sense danger,' he said, stopping. Athennar halted as well. Another ripple passed along the wall. Athennar felt as if they were stuck in the throat of a great worm. Looking ahead, he suddenly realised that the passage was getting narrower.

'Let's get out of here!' he shouted, and started to run back along the tunnel. Merric followed him, glancing over his shoulder as he did so. The convulsions in the wall of the passage were growing stronger.

Athennar, too, peeked back as he raced along the tunnel. In the distance behind them, the tunnel had almost closed. Another large ripple spread along the walls. 'Faster!' he shouted, as he willed his legs into greater efforts. Merric now ran alongside him, matching his speed with ease.

Yet another ripple came along. The tunnel grew narrower as it passed. Merric now had to fall in behind Athennar—there was no longer enough room for them to run side by side.

A further convulsion—even larger than before— swept along the walls. As it passed Merric, the tunnel wall bulged out and caught him, jerking him to a halt. His arm and side were trapped by the sticky moss. Struggling to free himself, he let out an involuntary shout.

Athennar heard the cry. Skidding to a stop, he rushed back to help the minstrel.

'No!' Merric called. 'Save yourself, my friend!'

The Animal Crafter ignored him and grabbed his free arm. Beyond Merric, he could see another large ripple heading towards them. Trapped, like a fly in a spider's web! He heaved with all his might, and Merric pulled as well. There was a loud sucking noise, and the minstrel tore free from the moss. They both tumbled to the ground, but rapidly regained their feet, taking care not to collide with the opposite wall. Then they were off, running, running.

The ripple raced towards them. Athennar looked back once more. It was no use—this time they would be trapped for sure, squeezed to death by the contracting tunnel. The wave of motion swept up behind them. He was knocked against one wall.

To his surprise, there was no moss to trap him. He continued to run, expecting to be squeezed by the tightening passage. Then he realised that the motion in the wall had stopped. They were free!

Just ahead of him Merric had stopped. Athennar clapped him on the shoulder in relief. Then, turning, he looked back as he regained his breath. A few yards away, the tunnel had been reduced to a small, moss-filled hole. On their side of the hole, however, the walls were bare.

The two friends sat down while they recovered their strength.

'Another—of—Dargan's—illusions?' panted Merric.

'Possibly,' replied Athennar. 'If so—it was still—real enough—to have—killed us.'

The minstrel nodded, and took a few deep breaths of air.

After a few minutes, Athennar rose to his feet, and helped Merric up as well. 'We must return and find out if the others have had any success,' he said.

Merric stared at the closed tunnel behind them. 'I trust they have fared better than we,' he said. 'Even more, I hope that they are safe. This place is evil, like the heart of its Master.'

'Yes, and this is just a small foretaste of what we may yet have to face,' muttered Athennar. The thought worried him. If Dargan could do this when not even present, what would he do when they eventually met him once more? Were they too late? Was he already too powerful?

27

Struggles and Statues

Gatera strolled along the right-hand passage, Rrum trotting along at his side. At first, the hard earth floor dipped and rose in gentle slopes. It was as if they were travelling over a series of small hills instead of walking along an underground tunnel. Then it flattened out, the passage curving first to the left, then to the right. Finally, they reached a straight stretch. In the distance, just within reach of the torchlight, Gatera thought he could see a door blocking the passage.

He stopped—something about the tunnel worried him. He could sense it through his bare feet. Motioning Rrum to walk behind him, he crept slowly forward, holding the torch at waist level so he could see the ground more easily.

After a few yards he stopped again. Just ahead, the floor changed—it became a shimmering, shifting mass. Gatera edged forward and tested it with his staff. It seemed solid enough, despite the way it appeared to move back and forth. Although he was well aware that he could be seeing an illusion created by Dargan, he wasn't happy. His Land Crafter instincts warned him that something still seemed wrong.

As he pondered, he felt Rrum tugging at his hessian doublet. 'I will testt itt,' he said.

'No!' rumbled Gatera. 'If anyone should test it, it should be me.'

'Butt I am lightter. If you tie a roppe to me, you can pull me backk if there is danger.'

Gatera scratched the back of his head, recognising the sense behind the little Rrokki's suggestion. 'Very well,' he agreed reluctantly, 'but be careful.'

'Butt of course!'

The Land Crafter tied a rope around Rrum's waist, and handed him the torch. He held on to the other end of the rope as the Rrokki slowly made his way forward. As Rrum moved on to the shifting floor, Gatera held his breath. Nothing happened. So it was just an illusion! Then why had he been so troubled?

Rrum walked forwards a few more steps. Gatera was just about to start following him when suddenly the floor beneath the Rrokki trembled, shook, and vanished. Rrum plunged headlong into the great hole that had suddenly appeared. Gatera felt a hard jerk on the rope, and it was almost pulled from his hands. Simultaneously, the air grew dark as the torch disappeared with Rrum. Just a faint glow came from the chasm.

Gatera held on to the rope and began to pull.

'Hold on, little friend, hold on!' he called. There was no answer. He kept pulling until eventually the little round figure of the Rrokki—still clutching the torch—was hauled back over the lip of the chasm. Rrum struggled to his feet, brushed himself down, and trotted back to join Gatera.

'Thankk you!' he said.

'I only just managed to hold on to the rope,' said

Gatera, checking his friend for any signs of wounds. The Rrokki seemed unhurt.

'We will nott gett any further this way,' Rrum said.

'No,' agreed Gatera, holding up the torch. He could no longer see a door at the far end of the tunnel— just a solid rock wall. 'Let's get back to the others!'

Hesteron and Vallel had encountered a different kind of obstacle on their journey along the central passage. The tunnel was fairly narrow, and soon began to slope downhill. Walking around a corner, the elves came face to face with a strange sight. The corridor ahead was closed—by a curtain of fire and water. Flames flickered upwards from the entire width of the tunnel floor. At the same time, a continuous sheet of water flowed down from the roof. Where the flames and water met—at about chest height—they formed a thin, yellow horizontal line of sizzling fire.

'What in the Realm—?' said Hesteron.

'It's as if the water and fire are cancelling each other out in the centre,' said Vallel, fascinated by the sight. 'I wish Fashag could see this.'

'Perhaps it's all just an illusion.'

'Perhaps.' She moved forward and reached up to test the water. It spilled over her hand, yet none of it reached the floor. 'The water certainly *seems* real; and I can feel the heat of the flames from here.'

'It appears that our way is blocked.'

'I could probably climb through the water if you helped me.'

'No—I think we should return to the others first and see if they have found an easier way forward.'

The two Crafters turned and retraced their steps. When they reached the company, the other search parties still hadn't returned. But after a short while, Gatera and Rrum emerged from one tunnel, followed shortly by a tired Athennar and Merric from the other.

Once all the friends had recounted their experiences, Athennar said, 'It seems that we have little choice but to try and pass the barrier in the central tunnel.'

'What if that is blocked as well?' asked Melinya.

'I think we'll find a way through—I suspect that this is just a series of illusions left by Dargan to test the strength of any unwelcome visitors, or to impress them with his powers. He probably thinks that those who are not worthy of his attention will give up before going any further—or that they will perish in the attempt! I'm sure that he also has more imaginative delights in store for those who pass this first test!'

'Dargan's ready for us!' wailed Bar'drash. 'We've got no 'ope!' He was rewarded by a cuff round the ear from Gur'brak.

Once the friends had all recovered, they began to troop down the central corridor. When they reached the curtain of flame and water, Athennar moved forward with Vallel and Hesteron to examine it.

Vallel puckered her lips, then said, 'Hesteron, if you kneel down, I should be able to stand on your back and poke my head through the water to see what's on the other side. At the moment, I can't quite reach without getting too close to the flames.'

Hesteron looked a little dubious, but agreed to the plan. 'Take it carefully,' he warned. 'If there's any sign of danger on the other side, pull your head back immediately!'

'I'll support you, so that you don't topple forwards,' added Athennar.

Hesteron knelt down and Vallel climbed carefully on to his back. She wobbled slightly at first, but Athennar clutched her arm, enabling her to regain her balance. When she had steadied herself, she bent her head and eased it forward through the curtain of water. The rest of the company watched in silent anticipation.

After a few seconds—a seemingly endless time to Hesteron—she emerged back out of the water and jumped down to the ground, shaking her head.

'Why are you doing that?' asked Hesteron as he climbed to his feet.

'To get rid of the— Oh! My hair isn't even wet! Yet it felt like water all around me!'

'Passing strange indeed,' said Merric, who had walked forward to join them. 'It is not right. It defies the laws of Toroth!'

'What's on the other side of the barrier?' asked Athennar, a little impatiently.

'Oh, sorry—nothing unusual. The corridor seems to continue quite normally.'

Athennar paced up and down for a moment and then said, 'Well, we must try it. The heaviest must go first—Gatera, that means you—so that we have enough people this side to help you through. If we form a short line on either side of him, we can support him as he lies down, and pass him through the water feet first. Gatera, we'll have to give you a heave through, and hope that you can land safely on the other side.'

'I'm not worried about that part—I'm fairly sure-footed. After all, I am a Land Crafter! I'm more worried about whether you'll be able to lift me high enough to avoid the flames!'

He lay down rather hesitantly, trusting himself to his friends' waiting arms. It took five of them to manage it: Athennar and Merric on one side, and Hesteron, Vallel and Melinya on the other. Rrum and the two Zorgs were too short to be of much help.

'Push your hands through the water when you are ready for us to pass Valor through,' Athennar said.

Then they moved closer to the curtain, taking care not to get burned by the flames. They began feeding Gatera's legs through the water, then gave a big heave. There was a muffled thump on the other side of the barrier.

'Are you all right?' yelled Athennar.

'Aye,' came a muffled rumble. Athennar was relieved—at least they could communicate through the sheet of fire and water.

'I'm ready for Valor,' continued the muffled voice. Two huge hands came through the water, ready to collect the Mountain Guard. Athennar and Hesteron carefully passed him over to the Land Crafter.

The next moment there was a deep-throated growl from Gatera.

'What's the matter?'

'I stood a little too close to the fire—it singed my doublet!' the Land Crafter boomed. Athennar chuckled in response.

One by one, the company passed through the water—Rrum, Gur'brak, Bar'drash (with much complaining), Melinya, Vallel and Hesteron. Sash, prompted by Athennar, leaped nimbly through the water. Only Athennar and Merric were left.

'Climb on to my back and leap through,' Merric said.

'No—you first.'

'Then how will you pass through? No, you forget that I am an elf. We are well known for our lightness of foot. When you are safely on the other side, I can leap through. I would ask merely that you request our friends to stand by the sides of the tunnel lest I land on them!'

'Very well.' Athennar climbed onto Merric's shoulders and with some awkwardness was helped through the shield of water.

'All clear!' he shouted from the other side after a few seconds.

Merric paced back down the corridor. Then he ran, swift and light upon his feet, straight towards the curtain. At the last moment, he sprang forwards and dived head first through the water. Curling his body in mid-air, he then straightened out and landed nimbly on the other side.

'Well done!' said Athennar.

At that moment, Vallel shouted, 'Look! The fire and water—they're disappearing!'

Sure enough, the curtain faded gradually until it had completely disappeared.

'Surely we didn't go through all that performance for nothing!' groaned Hesteron.

'No,' said Athennar. 'The barrier has achieved its function. There is no longer anyone on the other side, so it has ceased to exist. Come, let us explore the rest of this passage. But keep alert—you can be sure that there will be more dangers ahead!'

They eased their way step by step along the corridor. After rounding the first corner, it continued to twist and turn. In the torchlight, they all leaped back as they were confronted by an evil, twisted face. It was hideous—half human, half beast. Large bulbous eyes stared out, and a harsh leering grin mocked them.

'Huh?' gasped Hesteron, then smiled. 'So that's what it is!'

Bar'drash peeped out from behind Gatera as the others moved forward to examine the creature. Half hidden in a recess, the torchlight revealed it as a crude statue. Rrum touched the cold, roughly hewn stone. 'Very oldd,' he said.

'Probably made by the original occupants of this place,' muttered Gatera.

As they proceeded, they passed other statues—grim-faced men and women; various goblins; and other creatures more animal than human. The passage turned another corner and opened into a wide circular chamber. Statues were arranged all around the walls. Fierce warriors battled with strange beasts; wild-eyed horsemen were frozen in mid-leap.

Halfway around the room, the statues changed. Proud people of regal bearing leaned on their swords or stood proudly, stone crowns adorning their brows.

'What is this place?' breathed Merric.

'Perhaps a memorial for some ancient race, in memory of their battles or their heroes,' replied Athennar.

'But why are there so many statues—and why here?' asked Vallel.

'Perhaps a whole community once lived down here; it would be a useful hiding place. Any enemy would soon be lost or discouraged in the darkness.'

'And the illusions?'

'The illusions were no doubt created by Dargan or an earlier Dark Master. I would doubt that these people would have had the skill—or the inclination—to create such images.'

There was only one exit from the room, so they all filed through it into another cold and narrow passage. A slight breeze trickled along it, almost as if someone had left a door open somewhere.

Athennar suddenly held up a restraining hand. In the darkness, a little way ahead, the torchlight had reflected off something large. There was little point in dousing the torches now—if some creature awaited them, it would already have seen their light.

Creeping slowly forward, Athennar motioned Hesteron to accompany him. The passage led to another circular chamber. In the centre was a huge stone statue—the object that had reflected the torchlight. It was carved from a yellowish-white rock.

Athennar moved around to the front of the statue. Like Linnil, many weeks before, he was startled when its eyes grated open and its long tongue uncoiled from its mouth, oozing with evil-smelling liquid. Peering closely at the statue's head, he realised that it had probably been activated by some hidden mechanism; he remembered his father and Meltizoc discussing such things. Dargan's work again, no doubt!

Athennar sent Hesteron back to fetch the others while he looked around the rest of the chamber. There was little to see, except for the numerous passage openings all around its edge, and nothing to show which of the many exits they should take. While he waited for his friends, he pondered the problem. He was only too aware that a wrong choice could lead them into immediate danger—even death.

In his room, Dargan was disturbed from his experiments. Over in one corner, there was a slight noise from a tiny statue—a copy of the one in the circular chamber. Looking deep into its eyes, he gave a grunt of annoyance, then chuckled.

'It appears that one of your friends has arrived at last,' he said. 'I'm surprised that he has come this far. However, his quest will soon come to an abrupt end. So far he has only seen glimpses of my power—soon he will experience its full might!'

Kess stared back with unseeing eyes. Dargan cackled again, and began to untie the young man's bonds.

28

Fighting Illusions

The company assembled in the circular chamber, keeping their distance from the drooling statue. Gatera produced a lump of limestone from his backpack. 'I'll mark the passage we came through,' he said, 'so we can find it again if we're in a hurry on our way out.'

'Yes, but which tunnel do we take now?' asked Vallel.

'I think I know,' replied Athennar slowly. 'I suspect the statue is another object that Dargan has twisted to his own use. However, like those in the other chamber, it was obviously carved long ago. I think that the original sculptor would have built this one to face the tunnel that links this chamber with the main living area, now taken over by Dargan. That passage should lead us to him.' He pointed to one of the openings. It looked identical to the others.

Merric nodded his agreement. 'Let us continue with our quest. I can almost sense the evil of Dargan as it seeps through these passages.'

With Athennar again leading the way, the company stepped into the new tunnel.

This time, the passage was short, and led to a large platform. A dark underground lake lapped at its edge. Across the centre of the lake was a wide walkway, at the far end of which they could see the distant glow of torches.

'If we can see those torches, any of Dargan's guards will be able to see ours,' whispered Hesteron.

'There is little we can do about that,' replied Athennar. 'I expect that he has probably been warned of our presence already.'

Their conversation was brought to an abrupt end. Strange signs of activity began to burst out all around them.

The first threat came to Rrum. Out of the darkness, just at the fringe of the light from Hesteron's torch, the little Rrokki noticed a movement. He was about to shout a warning when he froze, unable to speak. There was something horribly familiar about the shape coming towards him. Then he recognised it— a cave-warg! The creature shuffled forward a few feet, then stood still. Rrum knew it was waiting—waiting for him! His hour of destiny had come. He wanted to cry out; wanted to flee. But when he looked back, the entrance to the platform had disappeared. A blank wall stared back at him. Trapped!

Rrum looked for his friends, but they were all now under attack as well. This time, there was no escape for him. This time he would have to face his tormentor.

Gulping a deep breath, the little Rrokki braced himself. He thought of his family, of his friends, of Kess. He realised that the warg was probably another of Dargan's tricks, an illusion, but one that was still real enough to hurt—and kill—him.

The cave-warg took another step forward. Rrum still couldn't see it clearly. It was just a large, black, threatening mass. It represented all that he hated, all that he feared. He remained frozen as it again moved towards him.

Melinya was meanwhile battling against a huge thunder goblin which had materialised on the platform in front of her. The sight of the creature brought back the memory of her time of imprisonment underground, held by Ganniwaggik and his goblins. The creature that faced her now was far more fearsome, however, and towered over her.

Unlike Rrum, she didn't freeze, but drew her sword and attacked. The thunder goblin stepped back, momentarily surprised. Then it strode forward, brushing her slim elven blade aside with its own enormous sword. It bore down upon her, knocking her to the ground. Giving an evil smirk, the goblin lifted its sword arm. Melinya saw the flash of a blade, and then . . .

And then the blade scudded harmlessly by her shoulder as another sword knocked it aside. A short, stocky figure stood next to her, brandishing his weapon at the towering outline of the thunder goblin. 'First you've got to deal with me, you festering toad!' Gur'brak shouted, bravely shielding Melinya.

'Yeah, and me too!' added Bar'drash, who had come to his captain's help, and now stood beside him, knees knocking.

Some way beyond the two Zorgs, Gatera also faced a fierce challenger. The moment he had sensed danger, the Land Crafter had gently laid Valor next to the cave wall. Returning to his friends, he had come face to face with his own opponent. It was the only creature that had ever defeated him—a tadrat. But this one was a far greater size than the ones he had faced in Dargan's stronghold. It was also more dangerous. At the stronghold, he had fallen and had lost consciousness. This time he risked a greater loss—his life.

As the creature snarled at him, he readied himself. The tadrat's sharp white teeth gleamed in the torchlight. Sparks of flame glinted in its cruel eyes. Then it rushed at him. Gatera dodged, and rammed his torch in the creature's face. It gave a high-pitched scream, and a smell of scorched fur filled the air. The tadrat turned and sprang at Gatera. As it attacked, the Land Crafter swung his staff as hard as he could.

The tadrat was knocked sideways by the force of the blow. However, it soon recovered its feet, and began to circle him. It seemed barely affected by the hard knock.

To one side, Gatera could hear Vallel screaming. The Water Crafter had been walking towards the lake to examine it when her own opponent had sprung up—a hideous face from the past. Vile and bloated, the huge head reared above the lake's surface as she approached. A Scorbid!

'No!' she screamed. A thick, tentacled arm shot out to grab her. She dodged, but slipped on the wet ground. Another tentacle crawled over the edge of the platform and began to worm its way towards her. Vallel rolled away, but a third one appeared above her, its moist suckers pulsating. It hovered above her for a moment as if taunting her.

Trapped between the tentacles, Vallel cried out once more. Visions of Vosphel swam before her mind. They mingled with echoes of the nightmare she had experienced in the Vale of Miscreance. But this was no nightmare—it was real!

Where was Hesteron? She looked around, but all she could see were tentacles, and the fat, slimy head of the Scorbid. Desperately she tried to edge away from the fleshy arms, but there was nowhere to go. This time there was no escape.

Hesteron was too occupied with his own problems

to see Vallel being attacked. Along with Merric and Athennar, he faced a trio of opponents, each an identical figure of fear: Dargan! The Dark Master had somehow projected three very real images of himself; one to face each of the three friends. The triple images cackled in unison, and then advanced.

Hesteron drew his sword, and sensed Athennar and Merric doing likewise. The three Dargans drew back their cloaks to reveal that they were also armed. Hesteron tried to concentrate on his immediate opponent—his friends would have to do their best to defeat the other two. Circling the first Dark Master, he made a sudden sword thrust. The cloaked figure laughed as he countered with his own blade. Dargan continued the movement by flicking his wrist, sending Hesteron's sword flying into the air.

Meanwhile, Athennar was struggling with the second Dargan. The Hallion man was more cautious than Hesteron in his approach, but was still taken by surprise by Dargan's excellent swordplay. He tried to force the Dark Master back, but Dargan just grinned and stood his ground.

Athennar suddenly faked a stroke, then slashed upwards at Dargan's hand. His opponent's sword was knocked from his grasp, and clattered to the ground some feet away. Athennar stepped forward to finish the Dark Master. To his alarm, Dargan grasped the blade of the sword with his bare hands. Wresting it from Athennar's grip, he flung it to one side. Then he closed in on the Animal Crafter.

Athennar swung a hard punch, but Dargan took the blow without flinching. He responded by tapping Athennar lightly on the stomach with the back of his hand. The Animal Crafter felt as if an iron fist had crashed into his midriff, and he crumpled. Dargan allowed him to regain his feet, then hit him again, knocking Athennar off his feet as easily as if he was swatting a fly.

Alongside Athennar, Merric was faring little better. Although light on his feet and able to avoid or parry the third Dargan's blade, he was starting to tire. The Dark Master, however, was not even breathing heavily. He seemed to be enjoying the contest, as if it was some form of idle amusement.

Merric dodged another sword thrust, Dargan's blade skimming past his body and slashing the edge of his cloak. Behind him, the minstrel heard a groan, but he couldn't afford to turn and see which one of the company was in trouble.

The groan had come from Bar'drash, who had been flung to one side by the giant thunder goblin attacking Melinya. The intervention of the two Zorgs had given her time to regain her feet, and she now stood side by side with Gur'brak, as the goblin mounted another attack. This time it had two foes to face—foes who knew its strength, and were wary of being caught by its powerful arms.

The elf woman and the Zorg danced from side to side, desperately trying to avoid the thunder goblin's grasp. Despite its size, the creature was quite agile, and soon caught Melinya, lifting her off the ground.

The next moment it dropped her as a sword bit deep into its leg. It swung out blindly, roaring with pain. Gur'brak leaped back, but was caught by one arm, and sent crashing against the cave wall. Sliding down, he landed in an unmoving heap on the floor. The thunder goblin, having rid itself of the trouble-some Zorg, now grasped Melinya once more. The next moment, it again yelled, dropped the elf woman, and started leaping about in agony. Something had stabbed its foot!

Bar'drash glared up at it, and shouted, 'You've killed my boss, you—you—'orrible, 'orrible beast!'

The goblin, still hopping, picked up the hapless Zorg and sent him flying into the lake. Then, his face contorted with pain and rage, he again turned his attention to the elf woman. By this time, however, another friend had arrived to help her—a lithe, black leopard that snapped and snarled at the creature's wounded leg.

To one side of the thunder goblin, the awesome shape of the cave-warg towered over Rrum. The little rock man looked up to see dark holes where the warg's eyes should have been; dark holes that seemed to grow and grow, merging with the beast's cavernous mouth.

He felt himself begin to quiver. What *was* this creature? It seemed to have such a hold upon him. Forcing himself to look away, he thought again of his friends and family—and of the need to defeat Dargan. He suddenly remembered, too, the rainbow cavern. The memory rekindled his hopes, and gave him the courage he needed. Not daring to look up, he shuffled forward, each step seeming to take an eternity. Then he deliberately bent down and clamped his jaws on to the cave warg's leg. The creature screamed: not an audible scream, but one that Rrum could sense in his mind. Then the Rrokki felt his jaws being prised open by two great hands. He began rising through the air, borne up by one of those hands.

Rrum began to struggle, but he could do nothing to stop the warg as he was lifted towards its cavernous mouth. Awaiting him was a vast hole, blacker it seemed than the impenetrable darkness of the black fog. Slowly, he was drawn nearer and nearer to the great maw.

On the far side of the platform, Vallel froze in fear as one of the tentacles brushed across her ripped tunic.

This was the end! Killed by the same monster that had destroyed her sister! She cried for help, but all she could see were the tentacles, as they closed in upon her with a terrible, unavoidable embrace. She thought she glimpsed the sudden flash of torchlight reflecting off metal; but perhaps she had imagined it.

She closed her eyes, awaiting the creature's touch, but it never came. Opening them again, she gasped as she saw the tentacles flopping on the ground, being dragged slowly back towards the lake.

She turned to look at the Scorbid. Protruding from its eye was a double-headed axe. The beast sank slowly, and was soon swallowed up by the dark waters.

Gatera smiled grimly and returned to his fight against the tadrat. It was fortunate that he had seen Vallel's plight. Without hesitating to think of himself, he had thrown his axe straight and true. His satisfaction at seeing it hit its mark was marred by the realisation that he now had only his staff with which to defend himself. He had already learned that it would afford little protection against such a fearsome creature.

The tadrat charged. Gatera sidestepped, swiping at its front two feet. The creature stumbled, but soon regained its footing. Then it charged him again. He swung the staff, but this time failed to stop the creature. The next moment, Gatera was knocked to the floor.

The tadrat pounced on him, two clawed feet digging into his chest, pinning him to the ground. The creature was incredibly strong. It lowered its face towards his. Desperately, he grabbed its neck. His huge hands tightened, and his arm muscles knotted with strain.

Unfortunately, the tadrat was stronger. It gradually

forced his hands lower and lower, until its teeth were inches from his neck.

Back in the centre of the platform, Athennar, Merric and Hesteron were still battling with the three Dargans. Merric saw Hesteron struggling on the ground with his adversary, and noticed Athennar being knocked off his feet for the third time. He heard the Animal Crafter utter a strange, snarling cry. Then Sash leaped forward out of the darkness. The minstrel had no time to see any more. His own assailant, seeing him momentarily distracted, drove home his advantage and tripped him up. Merric lost his sword, and felt one arm clamped by Dargan's foot. The Dark Master stood above the minstrel, sword poised to strike.

'Farewell, my brave enemy,' he said. 'Now, breathe your last!' He brought the sword down, putting all his strength behind the blow.

29
Face to Face

At the last moment, Merric rolled to one side, yanking his arm from beneath Dargan's foot as the sword descended. The weapon clanged harmlessly on the bare rock floor. Dargan staggered, but came towards Merric once more before he could regain his feet.

The minstrel had no time to find his own sword. Dargan was going to defeat them all! From the depths of his soul, he gave a piercing cry for help: 'Toroth, aid us now!'

The air in the cavern went suddenly still. At the same moment, Sash sprang at the Dargan who was attacking Athennar. The cloaked figure fell to the ground. Athennar leaped to his feet, retrieved his sword, and plunged it into the prostrate figure. Even as he did so, the Dark Master's image faded. Within moments it was gone entirely.

Cries of surprise came from all around the platform. All the assailants had faded into nothingness. Rrum fell to the ground, no longer held in the grip of the cave-warg. Vallel, who had rushed over to help Gatera,

230

saw the tadrat vanish before her eyes. Gatera's hands
were left wringing the air.

The friends slowly began to gather together.

'Look!' shouted Vallel, glancing back at the lake. A
wet hand was grasping at the side. A soaked,
bedraggled figure pulled itself on to the platform.

'Bar'drash!' chuckled Athennar. To his surprise,
Melinya ran past him and helped the Zorg to his feet.

'Uh—thanks. 'As it gone?' Melinya nodded.
'Where's the boss? Is 'e really dead?'

A groan came from a figure by the cave wall, and
Gur'brak staggered to his feet. 'Where am I?'

Melinya and Bar'drash went to help him. Gur'brak
was dazed and bruised, but otherwise all right.

'Thank you both,' the elf woman said. 'Your bravery
saved my life!'

'What do you mean?' asked Athennar, who had
joined her. She explained, then unexpectedly turned
to the Zorgs and kissed both of them on their leathery
brows.

'Yuk!' said Bar'drash. Gur'brak flushed, muttered
something, and looked away.

'I could almost kiss them myself for saving you!'
said Athennar. Seeing the Zorgs' worried looks, he
hastily added, 'But don't worry—I'm not going to.
However, you have my heartfelt thanks.'

They returned to the rest of the company. Vallel
was still recovering from the shock of her encounter
with the Scorbid, and Hesteron, bruised from his fight
with the Dargan image, was comforting her. Gatera
and Rrum appeared drained, and were lying on the
cavern floor recovering from their battles. Remembering Valor, the Land Crafter heaved himself to his feet,
and went over to the cave wall to check on the
Mountain Guard. Fortunately, the fighting had passed
him by. He was unharmed, but still unconscious.

Merric stood by the edge of the lake, peering across at the distant torchlight, wondering if Dargan was standing in the gloom on the opposite side, peering back at them. Even the minstrel's keen eyes could make out few details.

'Athennar!' Hesteron's call disturbed Merric's thoughts. He joined Athennar as he walked across to the Air Crafter, who was now kneeling by a dark shape.

'Sash!' exclaimed Athennar. 'Is she—?'

'She's still alive. Stunned, I think. How did it happen?'

Athennar shrugged, puzzled. 'I've no idea. When she leaped at Dargan, I was too distracted by what was happening to him. Perhaps she banged her head, or possibly it was just the impact when she hit him—he has strange powers.'

'I think she'll recover,' said Hesteron, as the others joined them. 'But we'll have to leave her here.'

'Gur'brak and Bar'drash should remain here as well,' added Melinya. 'They are both worn out. This is not their battle, yet they have already helped us.'

'Indeed,' replied Athennar. He looked kindly at the two Zorgs. 'Stay here with Sash. Don't worry—she will not harm you if she regains consciousness. We'll leave you some firelighters and a torch. I suggest you keep it unlit for the moment to avoid anyone paying you attention while we're gone. If we do not return, you will have to make your own way back to the open air.'

The Zorgs looked dubious, but agreed to wait on the platform.

'What happened to all those creatures that were attacking us?' asked Vallel. 'What made them disappear?'

'I believe we have Merric to thank for that,' answered Athennar. 'He called out Toroth's name.

Both Toroth and Elsinoth are names of power. They embody the truth and light of the Mighty One. As we saw with the Globe, truth is ultimately stronger than falsehood. I think that is why the power of the name of Toroth shattered the illusions, causing them to crumble and fade.'

'Would it have the same effect on Dargan?'

'No. Although he is a deceiver, he exists. The Dargan images we faced were not real, but he is. Words, however powerful, will not change that. I fear that we must find some other way to defeat him.'

'Why weren't Gur'brak and Bar'drash affected by the illusions?' Melinya asked suddenly.

'I don't know.'

'Probably because they're too stupid to be affected by Dargan's mind games,' growled Gatera. Bar'drash started to complain, but Gur'brak gave him a warning kick.

'Whatever the reason, they have still shown great courage,' replied Athennar. Looking thoughtful, he continued, 'We should leave Valor here with them.'

'No.' Gatera's voice was firm. 'He is part of our company. Along with Kess and Linnil, he was the first to start off on this quest. I will not cast him aside this close to the end of our task.'

'But he could get hurt!'

'I will protect him.'

Athennar sighed. 'Very well. My friends, I suspect that the walkway across the lake is all that now divides us from Dargan. I pray that Elsinoth will strengthen and guide us now.'

'Have you a plan?' asked Merric.

Athennar shook his head wearily. 'No. How can we plan when we don't even know what we're facing? We must trust Elsinoth to see us through. Courage and faith, my friends—those are our secret weapons. Courage and faith.'

'And if we still fail?'

'Then it is the beginning of the end for the Realm.'

It was a quiet but determined group that made their way across the walkway to the far side of the dark lake. Vallel kept glancing around nervously, fearful of the Scorbid's return. Few of the others took their eyes away from the growing glow ahead of them.

As they approached the platform on the opposite side, they could all see the outline of a great stone throne. Behind it, a waterfall spilled down and split into two channels that flowed past either side of the throne. The spray from the water glistened and sparkled in the low light from two torches.

From the heart of the throne came a deep, cold laugh, echoing around the chamber. As the friends stepped on to the platform, the flames from the torches on either side of the throne sprang higher, illuminating its occupant.

'Dargan!' Athennar said. 'Is that really you? Or do you still hide behind your illusions?'

A scowl crossed the Dark Master's face. 'There will be no more hiding, as you call it. I am real enough—and so is my power. Having tasted it once, I am surprised that you return.' Settling back into his throne, he gave a mocking grin. 'But I don't even need to lift a hand to defeat you. I am in a mood for amusement. You battled well enough against my illusions, but how will you fare against something real? Some of the Zorgs from my old stronghold, plus a few other stragglers, have recently arrived here.' Snapping his fingers, he watched with contempt as the company looked around for this new danger.

Athennar, however, ran towards the throne. 'How

about you, Dargan?' he shouted. 'Have you the courage to fight me hand to hand?' Reaching the front of the throne, he stopped. It was as if he had run into an invisible barrier. 'So, you *are* afraid!' he called.

Dargan laughed. In one hand he held the Sceptre: he stroked it with the other, almost teasingly. 'Afraid—of you? Hardly, my persistent friend. I just want to sit here in peace and watch the battle unfold. It should prove interesting!' He pointed to the walkway. A group of a dozen Zorgs was approaching. 'A small initial trial of strength,' he jeered. 'Though I assure you, this is just the start of my plans for you!'

Athennar ran back to rejoin his seven friends. Gatera laid Valor down, and stood guard over him. There was little time to prepare. The Zorgs attacked in a noisy mass. Gatera wished he still had his axe. However, these squat creatures caused him little fear. With a quick flick of the wrist, his staff thudded against the skull of one, then into the stomach of another. Looking around, he grabbed a third by the neck and swung it far into the lake.

The remaining Zorgs were also faring badly. They were a poor match for the fighting skills of Athennar and his friends. Soon the platform was littered with their bodies. Gatera hated to see such a waste of life, but knew that the company had to fight to survive. Sometimes even peace-loving people had to take up arms to resist evil.

'What now, Dargan?' called Athennar. 'What other evil plans are festering within your mind?'

The Dark Master glared at him, then smiled again. 'As I said, a small initial test. We will now see how you cope with twice the number of opponents. After they have weakened you sufficiently, perhaps I will add more details to this amusing game.'

'Game?' snorted Gatera. 'You call death a game?'

'He does,' said Merric quietly. 'Yet he knows that it is a game he must lose at some time.'

'But not now!' snarled Dargan. 'Let the battle continue!'

This time, two dozen Zorgs came across the walkway. The battle was much fiercer, although the Zorgs helped the company by getting in each other's way. Rrum fell, having been stabbed by a large, brutish opponent. Gatera brought his staff down hard on the creature's head, and it crumpled. In his anger, he flailed around with the staff, and several Zorgs were sent flying into the lake. Others dived in voluntarily to escape his wrath. The remainder went scuttling back down the walkway.

Gatera bent down to examine his friend. The Rrokki was still breathing. The Land Crafter laid him carefully next to Valor, and stood guard, grim-faced, ready for any further attacks. Hesteron was busy tending Melinya and Merric, who had both suffered slight wounds. When he saw that Rrum had been hurt, he ran over to join Gatera, accompanied by Vallel.

'One or two casualties?' mocked Dargan. 'There will be more soon—I have further Zorgs awaiting your pleasure.' He glanced meaningfully to his right and left. In the darkness, some distance away, Zorgs were gathering on either side beyond the bridges that spanned the water channels.

Dargan continued to taunt Athennar. Taking advantage of this distraction, Hesteron whispered to Vallel and Gatera. 'I can do little to help Rrum here. None of us will live anyway unless we can stop Dargan. It is time to unite our crafts. We must prevent those Zorgs from reaching us. Perhaps we will be able to put an end to Dargan as well, though we may die doing so.'

'What do you have in mind?' whispered Vallel.

'We must destroy this place—starting with the bridges. The Zorgs will then be unable to reach us. Then aim your efforts at the throne—let's bring this place down around Dargan's ears!'

'But—'

'We have no choice. Dargan is too strong. We must act now, while he is talking. I will distract him first with a little wind, while you two get to work.' After a few more whispered instructions, he left them and walked to the centre of the platform, a little way behind Athennar. The Animal Crafter was still arguing with Dargan.

Moving slowly at first, Hesteron coaxed the small breeze that wafted around the cavern. His two hands making circling motions, he called on all the skills and knowledge he had learned over the years. Remembering Merric's plea, he silently called to Toroth for help. The breeze grew into a wind, and he pushed it towards the throne.

'What are you doing?' shouted Dargan suddenly.

Hesteron ignored him. He couldn't afford to be distracted now. The wind grew stronger; tugged at the Dark Master's cloak.

Dargan gave a cold laugh. 'You think that a puny wind can affect me?' he asked. 'Your efforts are pathetic! I think it's time you faced my other Zorgs.' He clapped his hands.

While he had been speaking, a crack had appeared in the ground at either side of the platform. Gatera continued to stamp his feet in a strange, uneven rhythm. The cracks spread rapidly. At the same time Vallel had been stroking her hands through the water in one of the channels. The falls seemed to increase in ferocity, sweeping down the channels, smashing first into one bridge, then the other. Some of the water also swept towards the back of the throne, crashing against it even as the wind's strength increased.

Stones from the two bridges began to fall into the channels. The two groups of Zorgs waiting on the other side hesitated, unsure what to do. Cracks began to creep across the ground on which they were standing, and then both bridges collapsed into the water. The Zorgs fled for their lives.

Dargan's throne, buffeted by wind and water, began to shake, and the Dark Master leaped to his feet. 'Halt!' he cried. The company was instantly immobilised. The roar of the water died away, and the wind fell still.

Reaching down into the shadows by the side of the throne, Dargan pulled out a huddled figure. Holding a torch in front of it, the vacant, staring face of Kess was revealed.

Athennar struggled against his bonds. He had to help Kess—he had to defeat Dargan. It mustn't end this way!

'So far,' the Dark Master snarled, 'you have barely seen the fringes of my power. Now you will experience it in all its fullness. Prepare to die!'

30

A Desperate Battle

Smirking at the frozen forms in front of him, Dargan turned to Kess. 'Collect their weapons!' he barked.

Kess struggled down the steps and across the platform. His mind was reeling with a jumbled assortment of images. Where was he? What was he doing? All he knew was that he had to obey the nagging voice in his mind. He wandered across to the first of the figures. The face looked familiar, but who was it? His thoughts in a whirl, he strained to make sense of it all.

Athennar! The name came abruptly into his mind. It seemed to unlock his awareness. Slowly he remembered: Falron's betrayal; imprisonment by Dargan; the Dark Master beginning to experiment on his mind; then a strange interruption.

Now he remembered, he could see clearly. His friends were standing around the platform. Two figures lay on the ground, unmoving. *We've failed!* he thought. Anger surged through him. *I've got to break free!* He strove against his bonds, but Dargan's hold on his mind was too strong. Kess couldn't remember how he and Linnil had originally broken the Dark Master's power—he was still too angry and frustrated by the sight of his immobilised friends.

Disturbed, all he could do was watch as his hands relieved Athennar of his sword. Against his will, he walked on and collected all the other weapons. Then he returned and dropped them in a pile at the base of the throne. Reluctantly he climbed the steps until he again stood at Dargan's feet.

'Excellent! Now, I think you all deserve a small lesson in manners. There are six of you still on your feet. I shall teach each of you what I was about to show your young friend here: that you can soon learn to hate those you love. Now I must concentrate.' He fingered the Sceptre and fell silent for a few minutes.

To the watching company, it seemed almost as if he was struggling with himself. He seemed to grow old and tired. Then, after a short pause, another change came over him: he grew younger and stronger.

Opening his eyes, Dargan surveyed the waiting company. 'As I said, I am going to make you hate each other. Your hate will become so strong that you will want to kill each other. None of you will be allowed a weapon; you will have to survive on wits and strength. You will continue until only one of you is left. I will keep that person as my own personal slave. His or her first task will be to kill this young man, who has outlasted his usefulness. I have decided I no longer need to conduct any more experiments. As soon as I have dealt with you all, my conquest of the Realm will begin.'

Then he began, slowly and persistently, to convince them of their hatred for each other. His tones were insistent; his voice seemed to continue repeating the same message in their minds even after he had finished speaking.

Finally he was ready. 'Ah, yes. I think we will start with the two females on opposite sides; then the two elves against each other; and finally the giant against you, my friend.' His cold gaze pierced Athennar. 'You will at last learn to call me Master—if you survive that long.'

Clapping his hands, he called for some guards. Two Zorgs reluctantly trudged back along the walkway. 'Clear a space for the battle—throw some of those into the lake.' The Dark Master pointed to the bodies of the dead Zorgs, still littering the platform. The two guards commenced their grisly task.

Once a space had been cleared, Dargan turned his attention back to the six frozen figures. 'Now, let the sport commence. You have been given your opponents. You have only one aim—to kill them.' Chortling, he sat down on the top step of the dais to watch.

Vallel and Melinya began to circle each other. There had been insufficient time for Dargan to use all his power: although they were under his control, both of them could think clearly. That made the contest even more difficult—they were horribly aware of their own fight to destroy each other, but could do nothing about it. Melinya, despite her gentle nature, hated all that Dargan stood for. She was only too aware that it was his help that had enabled Zendos to keep her prisoner for such a long time. Now she was totally under the Dark Master's control.

The two women both leaped at once, and wrestled each other to the floor.

Meanwhile, Athennar was dodging a blow from Gatera. Remembering how Kess and Linnil had thwarted Dargan before, he had tried desperately to feel compassion or pity for the Dark Master, but had failed. Now it was too late; he had to concentrate on winning the fight. Dargan's instructions compelled him to try and kill his old friend. His mind screamed out against the command, but to no avail. Diving at Gatera's legs, he knocked the Land Crafter to the ground.

Merric, too, had remembered Kess and Linnil's success. He knew he could not bring himself to pity the Dark Master. Instead, he channelled all his concentration into one image—that of Linnil. He didn't know whether his ploy would succeed, but it was his only hope. As Dargan talked, instead of the Dark Master's chilling eyes, Merric envisaged Linnil's gentle green eyes gazing down at him with love.

Even so, he couldn't entirely block out Dargan's commands. He knew he would have to defeat Hesteron, or he would be killed by the Air Crafter. Before Hesteron could move, the minstrel raced nimbly across the floor, leaped high in the air, and felled him with a double kick to the head. The Air Crafter was knocked off his feet, crashed heavily to the ground, and lay still.

Hoping desperately that he hadn't killed Hesteron, Merric turned and forced himself to face Dargan.

'Kill him!' the Dark Master commanded.

'No—will not—refuse. You—evil.' The words forced themselves from Merric's mouth. Out of the corner of his eye, he saw a movement on the floor nearby.

'Then die yourself!' Dargan pointed one long, gnarled hand at Merric. A flash of white fire came from his fingertips.

The minstrel dodged, but was hit in the shoulder. He collapsed, a searing pain running through his body.

'You will not evade me a second time!' snarled

Dargan. As he aimed his hand, a figure struggled to its feet, defiantly blocking his view of the minstrel.

Kess, standing below Dargan, recognised the figure. He gasped inwardly. Valor! He hadn't recognised the Mountain Guard when he was lying unconscious on the ground.

'Another hero!' mocked Dargan. 'But not for long!' A blast from his finger flashed at Valor, knocking him off his feet. The Mountain Guard didn't rise again. Dargan gave a short, cold laugh.

No! screamed Kess inside his mind. *Valor! You can't die!* Great waves of grief swept through him. As the sorrow swamped all other emotions, he found he could move again. He quickly realised what he had to do. Keeping the picture of Valor clearly in his mind, he turned to the Dark Master. He was within the barrier Dargan had created around the throne, but would have to move rapidly while the Dark Master was still distracted.

Grabbing the edge of Dargan's cloak, he pulled with all his might. Taken by surprise, the Dark Master fell from his throne and crashed down the steps. Kess leaped after him, and grabbed the Sceptre.

'You dare to touch me?' screamed Dargan. Rising to his feet, he snatched the Sceptre back. Kess tried to hit him, but Dargan touched him with one hand. A searing pain shot through Kess' mind. The Quiet One dropped to his knees.

Dargan called the two Zorg guards. 'Keep hold of him,' he snarled, 'or you will be the next to die!'

Kess shook his head as he was dragged back to the steps below the throne. Looking up, he saw the green mask at the top. Its single jade eye stared back at him accusingly.

Still in a daze, he was startled when one of the two Zorgs hissed, 'Are you badly hurt?'

Kess turned to gaze at his captor. Gur'brak! The Zorg winked at him. Glancing at the other guard, he was greeted by the scarred face of Bar'drash.

'Who—what?' stuttered Kess.

Gur'brak leaned close to him, the drooling jaws not far from the Quiet One's ear. 'We're on your side,' he said. 'What can we do?'

Kess' mind reeled. Could he really trust the Zorgs? Even in his confusion, he realised he had little choice.

'Er, you must stop Dargan somehow,' he whispered, '—he's stepped outside his protective barrier. He's going to kill all the others!'

When Kess had attacked Dargan, the fighting had come to an abrupt halt. The figures on the platform were once again frozen in various poses; all except Merric, who was lying on the ground moaning and clutching his shoulder.

'Enough games!' Dargan shrieked at them. 'My patience has run out!' He raised his arms. Dazzling flashes of silver lightning shot across the cavern, lighting up the dark roof high above. Loud cracks and booms echoed around the chamber, and the air grew bitterly cold. Arcs of crimson fire streamed through the air above the Dark Master. He seemed to grow in size and strength. The whole cavern became a confusion of violent colour, noise and strange images. Dargan cackled triumphantly, and the sound hung in the air long after his mouth had closed.

'You want more illusions?' he shrieked. 'Then you shall have them!' Drunk—even mad—with power, he cackled again.

A monstrous figure materialised and shuffled forward along the walkway. The horrified onlookers cowered inside when they saw it, lit up by the bright flashes. The creature was both colossal and grotesque. A malformed shape, it edged its way forward on uneven limbs. Caught by the lightning, its eyes flashed with evil. The massive hands bristled with claws, and a huge drooling mouth hung from an outsized head.

At the same time, in the lake on either side of the walkway, the swollen bodies of two more scorbids burst up out of the water.

'Your doom awaits you!' screamed Dargan, a maniacal look in his eyes. Throwing his head back, he let out another ear-piercing laugh. It echoed round and round the cave. 'My power is total!' More lightning flashed from his hands, zig-zagging across the room as he waved his arms in exultation.

Lowering his hands, he commanded, 'Now, kneel before me, you worms! Kneel, before you die!' He turned to look at Vallel and Melinya. The next moment he crashed to the ground.

Gur'brak had run as fast as he could. Not daring to think about his actions, he had hurled himself at the Dark Master. Now the Zorg struggled to his feet and drew his sword. Before he could complete the action, he was grabbed by the neck.

'You snivelling traitor!' snarled Dargan. He threw the Zorg down, then pointed his hand at him. Before he could blast the Zorg, there was a flare of emerald fire from the throne. Splinters of the jade eye rained down upon the Dark Master. He screamed again, this time in agony. It was a terrible scream that seemed to tear the air with its pain. 'My eye! I can't see!' He fell to his knees, clutching his head.

Kess, having regained some of his strength, had followed Gur'brak. He had no weapon, but seeing the Dark Master collapse, grabbed the Sceptre. He felt its warmth; felt a sudden surge of power and strength running through his arms. As Dargan struggled to his feet, Kess swung the staff at his head with all his might. It thudded against the Dark Master's skull, sending him reeling backwards. Still holding his eye, Dargan staggered across the platform. He walked straight into a pair of huge, clawed arms. They tightened around him. Kess heard the cracking of ribs.

'No!' shrieked Dargan. 'You're an illusion! I'm your master! Release me!' The beast began to fade, but then grew stronger, then faded again. With a mighty heave, Dargan broke free and collapsed, blood trickling from a head wound. His arms thrashed around violently, scattering more of the silver lightning haphazardly through the cavern. The creature disappeared, and both Scorbids sank from sight.

The Dark Master gave a gasp of pain. Still stumbling blindly, he waved his hands in a circular motion. High above, the lightning and the crimson fire joined into a huge, multi-coloured fireball. 'Now you will see my revenge!' he screamed. He groped around for the Sceptre, not realising that it was the weapon that Kess had used to strike him. He couldn't find it.

'No matter!' he cried. 'Die, you pitiful creatures, die!' The fireball hovered, then began to arc through the air, gathering speed rapidly.

Dargan shrieked wildly, then gasped once more. 'Too much pain . . . too much power . . . can't control!'

With a great long sigh, the fireball swept through the air towards the staggering figure. Dargan lifted his arms to fend it off, but he was too late. 'No-o-o!' he screamed. For a brief second, his arched body was silhouetted as it was engulfed by silver and crimson flames. Then, with a final piercing wail, the Dark Master toppled into the lake.

For a second, there was stillness. It was followed by a tremendous explosion in the water. A plume of spray, tinged with scarlet, shot up towards the roof of the chamber, before falling back in a gesture of total submission. When the lake had stilled, all that remained was a dark stain on the water.

The cavern fell silent. Then, as they found that they were no longer under Dargan's spell, the friends all began to speak at once.

'I can move!'

'What happened?'

'Do you think Dargan is dead?'

'Are we safe?'

As realisation dawned, they began to hug each other. Vallel ran across to see Hesteron, and Gatera knelt by Rrum, lifting him gently from the floor. Melinya and Athennar helped Merric to his feet. Kess walked slowly across to Valor, afraid of what he would find.

Vallel joined him, supporting Hesteron, who was rubbing the back of his head. As soon as he saw Valor, however, the Air Crafter dropped to one knee to examine him. Valor had turned slightly as Dargan's firebolt had hit him, deflecting some of the force. However, the front of his tunic was scorched and there was a deep wound across his chest. Hesteron quickly retrieved his backpack, pulled out a small bottle and poured some thick, white fluid on to the wound. He asked Vallel to bandage the Mountain Guard while he went to check Rrum.

The Rrokki, like Valor, was still unconscious. Hesteron rubbed some herbs into the sword wound, then moved on to Merric. He gently dabbed the minstrel's shoulder wound with some of the white ointment. 'This will ease the pain,' he said.

'How are the other two?' asked Athennar.

'Rrum should recover after some rest. Valor is more seriously wounded. I have done what little I can. When we get back to the fortress, I will be able to treat his wound properly. I only hope he can

survive the journey. Both he and Rrum will have to
be carried.'

'Then it's all over?' asked Vallel. 'Dargan really is
dead?'

'He is,' replied Athennar as he helped Merric over
to join the others. 'Not even Dargan could survive the
power of that fire ball. It is ironic—he was killed by his
own illusions and power.' He turned to look at Kess.
'There is one thing I don't quite understand though.
Why was Dargan clutching his eye before you hit him
with the Sceptre, Kess?'

'I remembered his pain when Gatera smashed the
eye in his Throne Room, so I persuaded my accomplice to smash the remaining eye while I helped
Gur'brak.'

'Your accomplice?' Athennar asked, puzzled.

'Yes, he climbed to the top of the throne and
destroyed the eye with Gatera's staff.'

'But who—?'

Kess pointed. Athennar looked towards the throne,
and then chuckled. 'Well, life is full of surprises!' he
said.

Shuffling towards them, dragging Gatera's great
staff behind him, came the stocky figure of Bar'drash.

31

Return to the Fortress

The company collected their weapons from the base of the throne and prepared to leave. Low rumblings echoed around the great cavern.

'It sounds as if the place is about to collapse!' said Gatera. He winked at Hesteron and Vallel. 'Perhaps our work is continuing of its own accord!'

'With a little help from Dargan's lightning as well!' said Athennar, as they hurried along the walkway.

'What has happened to Dargan's Zorgs?' asked Kess.

'I think all those that tried to attack us have fled—either deeper into the caves or out into the open. Whichever way, there is little we can do. Who knows, were it not for Dargan, many might have trodden a different path in life—some might even have followed the heroic example of our two friends here!'

Gur'brak spluttered and looked very uncomfortable. A wide, crooked grin spread over Bar'drash's face. He had never been called a hero before.

The friends continued along the walkway. They were half way across when they saw a sinister, dark

shape creeping towards them. Kess' heart missed a
beat. What new enemy was this?

'Sash!' called Athennar. Kess smiled in relief as the
black leopard sidled up to the Animal Crafter and
nuzzled him. Then there was a loud crash from behind
them as the great throne split in two and smashed on
the ground. The waterfall splashed over it, as if
washing it clean. Lumps of rock started to fall from
the ceiling, and the ground began to quiver.

'Let's get out of here!' shouted Athennar.

The company raced down the walkway and across
the platform. Running down the tunnel, they reached
the chamber with the statue. The stone figure was
cracked, and the head had broken off and lay in pieces
on the floor. Stepping over it, they looked for the exit
tunnel. The one with Gatera's mark on seemed to have
changed position.

Athennar gave a wry smile. 'These passages have
all been jumbled up—no doubt by Dargan once we
passed through here. If it wasn't for your limestone,
Gatera, we would all have been lost!'

Behind them, they heard a great crashing rumble
from the main cavern. They continued their journey
with haste. Passing along the maze of tunnels, it was
with some relief that they reached the trapdoor and
emerged once more into the open air. The Zorg guard
attacked by Gur'brak had disappeared, and both the
huge doors to the tower were wide open.

'It seems that you were correct, Athennar: the Zorgs
have fled!' said Merric.

Athennar turned to Gur'brak and Bar'drash.
'And what of you two? Do you want to leave us
now?'

Both looked startled at the thought. 'Er—um, I
suppose so,' muttered Gur'brak.

'Aw, boss, can't we stay with 'em? At least we'd get

some good food—so long as they don't lock us up again!'

'That's a new one for you! You were the one who wanted to escape!'

'Yeah, but—'

Athennar interrupted the exchange. 'You needn't worry—you would be guests, not prisoners! If you would like to accompany us back to the fortress, you would be most welcome. You can stay with us for as long as you like—and I'm sure we could find you some work.'

The two Zorgs looked at each other, then both grinned. 'It's a deal!' said Gur'brak, offering his hand to Athennar. The Animal Crafter shook it warmly.

While Athennar had been talking, Gatera and Hesteron had found two long branches from a dead tree, and began to make a crude stretcher for Valor, using a leather blanket. When they had finished, Athennar said, 'Right! Let's go! We still have to find our way back through the Valley of Darkness.'

All the company shuddered at the thought.

'Do not fear,' Athennar continued. 'We may find that things have changed since Dargan's demise. If not, Gatera can lead us along beside the mountain stream until we have passed through the black fog. Ah, that reminds me!' Leaving them, he ran back to the castle courtyard, and returned bearing Falron's hunting horn. 'This should ensure our safety if we meet any more of those white creatures.'

Athennar's words proved true. With Dargan's death, the darkness had dispersed, and they had a clear walk through the mountain pass to the old wooden city. Their hearing was no longer affected, but Athennar blew the horn for good measure to ensure that any hostile creatures kept their distance. They saw none, and before nightfall had climbed out of the valley to the spot where the horses faithfully awaited them.

After camping for the night, the company set off for the fortress. One end of Valor's stretcher was tied behind Sundust, and the friends took it in turn to run or walk behind, supporting the other end. Gatera carried the still form of Rrum.

It took them eight long days to complete the journey. When they reached the fortress, Tolledon, Meltizoc and Whisper rushed out to meet them. The Guardian had Valor and Rrum taken immediately to a healing room. With the help of two other healers, Hesteron carefully tended their wounds despite his own tiredness.

When he had finished, Vallel put her arm around his waist. 'Will they be all right?' she asked.

Hesteron gave a weary smile. 'They should heal in time,' he said. 'They both have the strength of will needed to aid their recovery.'

Meanwhile, the rest of the friends made their way to the Dining Hall.

'How's Linnil? Has she recovered?' asked Kess impatiently.

Tolledon's face turned sombre. 'She still lives, but she grows no stronger.' Seeing Kess' face drop, he added, 'But give it time. It is only a few days since Dargan was defeated.'

'But surely she should be growing better by now!' said Kess. 'It's not fair! What is Elsinoth doing? Where is he—why doesn't he help her?'

Tolledon shook his head and looked questioningly at Meltizoc. The wise man replied, 'Do not blame Elsinoth, my young friend. Remember that it was Dargan who caused her illness, not the Mighty One! Have patience.'

Kess glared at him, but said nothing. *What now?* he

thought. *Why do I always have to wait?* Excusing himself, he left. He had to see his sister for himself.

After he had gone, Athennar gave a brief account of their adventures and then fell silent. Tolledon embraced each of the friends in turn, and shook the Zorgs' hands. 'Thank you all for your unselfish service to the Realm,' he said, his arm around Athennar's shoulder and his eyes gleaming with pride. 'You have won a great victory!'

Meltizoc, still puffing from the walk, added, 'Dargan never realised that love was so powerful. He thought hate was stronger. He was wrong. Hate is powerful, and drives someone on, but it only has one expression. Love has many outlets. Elsinoth's love is the strongest of all. Dargan underestimated it—and perished as a result.'

Tolledon nodded in agreement. 'I wish there was some way I could reward you all,' he said.

'Knowing that we have obeyed Toroth's will is sufficient reward,' Merric answered.

'The only other reward I need is a good night's sleep!' added Melinya.

'I'll settle for a meal first!' rumbled Gatera. Weary as they were, the company laughed.

When Kess reached Linnil's room, he knocked lightly on the door. A faint 'Come in' sounded from inside. He entered, fearful of what he might find. His fears were soon realised. It was even worse than Tolledon had said. Linnil lay in her bed, looking weak and pale. Kess could tell that she had faded even more since he had last seen her—it was as if he was looking at a living ghost.

'Hello, sis,' he said.

'Kess,' she whispered, giving a faint smile. 'It's so good to see you. Have you—were you successful?'

He nodded. Linnil reached out for his hand. 'I'm

so proud of you. Oh, Kess, what's happening to me? I feel so tired, so tired.' She closed her eyes and sank into sleep.

Kess sprawled on the bed beside her, holding her hand. It felt very cold. Tears trickled down his cheeks, but he too was tired, and soon fell asleep.

That was how Tolledon and Meltizoc found him; still clutching his sister's hand. The Guardian lifted him gently from the bed and carried him along the corridor to the Quiet One's own room. 'He is a brave one,' he whispered to Meltizoc.

'Yes. And his trials are not yet over.' The two men left the room, quietly closing the door.

A week later, the company gathered together once more in the Dining Hall. Much had happened in the intervening time. Valor and Rrum were both well on the road to recovery, and had joined the company for the meeting. Whisper and Kess had together alternated with Merric in keeping vigil over Linnil. The Valley girl had continued to weaken, however, like a candle slowly burning out.

Mardilla and the two children arrived from Kravos, seeking word of Gatera. The four spent many hours talking together and walking the plains around the fortress, accompanied on the shorter outings by Rrum. The little Rrokki had lost some of his former bounce and soon grew tired, but each time he did, Gatera or Mardilla would carry him for a while until he felt strong enough to walk again.

Gur'brak and Bar'drash initially spent their time strutting around the fortress, revelling in their new roles as heroes, and in the sideways glances from the other occupants of the fortress. However, for the seasoned elves and men from Hallion the novelty soon paled, and the Zorgs found themselves with little to do.

Bar'drash resorted to spending much time asleep. Gur'brak increasingly searched out Meltizoc, asking him many questions about Elsinoth, which the wise man answered with great patience. Eventually, the Zorg went to see Tolledon, and asked if he and Bar'drash could enter the Guardian's service. Tolledon willingly agreed, and they soon became the first Zorgs ever to join the forces of the North, and to swear loyalty to the Guardian of the Realm. Bar'drash did so with some grumbling; but was soon persuaded by a good-natured kick from Gur'brak.

Meanwhile, teams of Hallion men had been sent throughout the Southlands to hunt out any pockets of evil that remained. Other scouts were dispatched throughout the Northlands to tell the different communities of all that had occurred. Some of the returning scouts had relayed news to Tolledon which he now recounted to the gathered friends.

'It appears that the fading in Hallion continues,' he said. 'I'm sorry—I don't understand it.'

'So we failed after all! Dargan has won even though he is dead!' Kess scowled. 'It was all a waste of time—we will soon be living in a desert!'

'No, my young friend,' replied Meltizoc. 'Even if the Realm does fade, I am sure we can somehow work together to restore it. At least we are still alive, and have not fallen under Dargan's evil spell. That in itself is a victory. In the meantime, we will have to think of restoring areas once they have faded.'

'I hope it will not come to that,' Tolledon said. 'There must be an answer; something we have overlooked or missed. There must be!'

32

Looking for Answers

Kess was very restless that night. He tossed and turned, trying to think of any solution to the fading Realm—and particularly to Linnil's increasing weakness. His frustration turned to anger; anger at Elsinoth, at Dargan, at himself. Surely it couldn't end this way? Eventually, tired and bitter, he fell asleep.

Even in his dreams, however, the questions taunted him. Why had they defeated Dargan, only for evil to win in the end? Dark shapes flitted past the edges of his dream, mocking him. 'Where were you when we needed you, Elsinoth?' he cried. 'Why didn't you help us? Where were you? Why did we have to do it all by ourselves?'

His voice echoed round and round, just like Dargan's own maniacal laughter in the large underground cave. Then his dream began to change. The dark shapes retreated and patterns of bright, swirling colour flowed past him. The colours merged and became white. The light grew stronger and surrounded him, bathing him in its brilliance. Inside his spirit he felt a warmth, and he wanted to shout for joy. Music floated through the air: calm, serene music of a kind he had never before experienced. As the light continued to grow, he had to shield his eyes.

Then the music faded, and there was silence. Out of the silence grew a gentle whisper, a call that seemed to come from all directions at once: 'Where was I? Do you not yet know, Kess? I was in the wind, the water, and the earth. I grasped your hand and led you. I spoke to you through Meltizoc. I guided you through Athennar and Hesteron. I stood by you in Merric and Valor. I helped you through Vallel. I saved you through Rrum and Whisper. I shielded you by Gatera. I sent you hope through Melinya. I even aided you through Gur'brak and Bar'drash. And through it all, I was in you and encouraging the others through your love and peace. In your spirit you will still find me.'

'So you don't exist outside of us?' Kess heard himself say.

'I exist. I am Elsinoth, creator of the Realm, and of you. I am Toroth, by whose hands life was formed from light. I am no figment of the imagination, dreamed up to pamper you into a false sense of security. I am no illusion created by another. I am Elsinoth.'

The voice paused, then continued. 'But I choose to work through those who are willing to let truth, love and justice flow in their lives, and yet who still recognise their own faults. When they call on me, I am already there, before and after.'

'But we need your help now! My sister is dying!'

'Do you still not trust me, even after all this time, Kess?'

The question hung in the air, and echoed around Kess' thoughts. Ashamed, he bowed his head. 'I'm sorry,' he whispered. 'Please forgive me.'

The voice seemed to soften. 'I understand your pain. But those who follow me must suffer the same trials and illnesses as others in the world. Oh, how I grieved when Vosphel died; when Marason and Hinno died. How I grieve when anyone suffers. That is why you must continue to fight evil and suffering: and I will help you. Trust and you will find the way. Trust in me . . . .'

The voice faded, and Kess fell into a deep, dreamless sleep.

The next morning, Kess awoke feeling fully rested. Dressing quickly, he slipped out of his room and went in search of Meltizoc. He found the old wise man sitting on a bench in the courtyard, gazing up at the clear blue sky.

Meltizoc smiled when he saw Kess. 'Ah! Hello, young friend. How are you today?' The wise man patted the bench, and Kess sat down beside him.

'Meltizoc, I had a strange dream last night.'

The wise man raised one eyebrow in a query. 'Indeed?'

'Yes. Well, at least it seemed like a dream, but now I'm not so sure—it was all so real.' He related his night-time experience.

Meltizoc listened intently, then sat back and smiled. 'Elsinoth has revealed a great truth to you, my friend: he chooses to work through ordinary mortals, frail though they be.'

'But what does it mean? Why, despite his help, has evil triumphed?'

'Has it? Evil only triumphs when you allow it to do so. The followers of Elsinoth are not automatically guarded from all danger, as you have learned yourself. And yet, you must know that light is stronger than the darkness. Even though at times the darkness may seem physically stronger, light represents truth, and cannot easily be extinguished. Imagine a tiny candle in the middle of a huge, dark room: it is noticed by anyone in the room. They cannot avoid its light without closing their eyes. Would a tiny patch of darkness in a room filled with light have the same effect? I think not. Even a small light overcomes darkness; but darkness never truly conquers where there is still light—even the light in our hearts.'

Kess remembered the petals of light that had guided him through the black fog, and smiled. He thought he could understand what Meltizoc meant. 'But why must Linnil suffer?' he asked. 'Will she die?'

Meltizoc shook his head. 'I don't know. The followers of Elsinoth are not immune from danger or illness.'

'But surely he could help—doesn't he hear our prayers?'

'He does. It is just that we don't always receive the answers we expect. Elsinoth works in his own time: he allows us to learn and grow. Look at all the times you have overcome danger despite the opposition: in Dargan's stronghold; in the mists; the Jewelled Forest; the Black Caves; the Tower of Braggad. Need I continue? Was that not with Elsinoth's help? Or perhaps you thought it was just your own strength, even though it came as a direct answer to your pleas for help? Perhaps you failed to see Elsinoth at work, because the answer wasn't always easy, or didn't come at once!'

He looked Kess straight in the eyes. 'Don't let the light of your faith in Elsinoth die,' he continued. 'Nourish it and feed it; even though there are many matters you still do not understand.'

Kess looked thoughtful, then nodded. 'Thank you,' he replied. 'You are right. It's just that I've been

looking for someone to lash out at; someone to
blame—so I blamed Elsinoth. How easily I forgot how
he answered my cry and saved me in the Vale of
Miscreance.'

'And many times since!' chuckled Meltizoc. 'You
are called a Quiet One, my friend. Hold on, then, to
the quiet place within your heart—the place where
you know Elsinoth lives.'

Later that day, the company gathered together again
in Athennar's room. Kess explained his dream, and
how Elsinoth had described how he had worked with
them and through them, helping them at every stage
of their quest.

Gatera looked very thoughtful. 'Of course!' he
boomed. 'The Wanderer! He came at exactly the right
time to help Rrum and me to find Melinya! Could it
have been Elsinoth himself?'

'Who knows?' replied Tolledon. 'If not, perhaps it
was one of his followers. Kess' words give us much to
think about. However, for the moment let us return
to discussing ways in which we can prevent or slow
the decay in the Realm.'

Valor, his chest still heavily bandaged, suggested,
'Perhaps we could start by planting some trees in
Hallion to replace those that are lost.' He gave a slight
cough: a legacy of his heroic act when he had protected
Merric from Dargan's firebolt.

'You may be right,' mused Tolledon. 'Yet we don't
know if they would grow—they might fade too. Still,
I suppose we will only find out by planting a few.'

'There is another answer! There has to be!' Kess
stood, red-faced, and paced up and down the room.
'I don't believe that Elsinoth would readily let the
Realm—his creation—go to waste.' He paused by
Tolledon's seat and picked up the Sceptre, propped

by the Guardian's right hand. It was discoloured and marred—no longer a thing of beauty.

'Even Taz-i-tor, the Golden Sceptre, has become cracked and gnarled since Dargan used it. Everything he touched has been tainted. But I still believe that Elsinoth's power is stronger. It has to be!'

As he spoke, he felt a warmth grow inside the Sceptre. Surprised, he looked at it. Then a wild, strange idea suddenly leaped into his mind. 'Athennar! Do you still have the Globe of Truth?'

'Of course! It's here.' He moved over to a cupboard in one corner of the room, and fetched out the Globe. 'Why do you want it?'

'Never mind!' Kess took it from him. 'Follow me!' he said.

Without waiting for a reaction, he left the room. His friends hastily rose from their seats and followed him, curious to know what he had in mind.

Kess walked calmly along the passageway until he reached Linnil's room. Then, when all the company had assembled, he moved over beside her.

'How are you, sis?' he asked.

'Tired,' she whispered.

Gently, very gently, Kess lifted the Globe in his right hand. Holding the Sceptre in his left, he lowered the sphere slowly into the carved, cupped hand at the top of the staff. It fitted perfectly. Within seconds, both objects began to glow from within. The Sceptre seemed to stretch slightly. Its golden light pulsated for a moment, then steadied.

Examining it closely, Kess gave a smile of joy. 'It is restored! The Golden Sceptre is new and smooth once more!'

'And the Globe! Look how it changes!' gasped Merric. The friends crowded around. The green colours within the Globe were shifting and re-forming on its surface.

'What's happened to it?' asked Hesteron.

'From the maps I have studied, I would say that it has become a circular map of the world in which we live,' Meltizoc replied. 'Look! Here is the Realm as we know it!'

'But there is so much more!' breathed Tolledon.

'That must be my homeland!' exclaimed Whisper, pointing to part of the Globe. Tolledon and Meltizoc looked at her in surprise, but Kess smiled. 'I'll explain later,' he said.

A long groan came from the bed. Kess turned to look at his sister. Her eyes were closed. 'Linnil!' he called.

One eye slowly opened. 'Is there any chance of some food?' asked a clear, soft voice.

'Sis! You sound different!'

Linnil groaned again. 'It's strange—I feel released, as if I have just awoken from a long nightmare. I ache, but I feel a new strength seeping through my body. Kess, I think I'm starting to get better!'

Both Kess and Merric grasped her hands, and soon all three were weeping with joy.

Some time later, Kess again sought out Meltizoc. 'I know what happened,' he said, 'but I don't really understand how or why.'

The wise man smiled. 'There is a legend about the Sceptre that even I had almost forgotten. It is said that at a time of great need, someone with a gentle spirit would be given desperately needed wisdom. A legend can often conceal a basic truth.' His eyes twinkled. 'Let me explain more fully. I think the answer is within us; within you. You have been an example to us all in the way that you have held on to your faith despite great doubts and fears.

'When you joined the Sceptre and Globe together, you began the work of restoration—both in Linnil and the Realm. Yet it was not the power of either object that has begun the process: it is Elsinoth's power. He merely chose them as tools to teach us another important lesson. The Sceptre represents free will—the right to choose between good and evil. Similarly, the Globe symbolises truth. Elsinoth is showing us that only where, by our own free will, we choose to follow truth can we hope to fully conquer evil.

'Dargan's power was based on illusion. Perhaps he reached the point where to him the illusion became a reality. His power was so strong that he was able to force others to believe this too. I think that those things he caused to fade and vanish only appeared to do so; that too was an illusion. Unfortunately, when he experimented on people, his power was so strong that they—and any who saw them—believed totally in the illusion. In the end, they would fade away and die. So it would have been with Linnil. However, the one thing that could break the illusion was the power of truth. Our eyes were closed to this until Elsinoth, through your faith and actions, opened them again. Dargan believed he was using the power of the Sceptre; even we believed that. However, that too was an illusion. I should have known better. I should have realised that Elsinoth's power could never be used for evil purposes!'

'But what of the Globe and Sceptre? Why did they fit together so well?' asked Kess.

'I assume that was Elsinoth's original intention—to show that our world should be founded on freedom and truth. But at some point he must have decided to separate them—perhaps so we could eventually learn this for ourselves. He has now shown us that the two are inseparable. If our freedom does not lead us to follow truth, it may lead us to destruction.'

'Will Hallion also be restored, then?' asked Kess.

'Yes, I believe so. Indeed, I expect that a messenger will arrive within the next few days to tell us of the changes that have taken place; that it is once more a place of life and vigour.' Meltizoc smiled at Kess. 'Always hold on to the truth, my friend. We so easily build our own illusions about life. We form opinions about the Realm and its people, and sometimes they, too, can be an illusion.'

'Yes—like Falron! He fooled us into thinking he was good,' Kess replied.

'We all make mistakes. Acknowledging them is the beginning of wisdom. Now, enough of questions!'

'One last one, please! Will Linnil recover fully?'

'Very rapidly, I suspect. You have already seen the change in her. Now she needs to build up her strength. But with you to encourage her—and a certain young minstrel, of course—I would expect her to be in good form very soon. Now come, let us search out the others before you completely exhaust me!'

33

Together Again

Three months later, the friends all came together in the Great Cabin at Hallion. They were soon discussing all that had happened since they last met. Rrum, Valor and Linnil had all fully recovered. Indeed, Kess and Linnil had paid a visit to their Valley home, where there had been great celebrations. Elder Darron had heard the news of their deeds from messengers sent throughout the land by Tolledon. The twins were greeted as heroes; even Narfic and Rodik stood a little in awe of them.

Kess and Linnil had only stayed there a week. 'It's not the same any more, sis,' Kess said quietly on the second day. 'I don't feel as if I belong here. It's somehow—'

'Too quiet?' Linnil prompted.

They both laughed. 'Yes,' said Kess reluctantly. 'Oh, it's good to come back, but I couldn't stay. I think I'll take Tolledon's offer of a hut in Hallion!'

Linnil gave him a big hug. 'You too? Merric and I have already decided to make our home there. He doesn't feel it is right to intrude on his brother's rule as king of the River Elves. He will represent their interests at Hallion, and will call on them occasionally to keep them in touch with events in the rest of the Realm. Kess, I was so afraid you'd come back here to the Valley. I didn't want to lose contact with you!'

'Just because you're going to be joined with Merric, you needn't think you'll get rid of me that easily!' he teased.

Now they were back in Hallion with their friends, chatting excitedly and finding out what the others had been doing.

'So, it's going to be a triple ceremony, is it?' boomed Gatera. 'What did your Water Crafter community think of you joining with an Air Crafter, Vallel?'

Vallel giggled. 'Oh, they were horrified at first. But when I explained all that had happened—especially during our time in the mist, where our crafts overlapped, they began to listen. Since then, there have been several exchanges between the two communities. In fact, you might see one of the results at the ceremony. When I told them about the Ice Kingdom, with land made out of water, they decided that they should soon also contact your Land Crafters.'

'Ah, they show great sense!' grinned Gatera.

'And not before time!' interrupted Meltizoc. 'I am indeed pleased that each of the three main Crafter Groups is beginning to remember that it is just a part of the whole picture.'

'What do you mean?' asked Valor.

'Well, for instance, one could say that land is a life giver; water, a life sustainer; and air, a life renewer. They all represent a different aspect of our life together.'

'And what of Animal Crafters, my friend?' asked Athennar.

'Ah, well—er . . .'

The friends laughed. For once, the wise man seemed to have no answer.

'Are you nervous about tomorrow's ceremony, Athennar?' Valor asked.

'Nervous? A future Guardian of the Realm like me? Of course not—I'm terrified!'

Melinya gave him a playful poke in the ribs. 'I will soon put some courage back into him!' she said with a smile. 'He has grown soft since you all left, with no battles to fight!'

'Aye, we are unlikely to see another adventure like that again,' rumbled Gatera.

'Do not fear—there will still be challenges ahead,' Tolledon warned him. 'But for now, we can look to a brighter future. Come, I will toast you all with pulberry wine. To the brave company of the Sceptre!'

The friends all raised their goblets. 'To the company!'

As they drank, an embarrassed cough came from the doorway. A small yellow figure stood there.

'Fashag!' exclaimed Hesteron. 'Come in!'

'Oh, er, good meeting! As you know, I, er, don't really like company,' the gnome muttered. 'Can't stand throngs of people. But, well, I thought—'

'You've come for the ceremony! Welcome, old friend, it's good to see you. Come and join us!'

Fashag sidled nervously over to the table and sat down.

Tolledon poured him a goblet of wine, and patted him on the shoulder. 'I owe you my lifelong thanks, Fashag. I'm delighted you could come. It will give us all a chance to thank you properly for the brave part you played in the search for the Sceptre.'

'Oh, yes,' the Fire Crafter mumbled. 'What happened to the Globe of Truth?'

'Yes, where is it now kept?' asked Merric, his arm around Linnil's waist.

'Come, we will show you,' Meltizoc replied.

The company trooped out of the Great Cabin and followed Meltizoc and Tolledon. Just beyond the collection of huts was a small hill, ringed by a band of trees. The wise man wheezed and puffed his way to the top. There, on the crown of the hill, was a strong young tree. It had a beautiful, smooth, golden bark. At the top, the trunk split into five branches.

'Those were originally the fingers and thumb of the cupped hand at the top of the Sceptre,' Meltizoc explained. 'After we planted the staff here, it began to change, and gradually became the tree you now see before you.'

The friends moved forward to get a closer look at the tree. At the end of each of the five delicate branches was a single, pale green sphere.

'The Globe!' whispered Linnil.

'Yes. It, too, changed: there are now five globes to symbolise the spreading of truth throughout the Realm,' said Tolledon. 'This golden tree will stand as a reminder to all of your bravery, and of the freedom and truth which come from following Elsinoth.'

The next day dawned bright and clear; a perfect autumn day. White clouds chased each other across a sky of blue. Kess breathed in the freshness as he walked through the trees with Whisper towards the glade where the triple joining ceremony was to be held. It was the same clearing in which Dargan had started the blight of Hallion several months previously. After the uniting of the Globe and the Sceptre, the glade had returned to its former glory; indeed, some said that it was even more beautiful than before.

Kess and Whisper had grown closer since his return from the Southlands. The Quiet One still wasn't sure of her feelings, however, and wondered if they would ever find the same happiness as the couples who were to be joined together shortly. He hoped so. Whisper had changed since she had seen the results of their quest, and had pledged to seek and to follow the ways of Elsinoth.

The couple arrived at the glade and took their places in the front row of honoured guests. On one side of them stood Gatera, one arm around Mardilla, and the other huge hand resting on Rrum's shoulder. Fashag fidgeted nervously alongside Rrum. On the other side of Kess was Valor, and next to him, Meltizoc. Between the wise man and Callenor, Gur'brak and Bar'drash shuffled and muttered, self-conscious but proud of the new Hallion livery they wore. It had been specially tailored to fit their squat bodies.

'I don't 'alf feel 'ot, boss,' Bar'drash whispered, fingering his collar.

'Shh! And stop fidgeting!' hissed Gur'brak.

Behind the front row were lines and lines of people—Water Crafters; Air Crafters; Land Crafters; Mountain Guards; Hallion men and women; elves; Narfic, Darron, Rodik and Lorissa from the Valley; and representatives from most of the main towns in the Northlands. In the second row stood two special guests: Tessari, who had made the journey from the Ice Kingdom wrapped in strange clothes. Vallel and Hesteron had been particularly delighted that the Ice Kings had agreed to attend the ceremony.

All around the clearing, the tall, proud trees shimmered with the golds, reds and russet browns of autumn. To the delight of the onlookers, dozens of fountains suddenly sprang into life around the edge of the clearing—a display brought about by the joint

work of the Air and Water Crafters. The sparkling
arcs of water rose gracefully into the air, then fell in
cascades of crystal, the outermost droplets from each
fountain mingling with those from the next.

And then, to the gentle call of a dozen flutes, the
ceremony began. At the other side of the clearing,
facing the assembled crowd, was a short avenue of
silver-barked trees. Their branches intertwined above
the wide path, forming a line of arches. The grassy
path beneath the arches was covered with light golden
leaves.

On to the far end of this path stepped Vallel and
Hesteron. Vallel wore silver and blue, her dress
rippling like water as she moved forward. Hesteron
walked beside her, clothed in the forest green of the
Air Crafters. A gentle breeze teased his hair and also
fingered its way through Vallel's long flowing golden
tresses as they walked towards the waiting crowd. The
couple reached the clearing, and a light smile played
on Vallel's face. They took up their position on the
left of the glade, facing the crowd.

After a brief pause, Linnil and Merric came through
the arches, hand in hand. They both wore the colours
of autumn. Merric strode forward in shades of brown,
his lute slung over one shoulder. Linnil was clothed
in pale yellow, her auburn hair cascading around her
shoulders. Round her neck she wore the heart's-tear
pendant Kess had carved for her while she was still
ill. Kess thought he had never seen her look so
beautiful. She smiled at him as she and Merric moved
to the right of the clearing.

Athennar and Melinya were the next to walk lightly
down the path. Athennar looked resplendent in
scarlet, with the Guardian's emblem embroidered over
his left breast. Melinya seemed to float along; a vision
of loveliness in pure white, a ring of snow-flowers

entwined in her golden hair. Perched on her shoulder was a white hawk: Kal. At Athennar's side padded the black form of Sash. Melinya and Athennar took their position in the centre of the glade.

Finally, Tolledon came striding down through the trees. As Guardian of the Realm, he would officiate as priest at the ceremony.

The trilling of the flutes died away. A large white cloud moved slowly across the sun, blocking its light, but the glade still seemed to be bursting with colour and life.

'Let the celebrations begin!' called Tolledon. Music broke out around the glade, and soon everyone was singing and clapping.

After a while, Tolledon held up his hands, and everyone fell quiet. The Guardian spoke briefly about the part each of the couples had played in the quest to find the Sceptre. He told, too, of their strengthened belief in Elsinoth.

'Now, before the vows are made and the joining is complete, each of the participants is given the opportunity to say a few words to his or her partner. Vallel and Hesteron will begin.' He stepped back.

Vallel turned to face Hesteron. Her clear voice rang out through the glade. 'To you, my love, I offer myself: all that I am; all that I would be. Like the water I love, I offer you strength in your times of weakness; refreshment in your tiredness; and ever-flowing streams of love.'

Hesteron smiled, and took her hand. 'I, too, offer all that I am and would be. Like the air that is my constant companion, I offer to support you with the strength of a mighty wind; to care for you with the gentleness of a breeze; and to love you with the constant certainty of the air that we breathe.'

The two Crafters knelt down, side by side, facing

Tolledon. The Guardian then motioned to Athennar and Melinya.

Athennar was first to speak. 'Melinya, my heart has always been yours. As son of the Guardian, I ask you to share all my responsibilities, all my trials, all my joys, all my love—for without you, I am lost.'

Melinya's crystal tones seemed to float in the air as she replied. 'This and more I will do, for I truly love you.'

They, too, then knelt before the Guardian, who turned to Merric and Linnil.

The minstrel unslung his lute and began to play a soft and gentle tune. It was the same tune he had played so many months before, when alone at the fortress he had awaited news of Linnil. This time, however, it held an air of hope rather than despair, and the words had been changed:

> Features fair, lithesome grace,
> Float on by as on a breeze;
> I give to you my music, love,
> As floats the air among the trees.

> Green of eyes, smile serene,
> The beauty I have come to know;
> I give to you the songs of life,
> Of waterfalls, of streams that flow.

> The songs that I will sing to you
> Are songs of peace and songs of joy;
> Of faith in Toroth, and of hope;
> Of love that no one can destroy.

> True lady with your soul of peace,
> With russet hair and emerald gaze;
> I give to you my life, my love,
> From this time to the end of days.

Linnil lowered her eyes, then raised her head once more and replied, 'There are too few words to express my love for you. It is itself a melody; an ever-present song that will grow still more beautiful as the years pass.' Turning with Merric, they also knelt before the Guardian.

Tolledon walked forward. 'We will now seal the joining,' he said. Looking at each couple in turn, he said, 'Do you vow to walk the paths of light together; to seek peace in the Realm; and to remain true to one another?'

'With the help of the Mighty One, we do.'

'Then may Elsinoth the Mighty—Toroth the Light—grant you guidance, strength, wisdom and love. Two shall become one, with the strength of three.'

He lifted his head to address the crowd. 'Now rejoice! The joining is complete!'

The musicians struck up another lively tune, and everyone began to sing. As they did, the white cloud above parted, and a shaft of sunlight burst through. It fell upon all in the little glade, bringing warmth and life.

Remembering his dream, Kess smiled. It was as if Elsinoth himself was adding his blessing. As if in response to his thoughts, a soft voice echoed inside his mind: 'Truly, I am with you always.'

The voice died away as the singing around him rose to a crescendo. Turning to glance at Whisper, he felt her squeeze his hand. He looked at the three couples in front of him, and at Whisper. Then, shielding his eyes, he gazed up at the rays of light that shone down upon them all. The light seemed to be growing even brighter, and he felt it flooding into his heart, filling him with its warmth and strength.

'Thank you, Elsinoth,' he said.

Glossary

The following is a glossary of some of the people, places and things found in the Realm:

Air Crafters—those who devote their lives to studying the ways of the air

Animal Crafter—one who studies the ways of animals

Ateran—a Mentar, fellow-thinker with Nareta

Athennar—an Animal Crafter; son of Tolledon, Guardian of the Realm

Barak—a small, ferocious mountain bear

Bar'drash—a Zorg soldier under the command of Gur'brak

Black Caves—mysterious caves located in the north of the Realm

Blazer—Kess' horse, named from the white flash on his forehead

Bun'brid—a leader of the Zorgs based near the Land of Dreams

Callenor—a Hallion man; one of Tolledon's most trusted soldiers

Candra—a town on the slopes of Mount Tilt; home of the Mountain Guards

Carnak—the Keeper of Taz-i-tor, the Golden Sceptre of Elsinoth

Cave-Warg—an evil creature; feared especially by the Rrokki

Dargan the Bitter—one of the Dark Masters, who seek to spread evil

Elder Darron—one of the Valley folk; teacher of the ways of Elsinoth

Elsinoth—the Mighty One, creator of the Realm; known by elves as Toroth

Falron—a wandering poet who meets the company in the Southlands

Fangers—huge, bear-like creatures bred by Dargan

Fashag—a grumpy gnome; lives a solitary life as a Fire Crafter

Fenner-del—a young elf in Silder's group

Fether-del—one of the Air Crafters at Winderswood

Fetid Marshes—the swampy region that divides the Realm in two

Fingers of Dorphila—a gateway to the Land of Dreams

Fire Crafters—those who study the ways of fire

Fire Shadows—fiery servants of the Flame Master

Flame Master—a creature of fire, living deep in the Black Caves

Fortress of Fear—a huge structure straddling the Fetid Marshes

Galli-del—one of Silder's elves

Ganniwaggik—leader of the thunder goblins

Gatera—a Land Crafter from the Mountains of Kravos

Globe of Truth—a sphere crafted by Elsinoth to embody truth

Golden Sceptre—a staff crafted by Elsinoth to embody freedom of choice

Grey Runners—creatures of the Withered Wood; partnered by silver wolves

Gurags—hunting cats used by the Zorgs

Gur'brak—a Zorg captain stationed at the Fortress of Fear

Gwindirpha—wife of a former Guardian; Mistress of the Mists

Heart's-tear—a tiny flower found in the Valley

Hesteron-del—an Air Crafter (also a healer) from Winderswood

Hallion—a sheltered vale; the centre of the Realm's activities

Hinno-val—an elf leader, based at Hallion; trusted friend of Tolledon

Ice Kingdom—a city of ice, cradled in mountains in the north of the Realm

Ice bears—majestic white bears found in the north of the Realm

Jewelled Forest—a mysterious wood in the west of the lower Northlands

Jocale—a tree with multi-coloured fruit; found in the Jewelled Forest

Kal—a white hawk befriended by Athennar

Kessek—Kess, a Quiet One from the Valley; twin brother of Linnil

Land Crafters—those who study the ways of the land

Land of Dreams—originally a place of refreshment and pleasant dreams

Linnil—a Quiet One from the Valley; twin sister of Kess

Long Ravine—a chasm that splits the Southlands

Lorissa—one of the Valley folk; wife of Rodik

Marason—a Hallion man; one of Tolledon's most trusted commanders

Mardilla—a Land Crafter from the Mountains of Kravos; Gatera's wife

Melinya—an elf woman, raised in Hallion but taken away by Zendos

Meltizoc—a wise man whose counsel is often sought by Tolledon

Mentars—a gentle race of people with strengthened mental powers

Merric-mer—a prince of the River Elves; a troubadour and adventurer

Mistress of the Mists—Gwindirpha; imprisoned in the mist by a Dark Master

Moor Men—a strange, little-known race; distant cousins of the Rrokki

Mountains of Kravos—home of the Land Crafters

Nareta—a Mentar, fellow-thinker with Ateran

Narfic—one of the Valley folk; friend to Kess and Linnil

Parath—a town on the edge of the Inner Sea

Quiet Ones—the folk of the Valley; reputedly half human, half elven

River Crafters—Water Crafters who specialise in rivers and streams

Rodik—one of the Valley folk; a blacksmith, husband of Lorissa

Rrokk—Rrum's father; leader of the Southern Rrokki

Rrokki—a sturdy race of rock people

Rronadd—home of the Southern Rrokki

Rrudda—Rrum's mother

Rrum—one of the Rrokki, rescued by Kess at the Black Caves

Rustan—Valor's father; Captain of the Mountain Guards

Sash—a black leopard; friend of Athennar

Satta-del—one of the elves in Therrin's group

Scorbid—a legendary, bloated sea creature, 'recreated' by Dargan's powers of illusion

Sea Crafters—Water Crafters who specialise in the study of the oceans

Sellim—the town nearest to the Valley

Shorot—a strange, elusive, small and rather dirty animal

Silder-val—a leader of the elves seeking a way past the Fortress of Fear

Silrin-val—Silder's cousin, stationed at the Fortress

Simbrel—a small, enchanted horse found in the Jewelled Forest

Slipwort—a herb with healing properties

Splinter—Linnil's horse; has two white socks on her forelegs

Sundust—Valor's horse; a sleek golden mare

Targul—leader of the Tarks (others include Tarluk and Tarzil)

Tark—a winged creature; drains the mental energies of humanoid beings

Tarnock—Vosphel's home; a rocky island in the Troubled Sea

Tarrelford—home of the River Crafters

Taz-i-tor—the Golden Sceptre of Elsinoth; symbolises freedom of choice

Tessari—the Ice Kings; leaders of the Ice People (the Tissirim)

Therrin-del—a leader of the elves seeking a way past the Fortress of Fear

Thona-del—an elf prince; one of Tolledon's most trusted commanders

Tissirim—the Ice People; a peace-loving race

Tolledon—the Guardian of the Realm; based at Hallion

Tome of Neldra—an ancient book of wisdom

Tower of Braggad—sited in the Southlands; one of Dargan's key strongholds

Vale of Miscreance—a valley of nightmares in the Southlands

Vallel-val—a River Crafter, based at Tarrelford; twin sister of Vosphel

Valley, the—home of the Quiet Ones

Valley of Darkness—a dark pass through the Wailing Hills

Valor—a Mountain Guard from Candra; son of Rustan

Vesson-val—a leading River Crafter, based at Tarrelford

Venya-val—a leading River Crafter, based at Tarrelford

Vosphel-val—a Sea Crafter, based at Tarnock; twin sister of Vallel

Wailing Hills—a mountain range north of the Tower of Braggad

Water Crafters—those who study the ways of water

Whisper—a captive of the Mistress of the Mists

Whistling Waters—home of the Mistress of the Mists

Winderswood—home of the Air Crafters

Windrider—Athennar's faithful white stallion

Withered Wood—a strange, stunted forest in the Southlands

Zendos—a sorceror; apprentice of Dargan and cousin of Athennar

Zorgs—a brutish race of humanoid soldiers

The Will Of Dargan

by Phil Allcock

Trouble has darkened the skies of the Realm: the Golden Sceptre crafted by the hands of Elsinoth the Mighty has been stolen. Courageous twins, Kess and Linnil, team up with an assorted company of elves and crafters—and set out to find it.

Their journey takes them through rugged mountains, gentle valleys and wild woods to the grim stronghold of Dargan the Bitter. Will they win back the Sceptre? The answer depends on their courage, friendship and trust.

Phoenix
Published by Kingsway

In Search Of The Golden Sceptre

by Phil Allcock

The evil Dargan has stolen not only the Golden
Sceptre but also Linnil, who is locked in an
underground cell. Kess and his friends set off across
the Realm once again to search for both Linnil and
the Sceptre.

Through clinging, dangerous mists to the northern
kingdom of the extraordinary Ice People, and the
beautiful but treacherous Jewelled Forest—they
struggle onwards. Only the love of Elsinoth and the
strength of their friendship can sustain them, but will
these be enough to thwart the devious plans of
Dargan?

Phil Allcock is also the author of *The Will of Dargan*, as well
as short stories for BBC TV.

Phoenix

Published by Kingsway

The Book And The Phoenix

by Cherith Baldry

Times are hard for most of the Six Worlds. Earth is long forgotten, left behind in a past age when technology brought men and women to the stars.

The old tales tell how, generations ago, the colonists brought with them a belief, a faith, a way of life. But that's almost forgotten now, just a dream for old men.

Until now. Young Cradoc will see a vision of the legendary phoenix that will lead him to a Book. It is only when he discovers the power in the Book that he also learns there are many who will want to destroy it—and anyone who attempts to protect it.

Published by Kingsway

Hostage Of The Sea

by Cherith Baldry

They came from over the sea, a nation of warriors
intent on spreading their empire. When they
descended upon a small kingdom that served the
God of peace, the battle was short. And Aurion, the
peaceful King's son, was the ideal hostage to secure
victory.

Coming to the fearsome land of Tar-Askar, Aurion
meets the strong and proud son of the warrior king.
A most unlikely friendship develops—a bond of love
that will prove a greater threat to the Tar-Askan
empire than the weapons of war.

Also by **CHERITH BALDRY** in the *Stories of the Six
Worlds: The Book and the Phoenix.*

Published by Kingsway

The Muselings

by Ed Wicke

One day three scruffy children from an orphanage in the country have a surprise. Rachel, Robert and Alice fall *up* a tree into another world!

Why have they been brought into the land that scheming Queen Jess calls her own? The Queen and the children would *both* like to know, and as they try to find out, they stumble into hilarious and hair-raising adventures. Here we meet Lord Lrans, mad on hunting; the Reverend Elias, beloved but misunderstood vicar; Ballbody, a round, bouncy fellow…and the Muselings—kind, furry creatures whose world the children have fallen into.

Then Elias faces Queen Jess on a hilltop, and everything changes.

Phoenix

Published by Kingsway

Screeps

by Ed Wicke

'Up the tunnel was travelling something which twisted and slithered and slapped the walls with its scaly skin. It was several yards long, and its body was as thick as a man's. Its eyes were fixed on them, and its forked tongue flicked in and out as it writhed up the slope...'

They were meant to be on a walking holiday with Elias and Nobby, but somehow it had all gone wrong. So Rachel and Rob had to find the friendly Screeps themselves, braving first the Flitters and now the Kraal.

But why was the Queen of Avalon in the dungeons? How did Alice's ice cream end up in Lrans' pocket? What were these Daroks which the Screeps feared? And what was the answer to the worm king's riddle?

Phoenix

Published by Kingsway

The Curse Of Craigiburn

by Jennifer Rees Larcombe

They said that Craigiburn was cursed. The curtains were always drawn, and it was a sad family that lived in it.

James Brodie lived there now, with his father. What was the curse? Why would no one tell him? And why did the Ugly Man of the Forest send him away when he found out who he was?

Jamie was determined to find the answer to his questions. Little did he know how events would conspire to help him, especially once an old book came back from the distant past.

Phoenix

Published by Kingsway

THE PHOENIX
CHRISTIAN
FAMILY
C ★ L ★ U ★ B

If you've enjoyed reading this book, and would like to know more about Phoenix children's books, why not become a member of The Phoenix Family Club? Every two months in *Christian Family* magazine you can read two packed pages of news, reviews, jokes, and interviews about our books — hosted by the lovable Phileas Phoenix — and you'll have a chance to contribute something yourself. And if you become a member of the club, for the same price as most of our paperbacks you will receive a badge, a membership card, yet more regular news from Phileas Phoenix, a Phoenix book — *and* a special Free Token Form, exclusive to members of the club.

Below you will see a Phoenix savings token, which can also be found in other Phoenix paperbacks. Six of these tokens, stuck down on the Free Token Form, will get you another Phoenix paperback absolutely free.

For details on how to join the club, read *Christian Family* magazine, or send a stamped addressed envelope to: Phoenix, 1 St Anne's Road, Eastbourne, East Sussex BN21 3UN, England.

COLLECT SIX GET ONE
FREE
SAVINGS TOKEN
Cash value: 0.01p

Phoenix

Published by Kingsway